# Phantor_____

## A Novel By
# Diana Barron

**Published By**
**Barclay Books, LLC**

**St. Petersburg Florida**
**www.barclaybooks.com**

A Spectral Visions Imprint

PUBLISHED BY BARCLAY BOOKS, LLC
6161 51ST STREET SOUTH
ST. PETERSBURG, FLORIDA 33715
www.barclaybooks.com
A Spectral Visions Imprint

Printed and bound in the United States of America
Cover design by Barclay Books, LLC

ISBN: 1-931402-21-3

For Phil my rock, and our angels S & C

# Prologue

He was still alive and fully aware when she began to skin him.

His hot, burgundy blood mixed with her glistening saliva, splattering the ground and the grass, drenching them both. He was a macabre and grisly parody of a dancing Las Vegas water fountain glittering in the moonlight, as his veins and arteries ruptured and spurted, emptying themselves to the beat of his madly pumping heart.

Tearing off big wet chunks of his flesh with slathering gusto, she noisily peeled him, as if he were a pulpy red tangerine. Being shredded like newspaper in a gerbil's cage, his pain was blasphemous. Pinned underneath her massive powerful body, he thrashed and flailed around in his own hot sloppy soup. *God . . . no . . . n o o o . . .*

His racking screams tapered off to short, inarticulate, guttural bursts. *Uh . . . n . . . uh . . . n,"* as he gagged on the bloody saliva bubbling up from his throat, and on the gory snot splashing out of his nostrils.

With death hovering just beyond his reach, he looked down at himself through eyes swimming in a red haze, as the slimy ropes of his large and small intestines were dragged out of the ragged hole of his ravaged, steaming abdomen. The rank odor of fresh feces oozing out of the punctures and gashes, brought on a disjointed smell memory of the outhouse he'd used as a child on the family farm long ago.

Jerking and flopping in the throes of an agonizing death, his mind left him, and he floated up and up above the carnage that had been his body. He took his last gurgling breath, watching in horrified disbelief as his genitals were chewed into squishy crimson mulch.

*"Uh . . . n . . . uh . . . n . . . uh . . ."*

# Chapter 1

## Erin Wakes Up

Erin slammed back into her bedridden body with a jolt that snapped her eyelids open. Disoriented, she hastily looked down at herself and blinked around at her familiar frilly pink and white bedroom bathed in early morning sunshine.

"Damn. Just a stupid dream . . ."

She remembered no details about her nighttime excursion. All that remained was an elusive, wistful feeling of freedom. . . . Freedom. Something that was denied to her now, and had been for a long time.

The irritating ring of her bedside telephone dragged her back to full consciousness and the start of another day.

She was annoyed.

"Jeez, it's going to be a busy one and I haven't even had my coffee yet. No rest for the wicked." Erin was fond of joking that performing phone sex wouldn't have been a half bad way to make a living, if only she didn't have to answer the telephone all the time.

The phone was on its third ring when a fleeting thought occurred to her. *"Hm. That's weird. Not hungry. I'm usually starving when I wake up."* The insistent ringing interrupted her contemplation regarding the unusual absence of her appetite. "Oh well, down to business."

"Good Morning." Her voice rose an octave and took on a cheery lilt.

"Hey Baby!"

"Well, hey yourself! Darlin', would you hold for just a sec?"

"Why sure baby, but hurry back."

"You know it!" Erin placed a plump bejeweled hand over the mouthpiece, and bellowed for her protégé. "Mickey!" She figured she'd put her coffee order in now, so that it would be ready when she got off the phone.

Mickey skidded up to her bedside. "What'll it be this morning boss?"

"Mickey, would you bring me coffee please?"

He hesitated, expecting her to continue, which she didn't. *This is new,* he thought to himself. *No breakfast? She's always hungry . . .*

They blinked at each other.

"Off you go, Mickey . . . I've got a client." Erin nodded at the receiver in her hand, and then almost laughed out loud at the puzzled expression on her friend's face. "Yes darling, you heard me right. Now, scoot."

"Sure Erin, coming right up," replied Mickey, always eager to please as he turned on his heel, forehead wrinkled, and headed for the kitchen.

He loved Erin; always had. As he scurried to do her bidding, his mind flashed back as it often did, to the day they had first met.

As a matter of fact, now that he thought about it, next month would be the tenth anniversary of when he and Erin had crossed paths. It had been one single terrifying, but extraordinary day that had changed his life forever.

# Chapter 2

## Mickey

Even after ten years, the memory of that day remained as fresh in his mind as if no time at all had passed.

The kids, four boys and a girl, couldn't have been any more than thirteen or fourteen, but to him they were a dangerous mob. Mickey was no stranger to confrontation. He'd had to defend himself many times in his life, but this bunch had a dog. And that put an entirely different spin on the situation; a scary one, because Mickey was afraid of dogs.

The pooch belonged to one of the kids and probably spent much of its time curled up on the family sofa in a contented doze. But this day it had gone along with the gang in which it loved to be included, and it was having fun playing the game with them. *Bark, growl, bark, growl, strain at the leash, look ferocious, make my friends laugh*.

Mickey's dog-o-phobia could be traced back to his unhappy childhood. Never having had a real home or family to speak of, he'd never owned a dog, or had the opportunity to get to know one personally, and any of the canines he had ever run across in his lifetime had always seemed to be bigger than he was, and mean. The only dogs he'd ever had any dealings with were usually strays, like him. And they were none too magnanimous about sharing the wealth when he and they found a good food source at the same time. Wing Fong's Chinese Smorgasbord threw out lots of good, edible stuff on a regular basis, as did Vera's Café. Mickey and the other strays in town knew the circuit, but tried to stay out of each other's way whenever possible.

On this particular day, however, Mickey was cornered with nowhere to run—not that his stunted legs could outrun these healthy young hooligans and their hellhound if he tried. Plastered against a brick wall, his teeth chattered with fear, and his wide mouth was drawn back in a grimace that emphasized the deep creases in his high forehead, until he resembled an elfin Charles Bronson.

Almost wetting his pants, he wrapped his arms around his small chest, closed his eyes, and mentally willed the wall to magically swallow him up.

The kids fanned around him in a semi-circle, taunting and laughing. The red brick wall had been the back of a public school down the street from his home—really a cardboard carton in an alley—but he slept in worse places, and it was cozy enough, and he inwardly cursed himself for leaving to run an errand at that time of day. He was usually so careful about things like this, but for some reason that afternoon he was a bit distracted and not really thinking—not on his guard—and sure enough he was in that spot.

Then, just as he began picturing hunks of himself disappearing down the throat of the growling dog, a big black shadow crept menacingly up from behind the group of kids, growing larger and larger until it blotted out the sun.

And suddenly Erin appeared.

A voice boomed out of nowhere, so deep and loud and threatening that it sounded to him like the voice of God, an answer to his panicked prayers. Even the furry brown-spotted hound of the Baskervilles let out a squeak and ceased its histrionics to squat down on its haunches and look fearfully over its shoulder.

As Mickey watched, the little drama seemed to unfold in slow motion, right before his eyes. The thundering voice belonged to a woman. And what a woman!

"Get out of here you little bastards, before I bash your skulls in!" The wind actually whistled as she made a large swiping motion with the two-by-four for emphasis, her free hand balled into a fist and raised as if ready to finish off anything left when the lumber had done its work.

There was no need to tell the kids twice.

As one, they all turned and bolted, forgetting about Mickey. All flying Reeboks and Nikes, with the dog out in front, leash flapping, they ran screaming for home and their mothers.

It all happened so fast that Mickey could hardly grasp it, and while his mind caught up with what he'd just witnessed, he realized that someone was laughing . . . a lot.

"God that felt good! Ha ha ha!"

Mickey stared, his eyes almost bugging out of his head. The transition from stark terror to absolute amazement was almost too quick to handle, and for a minute he thought he might faint. But as he watched this incredible creature guffaw before him, he knew that he wouldn't faint because this was quickly becoming one of the most interesting moments of his life and he didn't want to miss it.

As his senses slowly returned, and the woman's laughter subsided, she spoke.

"Hi, I'm Erin."

Mickey's mind screamed out, *"I'm Mickey, and I love you, love you, love you!"* But his mouth, which at this particular moment was smarter than his mind, replied, "H-hi, I'm Mickey. Thank you for h-helping me."

"Happy to do it. Those little jerks. Maybe they'll think twice next time," Erin said, the corners of her mouth still twitching with mirth.

"I doubt it. Little jerks grow up to be big jerks," Mickey replied. And they shared their first laugh.

As they chuckled their eyes caught. And Mickey knew right then and there that he would love Erin until the day he died. He craned his neck way back to look up and into her eyes, and she smiled down at him. The brilliant sunshine that fell on her from behind made him squint, creating a glowing halo effect around her body, convincing him that she truly was his guardian angel.

Then suddenly, as he stared into those exquisite, bottomless sea-green eyes, he began to feel disoriented and a trifle confused— a little off kilter. He felt he was falling into them, and his heart leapt into his throat as he simultaneously experienced the different folds of emotions contained within.

The first layer was all warmth and compassion for another human being in trouble. But as if he viewed the layers being peeled away like an onionskin, he was almost overwhelmed by another, scarier emotion.

It was rage.

A rage so deep and rich, so dangerous that it almost knocked the breath right out of him, but he struggled to keep his composure.

Because, along with the knowledge of what lay behind those dazzling sea-green eyes, was also the certainty that the rage would never be directed toward him. He didn't know *how* he knew it, he just did. And so he laughed, with joy.

# Chapter 3

## Isolde

Erin smiled to herself as she watched Mickey exit the bedroom to fetch her morning coffee. Her lovely eyes shone softly with affection for him. Then she remembered the telephone in her hand.

Tossing her head to remove a sleep-tousled lock of her glossy, black hair from her eyes, she lifted her hand off of the mouthpiece, enjoying as always, the light show that happened whenever she wiggled her fingers in the sunshine.

Fiery glints and glitters danced off of ten deliciously large gold and gemstone confections that encircled every chubby finger and thumb. The rings were custom made for her by a gifted jeweler she had never met (at least not in person), but who knew her tastes better than anyone else on the planet, except of course for Mickey. As always, their beauty brightened her mood as she greeted her first client of the day.

"So sorry to keep you waitin' darlin'. Watchoo doin' up so early?"

Even as she asked the question, she smiled to herself because she already knew the answer. He called because he loved her voice, and loved the slight backwoods country accent that she affected whenever he called. Erin truly had a superb gift for voices.

And he loved the way it made him feel. There was a smoky, sensuous quality to it, like honey left to warm in the late afternoon sun and then slowly poured over his naked body. He could imagine himself stretched out in a field filled with wild flowers and waving green grass . . . impossibly green. So fragrant and green that the scent got into his head and took him to another place, where a hundred soft, tiny tongues licked the honey from every inch of his body.

"I couldn't wait to hear your voice today, and I was wondering what you were wearing." She could detect just the slightest hint of a tremor now.

"No hon, as a matter of fact I'm still in bed and hardly wearin' nothin' at all. Just a lil' ol' skimp of a thing that you could see right through . . ."

Erin paused for emphasis, and then continued to talk as she always did. Her client continued to do what *he* always did, and soon it was over.

"Th-thank you b-baby . . . th-thank you," he stammered breathlessly.

"Until next time darlin'." And Erin gently replaced the telephone receiver back in its cradle.

While Erin tended to her client, Mickey entered the large, homey kitchen.

"Isolde! Coffee!" he demanded with a grin.

Isolde was the cook for their little household, although the title really didn't do her justice. She had never trained in Paris or New York, had not in fact even finished the nightmare called high school, but she had a gift. Although God had not given her much when she was born, he had bestowed one very special talent— Isolde could cook.

It had been discovered very early in her sad childhood that in the kitchen no one could touch her when it came to food preparation. Isolde cooked by instinct—inspired and inventive.

When she was six years old, trying desperately to fit into a family that wasn't hers by birth, but by an unlucky roll of the dice, she got up early one Christmas morning and prepared the family breakfast as a holiday surprise. As each member was awakened by the delectable aromas emanating from the first floor of the house, they hurried down the stairs in their pajamas to see who was responsible for waking up their salivary glands. One by one they stopped short in the kitchen doorway, jostling and bumping into each other as they stared, sleepily dumbfounded.

"What the . . .!" her father exclaimed.

"Well I never . . ." came from the mother.

"Huh?" the big dumb brother who had made her life a living hell said.

And from the sister, who was ten years old and hated Isolde, presented a filthy withering look dripping with jealousy.

And there was little blonde Isolde, the mother's grown-up sized apron wrapped around her tiny body, twice at least, and crudely tied in the front. She was perched on a stool from the breakfast bar, a hand-held electric mixer clutched in both small hands. It whirred away as she'd whipped up the icing for the homemade apple and cinnamon buns, steaming in the muffin tin on the counter.

The mother was the first to snap out of her sleepy stupor, and she instinctively bolted toward Isolde to grab the mixer away from the tot, and give her a good smack to boot.

But something stopped her in her tracks.

With an insight the mother didn't usually possess, it struck her that Isolde knew exactly what she was doing. And from that day on, Isolde finally had a "role" in the family. A position. It wasn't love like the other kids had, but it would do. The mother took it upon herself to help.

She began dragging Isolde along every time she grocery shopped, teaching her about the different cuts of meat and how to judge good produce from bad. Isolde was a quick study, and pretty soon the mother would drop her off in the grocery store with a shopping cart taller than she was, and go shoe shopping for an hour or two. She would return to pay for the groceries, load them and the little girl into the car, and head for home.

Mickey met Isolde one day while she sat on a bus stop bench. She was crying and looked so pitiful that he felt compelled to stop and ask if he could help. When that offer elicited only another burst of heart-wrenching sobs, he put his arms around her. For the next three hours they walked and she talked.

She told Mickey that she was running away from home and why. She told him how her birth mother, only fifteen, had dropped her off in front of a Roman Catholic Church one day, never to return. Isolde had been four months old. Father Noone, the resident Priest, had found the baby and deposited her with an order of nuns who inhabited a convent not far from the church. After that, she became a victim of the system, and was shunted from foster home to foster home until she was five years old, at which time she moved in with a family who she knew would never love her, but who kept her as a curiosity and a conversation piece rather than a daughter. Now she was sixteen years old and had nowhere to go.

Mickey made a decision on the spot. "I want you to come home and live with me."

"What? Isolde thought she heard him wrong, and stepped back a pace, suspicion narrowing her sky-blue eyes.

Observing the distrust that suddenly clouded her pale pretty face, Mickey couldn't help but laugh. "I'm sorry. I guess that didn't come out right. What I mean is, my friend Erin . . . that's the lady I live with . . . came to my rescue once and took me in. We have a big house and a swimming pool, and it's really great there." Isolde just stared at him wide-eyed as his words gushed out, but she looked intrigued.

Sensing that he had tweaked her interest, he pressed on. "It's not how it sounds, Isolde. I'm not explaining it right. Erin and me, we're a family. We help each other. She needs me, and I need her. And there's lots of room; it's a big house. If it's privacy you're worried about, don't. You can have your very own bedroom and fix it up any way you want." When she heard the word "bedroom" Isolde looked suspicious again.

"Oh, and what would I have to do to earn this wonderful haven may I ask?" Isolde hadn't experienced much sincerity in her life, and it brought out her sarcastic side, her defense in a threatening situation. Crossing her arms over her bosom, she raised her chin and pointedly raked Mickey from head to toe with her eyes, hoping she appeared haughty and worldly. Assessing everything from the shoulder-length somewhat unruly brown hair combed straight back from his forehead, to the scuffed no-name sneakers on his tiny slightly pigeon-toed feet, she had to admit to herself that his appearance pleased her. *But, he is ten years older than me,* she thought, and she was afraid to trust her instincts.

The resident Memorial Park birds chirped and sung merrily in the canopies of the big oak trees overhead while Isolde waited for an answer.

"Cook!" Mickey looked like the cat that ate the canary.

"What?" Isolde was slightly nonplused by such an unexpected answer.

"Cook. You said you could cook, and me and Erin sure could appreciate that, let me tell you. That is, if you're really as good as you say you are." Mickey smiled even wider when he realized that he'd hit a sore spot.

"What do you mean if? If I say I can cook, I can. It's my best thing. I'll show you, you little twerp." Again Mickey burst into a belly laugh at her show of temper.

"Alright, show me. Let's go home." Mickey held out a hand palm up, and Isolde hesitated, but only for a second. Then she looked into his eyes, and took his hand.

On the day that Mickey met Isolde at the bus stop, he had been with Erin for almost five years. He thought it would be fun to have this pretty sprite around the house, and when she told him about her talent for cooking, he knew he had made the right decision.

For Mickey, Isolde's sweet open face and big blue eyes were icing on the cake, for there was a bigger more compelling reason why he was attracted to her. He had never met another person like himself before and he was entranced, for Mickey was a dwarf.

# Chapter 4

## Flower In San Francisco

Born to teenaged hippie parents in 1967 during the renowned Summer of Love, Mickey's unmarried mother and father, Susan and Scott, had been runaways. They had changed their names to "Flower" and "Cool" and spent the winter and spring of that year dropping acid and hitch-hiking all the way from Toronto to San Francisco—Haight-Ashbury to be exact—where the free love being preached and practiced by almost everyone usually came with a price tag and was rarely free.

Mickey was one of those price tags.

He was born with achondroplasia, or dwarfism. But his parents weren't aware that there was anything wrong with the baby, at least at first, because he was delivered in a flop house by a self-proclaimed midwife, who was just as stoned as Flower and Cool were on the day of Mickey's birth.

And when it became obvious that parenthood wasn't going to be the *gas* that Cool had thought it would be, he took off in search of more sex, drugs, and rock and roll, and he never looked back. So baby Mickey was left with his mother.

It didn't take long for Flower to become disenchanted with San Francisco. The stark reality of having to survive with a baby in tow had bashed head-first up against her dreamy teenage fantasies about living on her own in a hippie utopia, and the dreams suffered egregious damage, and finally died a pathetic death.

Flower became increasingly dependent on drugs to get her through her bouts of depression. And increasingly dependent on the men who had money to spend on her body and services in order to acquire the drugs she needed. Her shopping list included food only infrequently, and only when the teenager was lucid enough to remember that she had a hungry child to feed.

So around it went.

Little Mickey was left to his own devices much of the time. He was malnourished and left alone to wallow in his dirty diapers, in a cockroach infested second-floor walkup with no heat or running water.

Sometimes Flower would drag Mickey along with her when she forayed downtown in search of drugs, or handouts. They became a familiar sight to the locals. Flower in her ankle-length, dirty Indian cotton skirts and long greasy blonde hair, towing Mickey along in a rusty metal wagon she'd found in the trash. Her collarbones and shoulder blades stuck out of her baggy halter-top, which had no breasts to hold it up. Undernourished and anorexia-thin, she trudged along in her ragged leather sandals, stooped and beaten, and not yet out of her teens.

"Hi. Peace."

Flower glanced down to the sidewalk beside her, when she heard the female voice. Three girls were sitting cross-legged in faded, raggedy blue jeans, in a semicircle, and were smiling up at her. Angelic smiles.

By this time, Flower had folded in on herself, her dreams crushed and the weight of the world was on her shoulders. She extended a hand to no one, and was surprised when a hand was offered to her.

Looking spaced out and skeptical, she returned the peace symbol to the three hippy girls, making a V of her bony fingers.

One-by-one the girls rattled off their names, introducing themselves like the members of the Mickey Mouse Club doing roll call.

"Hi, I'm Sadie."

"I'm Leslie."

"I'm Katy. What's your name?"

Flower hesitated for a second as if she couldn't quite recall her name, and then glancing from face to smiling face, uttered suspiciously, "Flower."

"Well, hello Flower. And who's this?" Sadie reached out to little Mickey who was sitting in his wagon, staring fascinated at the three girls with their long hair parted in the middle, with his mouth open and big brown eyes wide.

"Mickey. He's my baby."

Mickey started to coo and giggle, reaching his thin little arms out wide to Sadie. Flower was neither a demonstrative nor affectionate mother, and Mickey was starving for attention.

Sadie uncrossed her legs and reached over to lift Mickey from the wagon.

"No!" Flower's reaction was immediately and noticeably hostile and possessive.

"Okay, okay, I won't touch him," placated Sadie before settling back down to the sidewalk and re-crossing her legs.

"Do you live around here?

"I got a place." Flower lifted her stick-arm to point vaguely down the street, and then dropped it loosely as if it weighed as much as a ten-pin bowling ball.

"You look like you could use a friend," Leslie piped up. "We were just about getting ready to head for home. Would you like to come for a visit? We live in a beautiful place in the desert with lots of great people. We're a family."

Flower stared at her but said nothing.

"You'd love it, and so would Mickey here," added Katy. "We've got plenty to eat, and lots of people to look after your baby."

"Yeah, and we know Charlie would welcome you," said Sadie.

"Charlie?" asked Flower.

"Charlie's like our father. He takes care of us. You'd love him," gushed Leslie. "We all do."

"No . . . No thanks. Gotta be going." With that, Flower picked up the handle of the old wagon and trudged off down the dirty streets of Haight-Ashbury into the July sunshine with her son in tow. Charlie's girls silently watched them go. It was 1969, but Flower wouldn't live long enough to recognize the trio from the Spahn Ranch on the evening news.

\*\*\*

A week later, Flower heard about an event being planned in upstate New York touted to be the biggest *happening*, the most fantastic *be-in* of all time. So she packed up little Mickey, bummed a ride with a group of "diggers" in a purple van slowly being eaten alive by creeping rust, and headed for Max Yasgur's farm.

But they never made it to Woodstock.

Halfway there, Mickey's mom tripped out once too often on a bad tab of acid. She threw herself out of the sliding side door of the "digger's" ratty van while traveling fifty miles an hour, and bounced down the pavement right into the path of an oncoming Peterbilt, which didn't leave much of "Flower" to identify.

The State Troopers in Wichita, Kansas took Mickey into custody, shocked at the condition he was in, and handed him over to The Department of Human Services. They tried to place him in foster homes, but no one wanted a little boy with his special problems, so off to the state orphanage he went, there to stay until he was eighteen years old. When the powers that be set him free, into a world he knew nothing about, he fled gladly.

# Chapter 5

## Erin Makes a Date

It didn't take long for Mickey to figure out that every city had a system of missions—soup kitchens and flophouses—for people just like him. People who fell through the cracks. No family, no skills, no incentive. People who no one had ever cared about their whole lives, and so had no expectations. Abused people, addicted people. Mentally or physically disabled people. People on the fringes.

This suited him just fine.

On the fringes he was barely noticed—let alone made fun of—and he blended into the warp and weft of the invisible underbelly of society . . . Until that fateful June day three years later, when Mickey, at the age of twenty-one ran afoul of a bunch of kids and a dog. And the rest, as they say, is history.

For the first time in his entire life, Mickey was truly happy. Erin was the first person who had ever really cared about him, so his gratitude and loyalty knew no limits. He would do anything for her.

Sometimes in rare moments of reverie, when he wasn't totally occupied by the daily routine of caring for Erin, he wondered if perhaps, just maybe her grisly demands went a little too far. But when these disloyal thoughts tried to insinuate themselves into his head, he quickly pushed them away and ran to ask Erin if there was anything she needed, *"Any tiny little thing; no, no, it was no trouble at all."*

In exchange for Mickey and Isolde's love and devotion, Erin took very good care of her companions.

She made an excellent living working out of her home as a phone sex operator. Even though her ad in the yellow pages was listed under "telephone dating," her product was verbal sex. The ad read:

"Kiss 'O' the Blarney Stone" telephone dates
    Live conversation - 24 hours - Adults only 18+
    Men call: 1-900-555-3746, (or 1-900-555-ERIN.)
    $2.99/min

Erin had always known that she possessed two outstanding features—her hands and her voice. Her hands she kept solely for her own pleasure, adorning them with the ten sparkling and expensive rings that she constantly switched from finger to finger. Her voice gave her clients pleasure and paid the bills. Nothing gave her more joy, or a sense of accomplishment, than to hold her hands out in front of her and admire them while she serviced some client with her words on the telephone. Often she would describe in detail, running her hands over her body, driving her caller wild.

In reality she could barely stand to look down at her grossly endomorphic body, let alone fondle it. *The fools!* The only real enjoyment that Erin achieved was watching the rings twinkle and wink as she moved them up and down and around, and she smiled.

Every once in a while, when Erin had known a particular caller for a while, she would agree to meeting in person—a date. Although eventually they almost all got around to asking, the client would have to meet her very specific criteria in order for her to accept.

And it had to be on her terms.

One, they had to be married. Two, they had to be childless.

Erin figured that if the man was married, there was little chance that he would tell his wife where he was going, and in fact, would likely go to great lengths to make sure he wasn't found out, thereby insuring her anonymity.

And this eliminated the risk of her involvement being detected when he turned up missing.

As for her second rule of making sure her victims were childless, she did not want to be responsible for leaving a child fatherless. Just because her own father was an abusive son of a bitch, didn't mean they all were.

It had been a long time since the last date, now that she thought about it, and the phone rang just as this occurred to her.

"Hello Kitten? That you? It's Rock, honey. I've been thinking about you all day, and couldn't wait to get home from work and into the shower."

"Why Rock, what a coincidence. I've been thinking about you too, and wishing you could see me now. I haven't been out of my bed all day, and I woke up with a tickly little feeling between my legs. Just before I came fully awake, I dreamed it was you down there with your tongue all warm and wet doing things . . ."

"Uhhnnn, ahhhhhmmm . . ." moaned Rock.

Erin could hear the shower running in the background, and knew that Rock (she also knew this wasn't his real name) liked to take his cordless phone with him while the pulsating water jets and his free hand did their thing.

Erin talked until she knew he was done, and waited while he caught his breath for the inevitable question that always came next.

"You're wonderful, Kitten. Can't we please get together in person? Karen works until almost seven o'clock every evening. I could come straight from work and pick you up. We could go anywhere you say, just name it. I promise you won't be sorry. Please?" begged Rock.

"Alright, Rock honey. You've finally talked me into it. But you must promise me something first," replied Erin with a cold glint in her emerald eye.

"Anything, just anything!" Rock could not believe his luck.

"Promise me you won't tell anyone about us. Okay honey?"

"Done."

Erin knew that Rock loved his wife and would never jeopardize his marriage by telling a soul about his planned infidelity, but she still wanted the guarantee in words.

"Alrighty then, I feel most comfortable at home, in my own bed, so here's my address. One week from tonight, okay?"

"Okay! God, I can hardly wait!"

"Me too. Bye bye Rock."

"Mickey!" called Erin, suddenly feeling purposeful and businesslike.

"Here I am Erin."

Mickey never seemed to be far away, and Erin realized absentmindedly that she never had to call for him twice.

"Mickey darling, I've got a date next week so we'll have to prepare."

The smile melted from Mickey's face like icing from the cake left out in the rain in Richard Harris's song, "*MacArthur's Park.*" He knew the drill. *Damn!* Now he would have to deal with that creepy little psycho, Beau. Oh well, it was a small price to pay to make Erin happy.

"You got it Erin! I'll get right on it!" He loved it when she called him "darling." Erin's sense of purpose was contagious, and with a spring in his step, Mickey whirled around and made tracks for the kitchen and Isolde. The two of them had better get cracking, he thought. They only had a week to prepare and there was a lot to do.

Also, he always took Isolde with him when he had to announce to Beauregard, the newest and scariest addition to their little extended family, that Erin had a date lined up. He knew this was cowardly on his part, and paranoid, as Beau wouldn't do anything to hurt him for fear of angering Erin. But having Isolde's company made him feel better just the same. After all, it *was* Beau . . .

# Chapter 6

## Beauregard

"Morning boss. I hear we're having company again soon!" Beauregard entered the room with his usual swagger and bravado.

"Yes Beau, in a week, and as usual I will be depending on you to see to it that everything goes smoothly."

"You can count on me boss!" And Erin knew this was true. As a matter of fact, if Beau weren't so damn dependable and competent, she would have gotten rid of him long ago. He was just over three feet tall, as mean as a wolverine with a screaming case of hemorrhoids, and she knew that the others were afraid of him. She also knew that he would never dare hurt anyone under her roof, because the other's fear of him was nothing compared to Beau's fear of her, and this kept him in line just fine.

Beauregard had come from down South somewhere—Mississippi or Alabama. His family was old money, and still lived on the plantation built by their ancestors around the middle of the eighteenth century, on the hefty proceeds from King Cotton. To a person, they all still wished fervently (and lamented privately) that slavery had never been abolished.

When Beau had been born, he'd had a full head of burnt orange hair and two perfect whorls on the crown of his head. Of course, Lila and Jackson Dupree had been told by the doctors immediately—the folds of loose skin and odd-shaped limbs being a dead giveaway—that the baby was a dwarf. This had not fazed Beau's parents, for he had been wanted and loved, and they were grateful for their new son. There had been some pretty strange family stories of other births, to other relatives, passed on in whispers through the generations, and they'd figured it could have been worse.

He had his mother Lila's red hair and his father Jackson's big brown eyes, and they were happy.

At first.

Lovingly they named him Beauregard, which means "Beautiful to look at" in French.

The doctors had said that Beau should have been born twins— ergo the double whorl on the crown of his large head. His parents had taken this as a good sign. They'd thought maybe that he would grow up to be twice as smart as other children, and that God indeed worked in mysterious ways, and this too had made them happy . . .

At first.

In his first year of life, his parent's hopes had actually seemed to be coming to pass. At seven months, Beau had been walking. At eight months he had spoken. As a rule, a child's first word is something to be celebrated with much ado by his doting parents, but as Beau's mom and dad found out with dismay, it sometimes depended on the word.

On a lovely summer day in June, Beau and his mother had been out wandering in her prized flower garden enjoying the sunshine and the lazy lulling drone of the bees as they floated from flower to flower. Beau had become distracted by a thing on the ground, and had squatted down inspecting the thing intently when the word had popped out of his baby's mouth as clear as a bell in the quiet of the country air. "Shit!"

"Oh my God! Beau? Did you say something, honey? Beau?" Beau's mother had been excited. Lila wasn't sure what she had heard at first because it had come out more like "thit."

"Shit!" The little boy was still staring at the thing on the ground, only now he was pointing his stubby little arm at the spot too.

Lila hurried over to see if her ears had deceived her, desperately hoping that they had. When she reached the spot where Beau was crouched between the rows of gladioli and bluebells, she peered down at what had captivated him so completely, and saw a steaming pile of poop. Obviously one of the family hounds had recently meandered past here and had left a calling card behind.

In a blink she snatched him up, and made a beeline for the house. This was an outrage to Beau that immediately triggered a full-blown tantrum. Little Beau kicked and screamed all the way back to the house, where Lila shoved him into the first arms she saw when she reached the big wraparound veranda. They happened to belong to Beau's nanny, who had come running when she heard the commotion.

"What's the matter Missus? What's happened? Is he hurt?" cried the startled nanny.

"No, he's not hurt! Brenda, have you heard anyone using bad language around Beau? I want you to tell me!" demanded Lila.

"Oh no Missus, never! Besides, I'm the only one he ever spends time with and I don't use the curse words!"

This was true. In all the time that Brenda had been in their employment, Lila had never heard a single swear word leave the girl's lips.

"Where's Jackson!" Without waiting for an answer, she stormed off to find her husband, leaving Brenda to cope with the still snuffling Beau.

The incident was only a portent of things to come. By the time Beau was five, he was a holy terror, and Jack and Lila were at their wit's end.

They tried valiantly to curb their son's behavior, including everything from child psychologists to drugs to a harness and leash. But their efforts were wasted.

By the child's tenth year, his parents were afraid of him.

They had been finding dead animals around the property for a couple of years, and some appeared to have been tortured before they died. Like the previous May when Jackson had come across one of their old house cats hanging by its neck on a skipping rope.

One end of the toy was tied around the hapless kitty's throat, and the other end around the part of the diving board that hung out the farthest over the deep end of the swimming pool. The rope was just long enough so that the cat couldn't reach the side to climb out, and also so it would keep its head under unless it treaded water. The poor thing had obviously been put out there when no one was around and had tried for hours to survive but simply ran out of strength.

The same could also be said of Beau's parents. They simply ran out of strength by the time their son reached his teens.

He had been expelled, removed or thrown out of every school he had ever attended, and there was nowhere else to turn. Jackson would dearly have loved to place him in the toughest military school available, but they all had rules regarding a minimum height requirement which precluded that notion, and Beau was denied admission.

On his sixteenth birthday, Beau was presented with a shiny new custom sports car, specially outfitted to accommodate his Physique. After learning how to drive it, he announced that he was taking a cross-country vacation and not to wait up.

Lila and Jack Dupree never saw their son again.

# Chapter 7

## The Digits Form a Family

Beauregard met Mickey in a grocery store one day, *accidentally* on purpose. His solitary adventure led him north until he reached the small town of Hester in New York State where Erin and her companions lived. It looked like a nice little burg, so he decided to spend a night or two, and besides, he was getting really tired of driving.

After renting a room with a kitchenette, Beau set out to find a grocery store and buy a few supplies. He spotted Mickey right off the bat, entering a quaint little food market on the main street of town, and he quickly parked his car out in front. Hurrying into the store, he scanned the aisles until Mickey came into view. Noting which corner would be the best for bumping into his quarry, he waited, and then, "Hey!"

"Excu . . .se . . . m . . . hey . . ." stammered a flabbergasted Mickey, when he realized he was face to face with someone who was almost exactly his height and had the same physical characteristics.

"Hi, I'm Beau!  Sorry 'bout that." Huge smile; angelic.

Quick recovery on Mickey's part. "No problem, no problem. Not at all! I'm Mickey. Pleased to meet you!" he replied enthusiastically, shaking Beau's hand.

The two small men bonded right away, and finished their shopping together, talking up a storm. They left the store, and Mickey hopped into the passenger seat of Beau's exotic-looking vehicle, and rode along to Beau's motel room. The southerner explained how he came from a wealthy family and was on an odyssey to *find* himself, and Mickey told him about his home and Erin. Within an hour, Beau had wangled an invitation for himself, and after having dinner together at Vera's Cafe, off they went.

Mickey knocked on Erin's door.

"Come!"

"Erin, there's someone I'd like you to meet" said Mickey, as Beau came into view just behind him. "This is my new friend, Beau."

The welcoming smile froze on Erin's face as the new *friend* stepped out from behind Mickey and snaked a hand toward her.

"Pleased to meet you ma'am," he drawled in his creamy Southern accent.

Erin shook his hand, and her blood ran cold. As they looked into each other's eyes, she knew what he was, and he knew that she knew. Under the fake *Southern Gentleman* facade beat the heart of a predator, and Erin sensed it. She recognized her own kind. His full-lipped smile grew wider and his dark Belgian-Chocolate eyes narrowed, crinkling into little mirth-wrinkles at the corners.

And even though their evil sprang from different sources, it made neither of them any less dangerous.

Mickey, of course, was oblivious to the volumes of information shared by the two strangers in a single instant. Mickey had a kind heart and he tried to always see the good in people, even though he had to look deeper to find it in some people more than others.

Covering her discomfiture perfectly, the lady of the house patted a spot beside her on the bed and the visitor sat himself down. After asking Beau a few questions about his background and future plans, Erin invited him to move in and join their little extended family. He promptly accepted.

Beau had another more sinister birth defect other than the

obvious one, and it was not visible to the naked eye. He had been born without a conscience. In earlier days they would have called him a psychopath or a sociopath, but these days the current terminology, according to the DSM-IV (the psychiatric bible of diagnosis), was antisocial personality disorder. A superior intellect combined with a lack of empathy was a dangerous combination, and Erin knew that Beau was going to come in very handy indeed.

Three years later, they really were a family—Mickey, Isolde, Beau, and Erin. Each had a special role to play that made the fabric of the group stronger and richer, and each one enjoyed their place in *the family.*

Erin admired and appreciated them all. Mickey, with a face like Charles Bronson on a bad day, but possessed of a heart as big as the Grand Canyon. Isolde, who could put any chef to shame, as well as having a talent for making even depressing days seem brighter, with her curly blond locks, twinkling blue eyes, and wide sunny smile. Even nasty little Beauregard, with his giant-sized ego, and as stuck on himself as cheap plastic wrap, had his endearing qualities, although Erin was usually the only one who could see them.

He kept his orange hair long at the back, and tied in a ponytail that looked like a curly carrot hanging down, thinking this made him look quite jaunty. When they were all together, Erin called them her digits. To her, they were an extension of herself, and since she was immensely proud of her hands, one day she affectionately started calling her little crew digits. They all liked it.

All, that is, but the twins.

# Chapter 8

## The Twins

Erin's mind began to wander as she lounged in her big king-sized bed and munched from a box of assorted chocolate-covered nuts, her favorite. *I wonder what mother would say if she knew what I did for a living?* she mused. Who am I kidding? I know exactly what she'd say:

*"Oh Erin, why are you doing this to me? What have I done to deserve this? This wasn't the way I brought you up. But then what did I expect? You're your father's daughter, that's for sure. Dirty dirty girl. Get upstairs now!"*

*"No mommy please?"*

*"Now!"* CRACK! goes daddy's belt. *"Now get!"*

*"Ow! Okay I'm going!"* Up the stairs, take off my clothes as I go, down to the end of the hall, naked now. One last appeal for mercy. *"Please mommy please!"* CRACK! goes daddy's belt again. At the closet door now. Into the little room with the mattress on the floor and nothing else.

Mommy turns the nightlight on. *"I'll bring you a snack. Your father can deal with you when he gets home."* Mommy shuts the door and mutters as she turns and heads for the stairs, *"Dirty dirty girl."*

A few minutes later mommy comes sack-toting something

good to eat, like a slab of cheesecake or a bowl of ice cream with nuts and chocolate syrup. The treats are a flimsy attempt by her mother to deflect Erin's attention away from the impending sexual abuse by her father. And she tells Erin how *very lucky she is to be spoiled so,* as she sits naked in the tiny windowless room, eating her ice cream and waiting for daddy to come home and "deal" with her.

Erin spent her unhappy childhood in the large house that she now shared with her friends. It was a good solid red brick home on a quiet suburban street in Hester, and it was set well back from the sidewalk. The large cedar hedge, almost seven feet tall, that ran all the way around the house, gave it a nice cozy sense of privacy. There was a wide, deep porch in the front, and at the very back of the property was a cute little cottage almost hidden from view by the mass of foliage that had rarely if ever been trimmed back.

Originally, the cottage had been installed to be used as a hobby shop, but her mother didn't have any hobbies and her father's hobbies didn't require a shop. Now it was the perfect haven for the twins.

Their names were Patrick and Sarah, and they had lived alone in the little house for as long as Erin could remember. This was not surprising, because the twins were her siblings.

Born almost five years before Erin, Frank and Marjorie O'Casey were devastated when the doctor announced upon their birth that they were midgets. A midget differs from a dwarf in that their limbs are straighter and more in proportion to the rest of the body, and they are usually taller.

Erin did not know her brother and sister well because, from the time they were infants, they had preferred their own company to anyone else's, and, so, mostly associated only with each other. Their little home was equipped with everything they needed to live a comfortable life all by themselves, and their parents were just as happy to leave well enough alone.

When Erin was born, and it was obvious that she would be a regular-sized child, her mother and father had been overjoyed. Not that they deliberately exhibited a preference for Erin, but it showed just the same, and early on the twins felt it and became reclusive.

As well as the twins' charming home away from home, almost hidden from view in a far corner of the big overgrown back yard, the large property boasted a kidney-shaped swimming pool that Erin no longer used. On hot days, however, the digits had great fun splashing and swimming in it, and floating around on inflatable toys and air mattresses.

Thinking about the pool reminded Erin of how lonely she was as a child. The twins had no use for her, and she didn't have friends the way other little girls seemed to.

She was never invited to pajama parties or sleepovers, and never had one at her house, convinced that no one would want to come. School was an ordeal for Erin and a torture that she had to endure every day. It was a nightmare because, not a day went by that she wasn't teased, and she couldn't wait until she was old enough to quit school forever.

In time, she became somewhat of an expert forger by writing notes claiming she was sick and signing her mother's or father's name. She also practiced her mother's voice hour after hour until she got it just right enough for variation so that she could telephone the school and get herself excused by saying a family member from out of state had died and Erin must attend the funeral.

Erin was extremely envious of the twins for not having to attend school. They were taught to read at home by their mother, and because she believed that they would never have to venture forth into the world to support themselves, they were left to their own devices after that.

Erin's face still burned with humiliation even all these years later, when she remembered the hated taunts in the schoolyard. *"Fatty fatty bubble butt, fell on the ground and couldn't get up!"* She would run home crying, and her mother would comfort her with whatever she had baked that day. There were always fresh pastries, cakes, or cookies to be devoured after school in her mom's kitchen. Then, more often than not, when she had stuffed herself, mother would find fault with some little thing or other until she worked herself into a frenzy and went for daddy's big leather belt. Once again, up the stairs, undress on the way, and into the closet at the end of the hall. Wait for daddy.

Sometimes she had a long wait. A lot of time to kill.

So Erin played shadow puppets.

The small nightlight that her mother had left on in the windowless little box of a room threw a perfect glow onto the opposite wall. Over time, Erin became very proficient at portraying many characters and puppets.

Her favorites were the scarecrow, the cowardly lion, the tin man, and Dorothy and Toto from the Wizard of Oz, her favorite movie. She saw it every year at the Morgan Theater, Hester's only movie house.

*"We're off to see the wizard. We're off to see the wizard. We're off to see the wizard."*

*"Hey those aren't the right words!"*

*"You just shut up scarecrow, you don't even have a brain! We're off to see the wizard."*

*"Yeah shut up scarecrow!"*

*"You shut up tin man, you don't have a heart!"*

*"All of you shut up, you're scaring lion!"*

*"Aw, I ain't a-scared, Dorothy."* Erin sometimes amused herself for hours before the faint crunch of car tires on the gravel driveway warned her that her daddy was home.

*"Princess!"* he calls as he enters. *"Where's my princess?"* Footsteps coming up the stairs, closet door opens as Erin tries to cover her naked self. But it seems like it gets harder and harder to cover herself all the time. *I must be growing,* she thinks.

Daddy sits down beside her on the mattress and puts his arms around her, chattering away as he strokes her bare skin. Chatter, chatter, stroke stroke, holding her close. After awhile he shudders and announces, *"Well princess, me thinks it's just about getting to be your bedtime. Off with you now."*

By the time Erin was in junior high, she knew what daddy was doing, and she wasn't happy. She was also the biggest girl in the school, and the staring, teasing, and insults were starting to really get to her. Then, to have to come home and be fondled against her will became too much for her to handle as well.

Enough was enough.

# Chapter 9

## Mommy and Daddy Take a Swim

One lovely summer evening, just as the sun was going down, Erin emerged from the closet while putting her clothes back on. Her father had descended the stairs before her and was seated at the breakfast bar in the kitchen, sipping on a beer.

"Feel like joining me in a swim daddy? It's such a beautiful, warm night. Please don't say no."

"Why princess, that's a capital idea. Race you!" challenged daddy, pleased as punch.

Benign smile from mom.

The two of them splashed each other, laughing uproariously, and raced each other from one end of the pool to the other. After a while, daddy really started to gasp pretty hard, and suggested that they take a breather, but Erin said no, they were just getting warmed up.

"Not me, princess. Your old dad's getting too old for this much exercise." Her father panted as he made it to the ladder at the side of the pool, thinking he would climb out.

But Erin had other ideas.

Quicker than anyone could imagine for one so big, she got in front of him, blocking his route to the ladder.

"Now princess, get out of my way. I'm ready to get out," he

ordered, treading water and panting.

"No daddy," she'd replied. "I don't want you to get out yet."

For the first time, he noticed the odd look in her eyes, and he tried harder to get around her, all semblance of merriment gone.

"Erin. I said get out of my way!" There was an edge of panic in his voice now, and he was starting to tire more and more. But Erin kept him treading water, always slipping in front of his escape route.

Then he had a brilliant idea. "Marjor . . . ugh . . . glug . . ."

Just as he raised his voice to call her mother, Marjorie, Erin dived onto his head with her full weight, and pushed him under the surface. She then, at the age of fifteen, weighed three hundred pounds, give or take, and out-weighed her father by a hundred and fifty.

He didn't have a chance.

He splashed and struggled and choked, fighting for his life with everything he had, but it was no use. He was no match for his giant princess. Erin deposited her huge bulk on top of him and floated, keeping him trapped under the surface until she could feel the life go out of him and his struggling cease. Then she maintained that position for another five minutes just to be sure.

When she was certain that he was dead, she clambered out of the pool and went running for the house yelling, "Mom, mom, there's been an accident. Daddy's hurt! Come outside! Hurry, hurry!"

Marjorie came flying out the back door, apron flapping, "Erin what's happened! Where's your father! What do you mea . . .!"

The words died in her throat as she reached the edge of the pool and a realization at the same time. "Erin quick . . . get him out of there . . . hurry!"

"You get him, mom!" and with a mighty push, Erin hurled her mother into the water and dove in right behind her. When Marjorie shot back up to the surface, spluttering and gagging, Erin pounced upon her.

Soon there were two lifeless bodies floating in that suburban backyard swimming pool, and Erin felt light as a feather for the first time in her life.

# Chapter 10

## A Bonding Experience

For a while Erin just stood at the edge of the swimming pool, staring in amazement at what she had done. Her heart was pounding in her chest, mostly from the physical exertion of drowning two full-grown people. Yet, as the shock began to wear off, Erin felt a bit of an adrenaline rush from the dawning realization that she was finally free.

As she stood by the pool watching her parents float slowly and silently in the slight current created by the water filter at the base of the pool, she had a detached, almost surreal feeling. It was if she was seeing the whole thing from a spectator's point of view, rather than as an active participant.

Suddenly they looked no different from the inflatable rubber crocodile or hippo that were stored in the basement, and she almost laughed out loud. But her odd fugue was broken abruptly when the sound of whispering intruded on her musings.

It came to the young murderess quick as a wink that the whole incident had been observed. She snapped her head around just in time to catch a glimpse of the twins ducking back underneath the overhanging branches of a huge willow tree that sheltered the front of their cottage.

"Hey you two, get back here!" hollered Erin as she took off in their direction. There was a frantic rustle of bushes and underbrush as the twins scrambled to reach the front door. They were just about to bang it shut when Erin reached out a hand to stop it in mid-slam, and entered the room. She halted in the doorway and stared in surprise. She had forgotten how long it had been since she was there last, forgetting for a second why she'd chased the twins home.

Everywhere she looked, there were paintings. Big and small, they covered almost every inch of wall and floor space, and they were good! Really good!

"Wow!" She exclaimed.

Meanwhile, Patrick and Sarah huddled together in one of the few spaces in the room not yet taken over by works of art, and they were shivering.

"We're s . . . sorry E-Erin. W . . . we didn't mean to s-spy on you! We won't . . . tell, honest!" the twins cried in almost perfect unison.

"What? Oh . . . Yeah Right." Captivated by the scene before her, she had almost forgotten that her siblings had just witnessed her killing their mother and father. *What kind of a person am I?*

"No . . . no don't be afraid! I don't know what came over me. I . . . I must have been in a trance or something!" answered Erin, a touch of panic starting to creep into her chest, her heart beating a little faster.

Then, gathering up his courage, Patrick stepped out from the corner and walked right up to Erin where she still stood in the doorway, (which she completely filled), and planted his feet almost defiantly. As the oldest, almost two and a half minutes older than Sarah, Patrick felt that as the man and his sister's protector, he better face the situation head on. Sarah's eyes shone with admiration at this show of bravery.

"We saw what you did Erin, although we didn't mean to. It was an accident. But if you're going to be mad at someone, take it out on me. Please leave Sarah out of it. I promise she won't tell a soul," her brother declared.

For the second time that strange day, Erin felt like laughing. But this time it was partly out of relief, and partly out of real amusement. In that moment, she suddenly regretted not ever making more of an effort to get to know Patrick and Sarah better. It dawned on her, looking down into her brother's earnest and serious face, that these were two people she would very much enjoy making acquaintances. And with that thought she did laugh.

Then, to her utter surprise, two more voices joined her own, in a chorus of giggles. The twins were laughing too! If the afternoon events seemed to Erin to be somewhat surreal before, they were now becoming just downright bizarre.

Feeling like Alice through the looking-glass, she half expected a rabbit to run by exclaiming on his lateness, but reality re-asserted itself quickly when Patrick, still hiccupping with remnants of laughter asked, "So, what are we going to do with the bodies?"

*The bodies. What are WE going to do with the bodies?* He had said *we*. Feeling stunned, Erin asked, "You mean you'll help me?"

"Of course we'll help you," Patrick asserted. "We didn't like them any more than you did." And, for the first time in fifteen years, Erin felt truly related to these two little people who lived in her yard and who looked so much like her with their shiny black hair and green eyes, but yet were so different.

In charge once again, and without missing a beat Erin said, "Well, I guess we get them out of the pool." And the three conspirators shared a chuckle.

# Chapter 11

## Just a Nice Little Cottage

An event experienced and shared, whether it be an especially joyous one, or a particularly traumatic or frightening one, tends to create a bond between the people involved, and the killing of Erin, Patrick, and Sarah's mother and father was a perfect example. Straight away, Erin was graciously invited in to share a bottle of wine while the siblings formulated a plan on what was to be done next.

As the trio sipped wine, talked, and got to know each other, Erin couldn't help but cast surreptitious glances at the myriad paintings that decorated the small home. The combined effect of that many colorful canvases in such a confined space was almost overwhelming for the senses.

But it wasn't just the numbers of artworks that fascinated Erin and kept drawing her eyes to them, but the sheer explosion of colors, the enthusiasm with which they were used, and most of all the subject matter. There were animals. Everywhere.

All kinds of animals, but mostly exotic and wild, untamed beasts of the forests and jungles of the world. One in particular that she couldn't seem to keep her eyes off of—almost the size of an entire wall—depicted an elephant herd.

The herd looked so real that she could almost hear the

trumpeting, as if the great beasts spoke to each other. Another favorite subject seemed to be carnivores with lions, tigers, and all the other great cats represented, as were the grazing animals. There were vast herds of Wildebeest, Zebra, and Caribou, as well as small family groups of Giraffe and Rhinoceros. There were Killer Whale pods and mammoth flocks of pink flamingos. The skill of the artist was astounding.

For just as Erin would turn from one painting to more closely examine another, she could swear that out of the corner of her peripheral vision she had just missed an ear twitching a fly away, or the faintest of movement as a baby antelope moved just that much closer to its mother. Erin had become so captivated by the sheer glory of her surroundings that she'd forgotten for a moment where she was, and why she was there. Then she heard a throat clearing, and her name.

"Ahem, Erin? Do you agree?"

"What? Oh I'm sorry," she apologized. "I didn't hear you. I was so caught up in your pictures. They're magnificent."

"Thank you," the twins replied simultaneously. "But don't you think we better get on with the matter at hand? It'll be dark soon, and with just the three of us, the job will take a while," added Patrick.

"Yes, of course you're right. Now where were we?" asked Erin, as she tore her attention away from the animals with a sigh and not a little regret.

Within half an hour, a plan was in place. They would freeze the bodies for now, buying themselves time to decide their ultimate fate. Fortunately, there was a huge old chest-style freezer in the basement, and every autumn dad would buy a side of beef and a whole pig, cut and wrapped, from the butcher. Because it was late summer, the freezer was almost empty now and would serve their purpose nicely. So, for the next fifteen minutes, the three lugged the remaining packages of meat from the basement to the kitchen refrigerator/freezer upstairs.

That was the easy part. Now they had to fish their parents out of the swimming pool and get them down to the basement.

At this point, Patrick displayed a talent for innovation that he never knew he had. Sending Sarah scurrying for the little red wagon they had played with as children, he retrieved a garden rake from the tool shed at the back of the house where daddy kept the lawnmower, hose, and other garden tools.

Then Erin dragged her parents to the side of the pool with very little effort, using the rake to catch onto their wet clothes. It was then just a matter of hoisting them one by one onto the little wagon and pulling it to the back door of the house. Luckily, the entrance to the basement was not far from the back door, and with a bit of huffing and puffing, the three of them were able to push, pull, and drag the bodies down the basement stairs and over to the freezer, into which they were unceremoniously dumped. The freezer wouldn't quite close, so it took another few minutes to stuff the arms and legs that were sticking out, down into the crevices around the bodies at decidedly unnatural angles.

With the cadavers safely disposed of for the time being, the twins said their goodnights and headed down the narrow path that led to their corner of the family property to settle in at home for the evening. It was only then that Erin began to realize how tired she was.

It had been an eventful day to say the least, and fatigue was starting to settle over her like a heavy cloak. She stood watching the retreating forms of her sister and brother, momentarily lost in thought, before turning in the direction of her own back door.

That night Erin's dreams were filled with animals—running, galloping, leaping, and pouncing animals. Dozens, hundreds, thousands of them, and in her dreams, she was one with them. In fact, she seemed to be in charge of them, the leader, the alpha animal, and they all demurred to her. There wasn't a language as such, but a cacophony of sound. A thunderous roaring, growling, trumpeting, and howling mass of sound. A wall of sound, feral and wild.

And she was part of it.

She understood, and made music of her own. Erin dreamed that she was a predator, a top-of-the-food-chain predator, and she liked it.

When the sun began to rise on her first day of true freedom, she reluctantly floated back up the nighttime dream tunnel into early morning consciousness and found herself wishing she could go back. But it doesn't work that way she knew, and so Erin sat up in bed.

Humming a few off-key bars of "Little Children" by Billy J. Kramer as she prepared a hearty breakfast of eggs, bacon, sausage, and potato pancakes, Erin decided she had better get started on a to-do list right away. There were a lot of details to be taken care of now and no time like the present to get started.

The first day was spent mostly rummaging through paperwork, bankbooks, bills, and household account-type stuff. She knew she would have to familiarize herself with running a home, and to be pretty crafty about it. Using her mother's voice, which was almost perfect in pitch and inflection from years of practicing, she called in sick to school for herself. Then she phoned her father's place of employment and made an excuse for him.

Since her mother had never had a job outside the home, Erin was glad that for her there was no one to call. The fact that she had no friends, was not a joiner, and didn't belong to any organized groups such as bridge clubs or P.T.A. was a bonus. As a matter of fact, now that she thought about it, Erin realized her mom was actually pretty antisocial. No ladies luncheons, no neighborhood coffee klatches, no gossiping over the back fence. *"Hmm. Well,"* she thought merrily to herself, *"just that much easier for me,"* and went on humming.

Creating her father's exit from society would be a bit more complicated, but not much. He had worked for the same small insurance company for many years, never really making much of a mark, not a standout employee by any means. The fact was that he didn't have to work at all, really.

Her grandfather, her father's father, had left him well-healed when he'd died many years ago, including leaving him the house they lived in, but he felt useful having somewhere to go every day. He had never gotten close to anyone in his office and hadn't made much of an impression on them. He was just always there, like a piece of nondescript furniture; you would notice if it suddenly wasn't there any more, but you wouldn't miss it.

So the next day Erin called in to her father's office again, using her mother's voice, and quit his job, saying the family was packing him up and moving him to Arizona for his health, as he was quite ill and the doctor had ordered it. By the way, could you mail any back pay or other papers to be signed please, and they would be forwarded. Thank you so much, and no that's very kind of you, but we'll be fine, much
obliged though.

There was barely a ripple around the office over this news, and the co-workers had always resented him somewhat anyway, being well-off and keeping a job that someone with a young family could have used, times being what they were and all. And so, Erin paid the bills (forging mom's signature), bought the groceries, and things ran smoothly.

At first.

Then one night Erin had the dream again. Only this time, she could swear she wasn't quite asleep yet when the sound of the animals started up. But that was ridiculous—absolutely. Of course she was asleep. Wasn't she? It was just that the dream was so *real*.

This time there was more than just sound; she could swear she could detect *smells* now too! Here was the gamey waft of a wild creature who had never been to a pet grooming parlor, and then there was definitely a sudden whiff of animal excrement. A childhood memory of a family trip to the zoo suddenly came to mind. Yes, she was absolutely, *positively* dreaming, but it seemed so real.

Every time Erin had the dream, it seemed another element was beginning to be added to it, and one day she thought that if she didn't talk to someone about it soon, she would bust. So the next morning after a particularly vivid nighttime adventure, she left the house via the back door and headed for the twins' cottage.

As always, when Erin took the little path leading to the cottage in the back corner of the property and caught the first glimpse of the dwelling almost completely hidden by foliage, she was touched by a feeling of going back in time. It had been there for as far back as she could remember, and now that she was becoming familiar with the place as never before, she began trying to recall just when it had come to be.

A snatch of conversation between her parents many years earlier came back to her, and as she lumbered forward she dug into her memory bank and tried to remember just what had been said that day.

*"Frank, I just can't believe we got such a bargain! And in New York too! Although it kind of makes me wonder why they would let such a marvelous artifact go for peanuts. Glad they did though, because it will fit perfectly in that back corner that I've never known what to do with. Don't you think?"* gushed Marjorie.

*"Well, it was a bargain all right, but it kind of gives me the willies,"* answered Frank.

A week later a big truck arrived to deliver the *artifact* that the twins called home.

*Hmmm* . . . mused Erin as she ascended the first of three small weather-beaten wooden steps that led up to the door. She raised her hand to knock just as she reached the third step. Standing beneath the whimsical gingerbread overhang, she froze with her hand in mid-air, surprised by odd sounds coming from within that didn't seem right—that sounded weird and out-of-place.

Curious, she lowered her hand and quietly put her ear to the door to listen. The strange sounds came again, and now she *really* had to see what was going on inside, and so she knocked. Still with her ear to the door, while waiting for someone to answer, Erin heard the sudden frantic and hurried shuffling of feet and urgent hushed voices.

And there was something else.

*Was that a growl? No, couldn't be, I'm hearing things. But wait! There it is again!* And not just a single growl, but a lot of them, and low-throated purring. *Purring?*

When no one came to the door, she rapped again, and this time it opened.

"Hi Erin. Come on in," invited Patrick.

"Patrick, what's going on? I just dropped in to talk to you and Sarah, and I heard these weird noises . . ."

"Weird noises? Well . . . um . . . uh . . . well . . ." stammered Patrick.

While Patrick fumbled with his suddenly non-existent powers of speech, and Sarah hid behind him saying nothing, Erin surveyed the room that was so familiar . . . until now. Something wasn't right.

*What is it? Wait a minute . . . the animals. They're different! They've moved. They have definitely moved. But that's impossible. These are paintings. They can't move. And how come the house looks so small from the outside, but so spacious on the inside?*

The place was bigger than it was the last time she visited and there was room to spare, even though today there were three people in it. Granted, two of them were little people, but Erin herself had been getting larger every day, and now weighed over four hundred and twenty-five pounds. Plus, whereas the twins had previously seemed to have all the room they needed for their sparse belongings . . . *but only just* . . . now they could furnish the space in grand style, including king-sized beds, and still have room to spare.

And that smell. It was familiar; it was the dream smell.

While the twins shuffled their feet and milled about the cavernous living room, not quite meeting her gaze, Erin took a better look at the many paintings that surrounded her.

The change was so obvious now that she really focused on each individual painting until a chill shinnied up her spine and she stifled a gasp. There . . . there was the female antelope that she had first seen on her first trip to the twin's cottage on that long-ago day when she had drowned her parents. A baby had been cuddled up to the mother then, but now it was not in sight. There was a forest of long twisted horn, and many animals in the herd, including young ones, but not *the* young one who had made an impression on her years before.

And the lion pride had shifted too. Whereas the group had been lounging in the intense African midday sun under some meager shade thrown by a stunted Savanna tree, now all but two females were on their feet. And a huge male was looking right at her! There was intelligence there, and something else. Recognition? No, it couldn't be. Then through her confusion and shock, Erin noticed the silence in the room. Slowly she turned around and saw the twins just standing and staring at her. For several seconds, no one spoke, until . . .

"Erin, have you had any dreams lately?" asked Sarah.

Now the big girl *did* gasp.

"How do you know I've been having dreams? And these animals, they're different! And how can this house be so big inside?" stammered Erin, now close to hysteria.

Patrick spoke up. "Magic."

It was too much. Erin felt the blood in her head siphon down and drain from her face, and the room began to spin.

"Quick Patrick, get a chair, she's going to faint!" ordered Sarah, as she ran for a glass of water and a cold wet cloth.

Patrick came to the rescue, for he knew there wasn't a chair strong enough in the house to hold up to Erin's weight if she fell onto it. As she swayed on her feet, he quickly and neatly inserted himself under her arm just in time for her to lean on while she got some balance back, and Sarah hopped up on a stool to apply the cold compress to her forehead.

In a few minutes, the twins were able to lead her to a fairly sturdy wooden kitchen bench, upon which she gingerly deposited her bulk. In another minute or so, some color began to return to her face, and she was able to speak, though her voice wavered a little.

"Wha . . . wha . . . at happened?"

"Sorry Erin, I guess it's all a little much at first," said Patrick.

"It's always been our little secret, but now I guess it's yours too Erin," confided Sarah gently. "This house is special."

Erin was still a trifle stunned but she began to feel her senses coming back, along with about a million questions.

"It all started when Sarah took up painting," began Patrick, "Of course that was quite a long time ago. You remember, you saw them for the first time when we helped you . . . uh . . . helped you . . . well, you know."

Erin flashed back to the day she had eliminated Frank and Marjorie. Nodding she said, "I remember."

Patrick continued. "We've always known our house was trying to speak to us, but when Sarah picked up her brushes and created the animals, they became the voice. They wanted to live, Erin; they wanted to live!"

Erin just stared at him, speechless, her lovely sea-green eyes wide and sparkling like brilliantly cut, glittering emeralds.

# Chapter 12

## Hester On Edge

The first of the disappearances barely made a four-line filler in the small weekly newspaper. The "Hester Hallmark" served the small community its share of local events, going-out-of-business and seasonal sales, and reports on the latest crimes committed in and around the county.

A huge pool of congealed, sticky blood was found one Monday morning by a group of school children taking a short cut through an alley behind Monroe Street, just past the dumpster used by Wing Fong's Chinese Smorgasbord. *"ALL YOU CAN EAT! $5.95!"*

The police were called, and an investigation was initiated. The cops easily identified the missing victim when they found the old moth-eaten fedora swimming in the gore.

Everyone in town knew that that particular weathered and beaten-up chapeau had always graced the head of one Hector Hornby like a crown made of lumpy oatmeal.

"Happy" to his friends, and "Horny Hec" ha ha to the local kids, Hector had made the Monroe Street alley his home for as long as anyone, even the old-timers, could remember.

Happy had spent the better part of those years viewing the world around him from the inside of a bottle of Wild Turkey.

During the good times that is. When times weren't so good, there was that old standby, aftershave. Ol' Hec' got along.

Of course, when the grisly discovery was made, no one was surprised, and people nodded knowingly to each other while pontificating on the fact it was bound to happen some day.

Naturally, the cops were perplexed by the absence of an actual body, until the coroner examined the bloody, shredded hat and declared that the victim had been carried away, and was most likely attacked by a hungry cougar come down from the hills during the night, judging by the tooth marks.

"Only one predator in these parts has teeth that big, and that's a mountain lion."

This announcement set off a flurry of activity by the good ol' boys and hunters of the town, worried about their families.

"Jeez if it's got the Goddamn balls to march bold as you bloody well please right into town and carry off a full grown man, just think what could happen to the wimmin n' kids! Saddle up fellas! Lock n' load!"

There was a full week of excitement and free flowing testosterone in the air, while the hordes of local heroes convoyed with their pickups and four-by-fours, gun racks weighted down with every piece of deadly artillery the good citizens owned.

A lot of wives were surprised with spontaneous bouts of love making by their husbands.

"And on a week night mind you, Shirley!"

But by the seventh day, no trace of a cougar or Hector was found, and everyone shook their heads and said how it must have been that rainfall late on the evening after the killing, and that the cat would be hell and gone back up in the high hills by now.

"Shame about Ol' Hec' though. So Charlie, up for a beer?"

"Hell yes!"

The excitement died down as quickly as it had begun, and "Happy" Hector Hornby ended up like meatloaf filler in the local rag. His cohorts spent a few nervous nights looking over their shoulders, but they moved en masse to a new alley behind Division Street. *"Time we moved on anyway,"* and without much ado, life returned to normal for the winos and hunters of the nice little town.

One night in a dream, Erin thought she heard a man scream, was almost certain of it, but dreams were funny that way and after all, it wasn't real was it? So what did it matter. *Still* . . . When a rummy disappears and seems to have met with foul play, somehow it doesn't strike people as all that tragic.

\*\*\*

But it's a completely different story when it happens to a young person from a good home, and that's just what happened a few weeks later when Billy Tucker one eerie, shadowy autumn evening, disappeared without a trace while walking his dog, Buddy.

Billy and his best friend, a black Labrador retriever, were out for an after dinner constitutional. Billy's dad had presented a little six-week old black bundle of energy to him on his fifth birthday, and it was love at first sight. Since that day five and a half years earlier the two had been inseparable. Buddy considered it his personal mission in life to watch over and protect Billy from any and all threats no matter how small, be it a bumblebee or Aunt Mary's cat, "Dody." When Buddy was with him, Billy felt completely safe and indestructible.

It was October, and Halloween was fast approaching. On the last night of Buddy and Billy's lives it got dark early, which was normal for October, but the moon was in the final phase for its cycle. It was even darker than usual with no lunar glow to light their way, and the night had a spooky, shadowy quality to it as they made their usual nightly excursion across the little memorial park that evening. The kind of night that could make a not-quite-a-teenager-but-not-a-baby-either boy believe that there really *was* a bogey-man. Or zombies. Or werewolves.

Not even the faintest breath of wind ruffled the leaves that were left clinging to the black, spiny branches on the old oak trees over their heads, like the spindly grasping arms of the undead, waiting to snatch him and Buddy up, and drag them down into an open grave in Shady Hills Cemetery.

Billy stopped for a minute to switch the handle of Buddy's leash from his right hand to his left, so he could adjust the collar of his gray fleece sweatshirt with the little zipper under the chin and the New York Rangers logo on the front.

With a small shiver, he pulled it closer around his cheeks and almost right up to his nose. Buddy stopped too, and sat very close to Billy, leaning against his left leg as if loath to separate from his friend. As Billy fiddled with his collar, he looked down at his dog and realized that even in the hushed quiet of the park, he hadn't heard the familiar clicking of Buddy's toenails on the brick pathway.

Buddy was tiptoeing.

Now they were halfway across the park, and a funny, tingly feeling started to creep over him. Normally the boy knew this small oasis of grass and trees, benches and statues, in the center of town like the back of his hand, but tonight something was different. Billy could see that Buddy felt it too. Usually bouncy and inquisitive, the glossy black canine stayed very close, almost huddling against Billy.

Then Billy slowly lowered his arms and rested his left hand on Buddy's head for reassurance, scanning the ominous shadows of the park, swiveling his head around. Then as one, by unspoken agreement, Billy and Buddy arranged themselves back to back, on high alert, listening for the smallest sound out of place, the tiniest rustle that didn't fit.

The hairs on the back of Billy's neck were now standing on end, while Buddy's ears went back and he began a low growling deep in his chest. When Billy looked down, the dog's teeth were bared, and that's when he really got scared. Buddy's cherished protection had never really been put to the test, and they both knew that whenever the dog went into bodyguard mode, it had been in fun.

Billy had never seen his pal behave like this before.

It felt like the two were connected by an electric current, eerily aware of the menace suddenly hanging thick in the air all around them.

That's when they heard it. The ear-splitting, heart-stopping avalanche of sound bearing down on them like a freight train out of control, or a tornado touched down out of nowhere. It was the sound of a hundred wild creatures all roaring and screaming at once, either in rage or terror, or both. Billy's bladder let go as his terrified screams and Buddy's mad growling and barking melded with the other.

The ghastly shrieks of boy and dog were abruptly cut short by something unseen and savage. A shower of sparks and an acrid whiff of smoke would have been detected by anyone nearby who happened to be in the vicinity, but no one was.

All that was found the next morning when the search got underway was Buddy's red leather collar and little tin name plate attached with rivets:

BUDDY TUCKER, 237 Morninglory Dr.

Hester, N.Y. 555-8226

With the leash still hooked to it, the thick leather collar was discovered crusted with dried blood and bitten right in half. Again, as was the case with old Hector, the search and investigation produced no clues or evidence, and the citizenry became edgy and frightened. The police were stumped and called in animal experts, who concurred with the theory that a predator of the four-legged variety had definitely made off with the unfortunate victims, but without paw prints or hair, they couldn't be of much help either.

So people began staying indoors at night except when absolutely necessary, and didn't go out alone. Since there were no bodies, a memorial service was held for the boy, Buddy's leash gained a place of honor on the wall in Billy's perfectly preserved upstairs bedroom, and Mrs. Tucker cried for weeks.

# Chapter 13

## Digits in Love

Erin was roused from her nap and her sleepy dream memory of the first time she had seen Sarah's paintings, before she had ever met Mickey, or Isolde, or Beau, when she realized that Beau was standing in her bedroom doorway speaking to her.

"What was that Beau?" she asked as she shook her black curls and dragged herself back to the present.

"I said, we emptied the freezer boss. Now do you need me for anything else before I go and help the twins feed the animals?"

"No thank you, Beau. But could you please ask Isolde to come speak to me on your way through the kitchen?"

"Sure Boss."

With that, Beau turned and left, hurrying to his task. When he reached the kitchen, he found Mickey there as usual, keeping Isolde company while she prepared Erin's dinner. Erin ate several times a day, and Isolde was kept busy at the stove much of the time. And since Isolde spent a good portion of her time in the kitchen, so did Mickey.

She and Mickey always ate separately from the others, with Isolde preparing meals just for the two of them. Since Erin ate in her bedroom, their meals taken at the kitchen table were not an issue.

And Beau had his own system.

From day one, upon discovering that unused formal dining room with the large, oval mahogany table, and seating for eight, on delicate Queen Anne chairs, (another auction acquisition by Erin's dead parents), he'd laid claim to the room.

Alone he sat at the head of the table, and insisted on being served out of antique silver and china. This arrangement appealed to his delusions of grandeur, and he ate his meals in high style, like a little king on his throne.

Although she didn't complain about the meals she made for Erin and Beau, considering what they were very often comprised of, Isolde and Mickey could never bring themselves to partake in what they thought of as the *"nastiness."*

When cooking for the family, Isolde found a way to distance herself from the ingredients, and concentrated on the art and skill of food preparation and presentation. In this way, she was able to come to terms with her queasiness. And having Mickey by her side helped a lot, because when Mickey was happy, she was happy, and pleasing Erin made him happy.

For Isolde and Mickey were in love.

It had happened slowly, developing over time, starting with their friendship. At first Mickey was fond of Isolde with her sunny disposition and sense of humor, and felt very protective and brotherly towards her. Isolde admired Mickey's sense of responsibility and personal dignity, which she knew was very important to him. She also appreciated the fact that he disliked Beau as much as she did.

But both were glad that Beau was what he was, because the things he had to do for Erin definitely didn't appeal to them, and they were relieved every time Erin had a "guest," that their roles were not as drastic. In time, fondness grew into love, and they spent most of their time together.

"Isolde, Erin wants you!" bellowed Beau, as he burst into the room. Beau never simply entered a room, like other people. He loved to make everyone jump. He got a huge charge out of startling, or even scaring people. *Especially* scaring people.

"Okay, I'll be right there."

# Chapter 14

## Rock's Big Date

Across town, Rock was getting ready for his big date with Erin. His hands were trembling with excited anticipation as he got dressed, and he had to stop what he was doing and force himself to calm down.

He just knew Erin was going to be drop-dead gorgeous.

No one could have a voice like that, a voice that literally *dripped* sex and not be magnificent. As he put the finishing touches on his toilette, he fantasized a little about what they would do when they finally met and were free to revel in each other's bodies to their hearts content. As he turned to survey the final product in the freestanding oak-framed oval mirror that stood in the corner of his and Karen's bedroom, he saw (and felt) that he was already achieving a major erection at the thought of what lay ahead.

*Oh God, this is gonna be good! Can't wait, can't wait, can't wait!*

Then Rock forced himself to come back to earth a little. *Gotta be smart. If Karen ever found out! But she won't, she won't. I'll be home by eleven, alibi firmly in place. Yeah. Park the car a few blocks away, just to be on the safe side. Okay, one last mirror check, and here I go! Oh, boy!*

\*\*\*

It was fully dark when a nervous Rock climbed the steps leading up to the large shadowed front porch and pressed the doorbell of Erin's home, just as she had asked. His heart was hammering in his chest as the big wooden door slowly opened and . . .

"Hello?" The large cheesy grin he had adopted for his first impression faded and became quizzical when it seemed that the door had opened by itself. *There's no one here!* And then . . .

"Hi, you must be Rock. Erin's expecting you. Please come in." And Rock looked down in the direction from which the voice was coming.

There was Mickey, smiling a welcome, and gesturing for Rock to follow. *What is this?* he wondered, perplexed.

He was shaken by this somewhat bizarre turn of events, but made an effort to recover, unwilling to give up his fantasy. So he followed Mickey. With Mickey leading the way, they came to a closed door, whereupon the little butler-for-a-day gave two soft raps.

"Yes?"

Rock's equilibrium was instantly restored when he heard Erin's dusky voice issuing enticingly from behind the bedroom door. *Thank God!*

"Your guest has arrived, miss!" announced Mickey as imperiously as he had done so many times before.

"Show him in please, Mickey!"

"Yes, Miss!"

The last thing that Rock saw before he died was not the sexy voluptuous sex-creature that had dwelled in his imagination, but a veritable mountain—a mountain *range* of flesh.

The blow was swift, sure, and powerful, and Rock was dead before he even crumpled to the floor, like a worn out paper machè streamer after the parade has passed.

On a stepping stool, wooden club in hand, Beau grinned. Then he and Erin locked eyes, and together they went into gales of laughter. Fits of mirth. It never failed. How she loved the way their faces changed at the first sight of her in her king-sized bed, for she was huge . . . not just huge . . . she was *massive*. So massive that she had been unable to leave her bedroom for the past two years. So enormous that she couldn't walk, or make her way to the bathroom. So incredibly huge that the legs on her bed had had to be removed long ago, and the box spring too. The rolls of fat on her body, and soft, stacked layers of chins gave the impression that her face was floating in a sea of flesh-colored bread dough, a tiny little face just floating there.

The monstrous great rolls sprouted two plump, pretty hands covered with jeweled rings, and two chubby bare feet poked out of ankles twelve inches across, with deep, deep creases. They looked like someone had stuck them onto the wrong body by mistake. Her breasts were two great squishy pillows that spilled off to either side, and roiled like waves on the ocean when she moved even a little bit. Right now they were positively Tsunami-like as Erin laughed her contempt. *The stupid, lusting bastards,* she thought to herself. *"It serves them right."*

"Alright, get him out of my sight," Erin commanded when at last she was able to speak.

"Yes, boss."

So Mickey and Beau each grabbed a foot of the would-be lothario. With some measure of grunting and groaning, they each grabbed a corner of the thick blue plastic tarp upon which Rock landed, placed there earlier by Beau so as not to mess up Erin's pink shag carpeting. A slimy, thick river of blood was draining from the jagged hole in Rock's skull after Beau had smashed it in with his club, and when they were sure the mess was contained, they backed out with their dead cargo through the bedroom door.

The same door beyond which, only minutes before, Erin's victim had mistakenly believed lay a garden of earthly delights.

# Chapter 15

## You Are What You Eat

The door closed behind Mickey and Beau as they laboriously dragged Rock from the bedroom, and Erin's smile faded as she caught sight of her morbidly obese body, and her expression grew somber with the onset of bad memories that came to her unbidden.

Starting out in life as a plump and pretty baby, Erin soon grew into a chubby toddler. By the age of five, when she began her first year of school, her weight had ballooned to almost one hundred pounds.

From day one, because of the teasing of her classmates, the little girl had become an outsider. At first, more often than not, she would arrive home from school in tears. Her mother would soothe and comfort her with treats fresh from the oven, only serving to make her fatter.

Her obesity increased with the passing years, until the momentous day, at the age of fifteen, when she achieved her emancipation by drowning her parents in the family swimming pool.

After that incident, Erin began to pack on the pounds at an astounding rate. Even though she truly was a voracious eater, the bulk seemed to accumulate much too quickly, and her food intake, though large, still didn't account for the unnatural acceleration. By the time Erin was sixteen, she had exploded to an incredible four hundred pounds.

Astonishingly though, size was not an issue to Erin until the day came when she could no longer fit through the front door of Patrick and Sarah's cottage. She was twenty years old, weighed five hundred plus pounds, and was completely devastated.

Her favorite diversion—and one she looked forward to every day—had now been taken from her. Now she could not watch or help the twins feed the animals.

Since the day she had discovered the secret and almost fainted from shock in the small house, her life had changed. When her brother and sister had admitted that the meat they were "butchering" was actually the frozen bodies of Frank and Marjorie, existence suddenly became much more interesting. Especially when they demonstrated the reason:

She stared as the little red wagon was loaded down with chunks of frozen flesh and dragged into the living room by its long black handle. There was an audible chorus of lip-smacking, low growling, and throaty grumbling as the meat mountain approached the first of the paintings. Now she saw the massive male lion that had frightened her the first time, years earlier, appearing to be moving forward, looking right at her.

Only now its eyes were fastened on the load of food, and it was drooling open-mouthed, revealing the largest and scariest fangs she had ever seen. Fanned out around and behind the big male were the rest of the lion pride. An assortment of females and cubs, giving their leader first eating privileges, but staying close enough so as not to be left out when their turn came to eat.

The most startling part came when Patrick picked up a chunk of meat and tossed it right at the painting of the lions. Erin had gaped with wonder when the morsel being tossed sailed right *into* the canvas, landing at the front paws of the huge carnivore who pounced on it and began ravenously devouring it.

Tearing her eyes away from this incredible scene before her, and in wide-eyed disbelief, Erin looked around and became aware of the sights and sounds all around her. The room was alive with movement and sound. Behind and all around the lion pride were the endless, waving grasses of the African Serengeti, stretching as far as the eye could see. There was much rustling and scratching, as the predators moved forward, and the grazers retreated a safe distance into the background, within their own frames.

Here was a herd of elephants, moving off in a family group, their ears flapping and trunks swinging from side to side, as they followed a massive bull farther back into the scrub and bush land of the plains where they dwelled.

A sudden flash of color caught Erin by surprise as a huge Bengal tiger, with black and orange stripes, bounded into the foreground of a painting of an Indian rain forest, lured by the scent of food. *"Overwhelming"* would have been the understatement of the century to describe the tableaux taking place in the magic house.

Hippos wallowing in mud-holes, zebras jockeying for position at a watering spot, and a lone cheetah bounding straight out of the vast green grasses of the savanna towards the meat being thrown to the left, right and center, and right into the paintings to feed the wild creatures that Sarah had created.

Erin was speechless with awe. She thought she had never witnessed anything so beautiful in her life, and she now knew what her dreams meant.

The animals were hunting.

Sarah had, whether on purpose or not, designed it so that the predators could not hunt within the confines of their own frames. The carnivores and herbivores were separated, and so, not sated by the food the twins were able to provide during the day. The meat-eaters had found a way to leave their canvases at night to search for prey, although at first it was only an occasional thing—a few chickens missing here, a pig or two there—and was fairly unremarkable. But, as time went on, and Sarah's animals increased in number, a new delicacy was added to their menu.

Erin watched, fascinated, while the magnificent beasts of the veldt, savanna, jungle, and plain gorged themselves, and she understood. She knew what the taste in her mouth was on the mornings after a nightly sojourn, running with the pride. And she also knew that she was the leader.

By day, she too, just like the animals, ate to satiation, enjoying the delicious meals that Isolde made for her. And by night, she willed herself to sleep, knowing that the big male lion would come for her in a dream and lead her spirit out of its suffocating prison of flesh. Together they led hunting parties, out of their picture frames, and into the night, in search of more.

So people disappeared. They were killed on the spot, torn apart, and carried by the pack, back to the incredible gallery in the little house behind Erin's home. The bodies and body parts that were clenched in the jaws of dozens of wild beasts entered the paintings, where they could be eaten undisturbed, without fear of detection or interference. After a feast, only bones and rags were left, and these were easily hidden in the tall grasses, shrubs, and mud holes of the gallery. And so no bodies were ever left for the police to find, or citizens to stumble over. Only pools of blood, and question marks remained. The animals must eat.

When Erin ran with the big cats, she felt truly free, and was one of them. The big male lion in particular, seemed somehow familiar, and in time she began receiving messages from him—feelings. Many of the mental impressions at first were all jumbled up, and came at her, bombarded her, all at once, so that at first it was difficult to decipher their meanings. As she and her friends gamboled and galloped through deserted city streets, down dark odorous alleys, and across small wooded parks, violent emotions washed over her psyche. Erin wanted to understand what they meant, and felt that she was *supposed* to understand.

Sometimes there was an overwhelming sensation of stark Terror, and fear of the unknown, combined with feelings of confusion so profound that she felt almost crazed. And other times there was the rage. An anger so full and rich that it seemed her very soul would be consumed by it. Often, after the rage, there was the descent into despair, a black pit so debilitating that it made her want to lay down and die. And layered over all of these painfully intense, and heart-wrenching emotions was the utter feeling of powerlessness, of freedom lost. Of free will stolen. And so she ran, wild and unfettered through the night with her own kind, the way it was supposed to be. The way nature had designed it to be.

Erin delighted in the closeness and camaraderie of the pride. The oneness and the total acceptance. She reveled in the feeling of belonging, of knowing what she was and where she belonged. There was unparalleled joy in the way they functioned as if with a single mind. No words had to be spoken, no dissension or argument; there was just a wonderful wordless communication.

Sometimes after a successful night of hunting, the predators came boiling home in a tremendously good mood.

Like the night that seventeen-year-old Angela Neary and her boyfriend, the love of her life, Marky Barton, decided that they were sick of staying home under the watchful eye of their parents.

Marky was a star linebacker on their high school football team, and had been a member of the ROTC for two years. He was big for eighteen years, six-foot-two and almost two hundred pounds.

On the night Angela and Mark broke curfew, the moon was full and creamy and beautiful. And Mark thought that if he didn't get some soon, he would go out of his mind, so he convinced Angela to sneak out of the house to go parking up on the local lover's lane, Beacon View Ridge. *"The Ridge,"* as the locals referred to it, was a promontory at the highest point of an escarpment that ran along one side of the town of Hester, while the picturesque Hester River bordered the other side, running almost its entire length. Eventually it emptied itself into the Atlantic Ocean after passing through myriad small towns just like Hester along the way.

Angela had misgivings about breaking the curfew set by the local police until the killer or killers were caught, but she loved Marky, and was planning to marry him one day. And it was such a heavenly evening . . . Besides, Angela believed that her hero was so big and strong that he could, and would defend her against any attacker, man or beast.

And so she agreed to go.

Just to be on the safe side, Marky brought along his dad's hunting rifle, a big old, over-and-under shotgun which he had been taught to use when he was twelve years old, on his first foray into the high hills with his father, although he had never actually shot anything more threatening than a row of Budweiser beer cans off of a fallen log.

So, equipped with the gun, a bushel of raging hormones, and

the firm belief of the young in their immortality, the two teen-aged lovers snuck out of their comfortable suburban homes, and set out for their trysting place.

When they arrived on top of the ridge overlooking the pretty little town, Marky parked his eight-year-old rag-top jeep under the full, spreading branches of an old maple tree that had held its vigil as guardian of Hester since before his great-grandfather's day.

As the engine died and night settled around them like a velvety blanket, Angela felt that she was the luckiest girl in the world as she edged over to Marky's side of the jeep and snuggled up against him. After tuning in the radio to their favorite rock and roll station, and turning the volume down low, the teenagers admired the extraordinary moon that was filling the sky with a filmy glow meant just for them. Adding to the magic of the night was the sound of thousands of crickets chirping their joy at being alive on such a beautiful evening.

The sound added to the sexual electricity generated in the front seat by the clandestine nature of the date, and the feeling of danger, of tempting fate. Then, as Marky's big hand crept slowly around Angela's shoulder and slid gently down to caress a breast that was anxiously anticipating it, they began to kiss in earnest.

Within minutes, the outside world disappeared. All that existed for Angela and Mark were tongues tasting and probing, and hands fumbling and feeling and fondling. The windows steamed up with hot breath expelled, faster and shallower by the minute, while Angela's bra released her breasts, which now seemed too large for it as they swelled with desire as Marky undid the clasp. And Marky felt his whole being centered now on his crotch, where Angela's small, knowing hands had lowered the zipper of his Levi's. Now she was massaging and kneading his penis which felt red hot and ready to explode, so exquisite was his need.

They never saw a thing.

In the fervor of their passion, the young lovers didn't notice that the crickets had stopped their singing, and that a moving, shifting shadow had blotted out the moon. What they heard was a scream of rage to rival any that demons of hell could produce, and the violent ripping, tearing sound of the canvas roof over their heads being laid open to reveal the stars above. Daddy's gun never got off the back seat as torrents—geysers—of blood sprayed and splashed the interior of Marky's pride and joy.

As one, the teenagers were torn from their seats and dragged off into the warm autumn night, never to be seen again.

Angela's bra was found the next day, drenched in blood, in a rut made by dozens of tire tracks, ten feet from the grisly death car.

# Chapter 16

## Rudy Makes a Ring

Erin awoke feeling wonderful. She also had to pee.

"Isolde! Mickey!" called Erin.

Isolde and Mickey entered Erin's bedroom as they did every morning. It was their responsibility to help her perform her morning ablutions, as well as every other personal function that she needed to perform. The two digits were devoted and loving. They owed everything to Erin, including living in the first real home either one had ever known. Plus, if it hadn't been for Erin, they would never have met each other, would never have known what it was like to be in love. And so they tended to her every need selflessly and lovingly. And sometimes it hadn't been easy.

Like the first time Mickey had brought a wrapped roast up from the freezer for Erin's dinner, and Isolde saw that it was like no other meat she had prepared before. At first she had gone into immediate denial, but finally she had a quiet talk with Mickey, who reminded her of the great debt owed to Erin, and she'd succumbed. She'd even decided to make the best of it, and came up with even more exotic and delicious meals than ever before.

Isolde could do wonders with spices.

After the bedpan was removed, and her sponge bath was completed, Erin settled back against her many pillows in the big king-sized bed, and waited for the first call of the day from one of her numerous clients. She felt extraordinarily good this morning, and hoped it would be one of her favorites.

It was.

"Good morning my charm."

"Rudy! How are you this morning my darling?" bubbled Erin.

"I awoke with you on my mind, Liebchen! And little Rudy was standing straight up as I felt your lips on him, and your delicate little tongue licking at him," urged Rudy in his slight old world accent.

"Mmmm . . . how delicious you taste today, my sweet Rudy, and how hard you are! Yum . . ." Erin made licking and sucking noises on the telephone while Rudy's breathing accelerated and grew harsh.

In a few minutes, as always, the sound of Erin tasting, slurping, and moaning brought Rudy to a wrenching climax, and then ended in a shuddering groaning sigh. She gave him time to enjoy himself, and waited for him to speak first.

"Ah you are the best Liebchen. The very best. Now what can I do for you?"

Rudy was a jeweler. Over the years he had showed his gratitude for her services by creating the most magnificent and ostentatious pieces of jewelry that Erin had ever seen. Erin kept a post office box in town, under an assumed name just for deliveries from Rudy, and this morning she was ready for him.

"Rudy darling, I want a ring. But this one must be special. It must be the most spectacular lion's head ever created, with diamonds in the eyes and a ruby for the mouth. It must be splendid and ferocious. Can you do it for me darling?" cooed Erin.

"Done my little ivy!" promised Rudy. "You will hear when it is ready!" And with that Rudy said good-bye.

# Chapter 17

## Memories of Pain

On the nights after a good kill in town, the carnivores in Patrick and Sarah's works of art were content to lounge and munch in their frames for a while.

And, at those times when Erin had had a "date," and the twins had filled the freezer to capacity, the grazers in the collection took their turn. En masse, and in great noisy undulating herds, they would leap from their plains and grasslands under the cover of night, and roam the countryside.

There were elephants of every size, giraffes as tall as houses, and beautiful striped zebras. Gazelles leaped and gamboled together, while buffalo and wildebeest cut a swath half a mile wide. Snakes of every description slithered hither and yon, to return at dawn, tired and happy with the night's ramblings.

Although the animals remained unseen to the human eye, the obvious damage to the crops of surrounding farmlands was perplexing and frightening to the farmers who awoke to find the trampled fruits of their labors.

And always there was the lingering scent of something burning, although evidence of a fire was never found.

On these nights, hippos splashed and played in the Hester River, alongside other aquatic creatures normally found in salt water. There were leaping, frolicking porpoises, and graceful, massive white beluga whales.

The town was haunted.

It is believed by many that objects, places, and all manner of things can retain a "trace memory" of the beings which once inhabited or used them. And such was the case in Hester, New York.

When Erin's parents attended a long-ago auction while on a vacation in New York City, they had unknowingly acquired an object possessed by just such a "memory."

The twins home, the quaint little cottage behind the house in which Erin and the digits now lived had once been a "circus wagon." Or, more accurately, a "menagerie" wagon. If Erin had ever thought to pull back the high, thick overgrown foliage which hid the bottom half of the house, she would have seen wheels. Big, wooden wheels—two short ones in the front, and two large, higher ones at the back. Halfway through the last century, the wagon had been part of the traveling Circus and Menagerie owned by Phineas Taylor Barnum. The large, colorful procession had criss-crossed the country and carried many species of wild animals to put on display in the small towns and big cities along the way.

In those days, the unfortunate creatures were rounded up in the countries of their origin, and stuffed into cages, which were then loaded onto large ships bound for North America. At the time, most people had never heard of, let alone seen with their own eyes, the varied and spectacular kinds of wild creatures with which they shared this earth.

The captives were dragged from their families, transported to a far away, foreign place, and placed on display as "curiosities." They endured much pain, fear, abuse, neglect, and loneliness. And when they died, because P. T. didn't believe they had feelings or souls, they were simply replaced because they were considered "expendable."

And so it was the souls of the tortured and displaced wild creatures that spoke to Sarah and Patrick in their small "home," begging to be released from their pain and their bondage.

And the twins, knowing what they needed and themselves

understanding what it meant to be strangers, misunderstood and isolated, couldn't help but respond and bring them back to life—to the life from which they had been so cruelly kidnapped. Now they were back in the environments that they loved, and where they belonged—environments they would never again know in life, but had been returned to after death by Sarah's brushes.

The collective spirit of the beasts recognized early on that Erin was the leader in their new "territory" and, as such, she was allowed to join them on their sojourns into the night.

It was after her first "hunt" that Erin fully came to realize the responsibility that she and her family—the five digits—had toward their amazing charges. The need for food grew larger all the time, as the numbers grew with the normal breeding that animals do.

And something else. Upon waking on the morning following her initial dream hunt, Erin also acquired a taste for flesh—human flesh.

Although the bears, lions, leopards, and all the others were invisible to the naked eye, they could sometimes be heard, especially during an attack and kill, and usually the prey were the only ones to hear.

But, not always.

# Chapter 18

## Mrs. Stringer Meets Her Neighbor

Mrs. Stringer lived next door to Erin, a full driveway away, behind the dense seven-foot tall cedar hedge that separated their properties. But, on certain evenings when there was no wind and she was preparing for bed, Mrs. Stringer thought that she heard something. Just sometimes, after the television was turned off for the night, and she checked the back door to make sure it was locked, she would sometimes catch the faintest of sounds—animal sounds. Once she could swear a bear, or something huge, roared in triumph. She'd recognized the roar because two weeks earlier she had seen an episode of *National Geographic* about grizzly bears, and the noise from next door was eerily similar. But she shook her head and put it down to old age playing tricks on her imagination.

Another time, a trumpeting elephant had startled her into dropping the sweater she was knitting for the church bazaar rummage sale in November, and this time she hadn't been so quick to blame her age. *"They must have the T.V. on too loud over there,"* thought the lady to herself. So picking up her fallen knitting, she moved to another room, the hair standing up on her bony arms.

It wasn't until the morning that she couldn't find her beloved calico cat, Susie, that Mrs. Stringer began to get really creeped out.

After walking the entire outside circumference of the house in her robe and slippers, calling Susie's name over and over, and shaking a box of kitty treats that the elderly lady knew something wasn't right, she realized just how much of an understatement this actually was when she discovered poor Susie's partially devoured remains beside the back step that led to the mud porch, and was almost (but not quite) hidden under a large rhododendron bush.

After vomiting up her morning tea and scones into the bushes, Mrs. Stringer got an old towel from the laundry room. While trying not to look, she wrapped up what was left of Susie in it, and headed for the bus stop with her purse.

"Doc, what happened to my Susie?" Asked Mrs. Stringer, as tears edged down along the creases in her wrinkled cheeks, like little tributaries searching for the big river.

"Well Violet," began old Doc Blumberg carefully, "I haven't seen anything like this since medical school" (a long, long, time ago) "and of course I'm not a Veterinarian, but if I didn't know better, I'd say Susie's been swallowed by some kind of snake, and regurgitated. Big one too, looks like."

"A snake! What . . . !?" With that, Mrs. Stringer swayed on her feet, her eyes started rolling back in her head, and Doc Blumberg caught her just before she hit the floor, unconscious and as boneless as a jellyfish.

From that day on, Mrs. Stringer became what her long-departed husband Herb had hated most. A snoop.

With Susie gone, and her knitting forgotten, Violet pictured herself as Miss Marple and set out to get to the bottom of things.

*"There's something weird going on over there, and I'm going to find out just what!"* she thought to herself. *"My poor, poor Susie."*

Over the years the old woman had never given much thought to the neighbors to her left, since they had always been unsociable, and kept to themselves.

"And that big girl. What a lump," the old lady had grumbled to herself on more than one occasion.

But now, come to think about it, she hadn't seen her in a long time, and her curiosity was piqued. So night after night she sat up and listened. She heard different things at different times.

One night the cawing of wild birds, like parrots. Another, the howling of wolves, and still another sound like hyenas laughing. Eventually, Mrs. Stringer took to peering through the hedge. It was at least two feet thick, and so dense that barely a crack of daylight could be seen through it at any given point, but she would inch her way along, careful to be oh so quiet and not to make a sound, until . . .

"Peek-a-boo!"

"Eeek!" Mrs. Stringer was so surprised that she almost had a stroke right on the spot.

It was Beau peering back at her through his side of the hedge, and just about eye-to-eye since Violet had bent over double while she had crept along.

And he was grinning his usual arrogant grin.

"Why howdy there neighbor! Thought there was somebody looking at me! Caught sight of that pretty purple dress you have on through the leaves, and took myself a closer look! Sure enough, here you are! Lose something?"

"Why . . . why . . . y-yes . . . I . . . I . . . um . . . dropped an earring yesterday while hanging out the wash, a-and . . . well, that's what I was searching for just now . . ." replied the goggle-eyed Mrs. Stringer, as she started to straighten up and back away. *"What a strange little person,"* she thought to herself. Aloud she apologized, "I'm sorry if I disturbed you."

And with that, the surprised old lady turned and fled to the sound of Beau's hearty laughter.

That night, Violet was much too tightly strung to sleep—like a guitar string ready to snap—and she knew she would have a difficult time of it without a little help. So when the light began to fade from the sky, and dusk drifted down upon her house like a fine layer of gray ash, Mrs. Stringer changed into her ankle-length purple nightgown, topped off with her oldest, most comfortable dressing gown. She arranged herself in her favorite overstuffed armchair with a glass of sherry and a good book.

A couple of hours later the empty glass dangled from her hand

and the book lay open on her lap while she snored quietly.

*CRASH!* The sleeping old lady was jolted awake and half out of her skin by the sound that erupted from behind the swinging kitchen door. Sherry glass and book were thrown to the floor as she leaped out of her armchair.

*Oh my Lord, no! There's someone in the house! Please God, no! Cookie jar . . . that was the cookie jar! Hide . . . hide!"* Violet was so scared that her mind was skittering to and fro, searching for sense, trying to *make* sense.

Then she heard the *other* sounds.

First a heavy *thump!* as if someone, or some*thing* had jumped down from the counter in the kitchen and onto the broken shards of the ceramic cookie jar. Then there was a slow rhythmic hissing like steam being released from a teakettle a little at a time. And finally, along with the hissing, came the dry sand-papery whoosh-whoosh-whoosh, as if something heavy were being dragged slowly across the floor of the kitchen and was heading for the darkened living room where she stood quaking in terror.

Then the little voice of reason—what modicum of reason still remained in the mind of Mrs. Stringer—screamed *RUN!* And she did. Unfortunately, almost blind in the darkened room, she ran *smack* right into her overstuffed chair and almost lost her balance just getting a hand-hold on the upholstery when she was halfway to the floor, tearing two fingernails down to the quick. The hissing and whooshing sounded like it was getting closer, and whatever was bearing down on her and coming through the hinged, wooden swinging door that separated the kitchen from the living-room, would be on her any minute.

*"Dear God, no!"*

Finally, a toehold and a mighty push off the arm of the chair and she was in motion! With three locks on the front door, including a dead-bolt, Violet knew she'd never get out of the front door in time, so she bolted for the staircase.

There were only two telephones in Violet's home—one in the kitchen, from which she was now cut off, and a second one in her bedroom.

It was her only hope.

She made a crab-like, decidedly ungraceful scramble up the stairs—and would have made it too, but for the arthritis in her knees that prevented her from getting her right foot quite high enough to clear the first step. *Smash!*

Her toe caught the riser on the stair and down she went, face first. The wind was knocked out of Violet and she lay there for a second, her fragile heart pounding like a jackhammer. But only for a second, just barely long enough to grab a ragged breath, because the crack in the swinging door was opening steadily wider now, and the menacing hissing sound was louder, almost right behind her. *Please, no.*

Sobbing and babbling now in abject horror, and unmindful anymore of her torn, bleeding fingernails, with a superhuman strength she didn't know that she possessed, Violet made a frantic lunge for the second step.

The thing was right behind her now, and something whip-like and scratchy grazed her heel as she clambered spider- fashion up the stairs.

Yet, as heroic and impressive as the effort was, Mrs. Stringer didn't make it to the telephone.

Screaming in agony as a thousand white-hot needles shot through her, Mrs. Violet Stringer was unceremoniously dragged back down the staircase upon which she had made her escape halfway to the top. Something huge had bitten down on her left ankle and had sunk its fangs into it.

Gibbering and keening in pain and fear, Violet had to see what form of evil the devil had sent to end her life—and that was when the lady parted company with her mind completely.

*For there was nothing there.*

She could feel the fangs, and could feel the breath being crushed out of her as the constrictor wrapped its massive coils around her. Long gray wispy strands of hair fluttered wildly about her head, banging on every step as she was dragged by one of her skinny ankles down the staircase to her fate, but *she still saw nothing.*

Her last conscious thought, originating in that place where reason no longer resides was, *"Susie . . . I'm being swallowed whole."*

And so she was.

Had there been a witness present during the last few seconds of Mrs. Stringer's earthly existence, they would have heard the "zzzzt" and seen the puff of smoke that lingered for just a moment over the staircase. And they would have detected the stink of burning flesh.

# Chapter 19

## Mickey Goes To Town

The morning after the unfortunate Mrs. Stringer's demise, Rudy the jeweler, true to his word, called to say that Erin's new trinket was completed and ready for pick-up. Erin happily dispatched Mickey to retrieve the latest bauble from her post office box in town.

Jiggling with anticipation, Erin was in particularly good spirits, and Mickey set off for town with a bounce in his step because—when Erin was happy, he was happy.

Mickey always rode the bus when he went to town to do errands or to shop, and after ten years it had become a routine. He knew the scenery by heart and he, himself, was a familiar sight to his neighbors as he wandered up and down the main street and in and out of stores tending to Erin's and the family's needs. He had grown comfortable in Hester, New York, and now considered it his hometown and a pretty little place too. He smiled to himself, bemused as he rolled past the landmarks that he now knew so well. There was the Mom N' Pop Grocery where he had accidentally on purpose been bumped into by Beauregard. And across the street was the bus stop bench upon which his Isolde had been sitting and crying the day five years ago when fate had brought them together. He rode past old Doc Blumberg's Medical Clinic, Freda's Café—"Breakfast All Day! Bottomless Cup o' Java!"—and the tidy little

Police Station just one stop before the Postal Outlet where Erin kept her post office box. When the bus pulled up, Mickey alighted and paused for a moment. Something felt different . . . amiss. He looked back over his shoulder at the departing bus, a look of puzzlement beginning to creep over his features. Swiveling his head to peer down the street in the other direction, he took stock. It was a weekday, a weekday *morning,* and even though Hester, New York wasn't Manhattan, there should have been *some* hustle and bustle. But the street had an almost deserted look, as if people had slept in today, or it was a holiday that he had forgotten about. Then he saw that the shops and stores were open, and he spotted a few citizens here and there going about their business . . . but it was so quiet. Quiet and odd. Chewing his bottom lip, Mickey stood rooted thoughtfully for another minute or so, but seeing nothing obvious or out of the ordinary, decided it was his imagination and made tracks for the Postal Outlet.

"Morning lil' feller," said Mr. Wilton.

"Morning Mr. Wilton!" replied Mickey with a grin. Mickey never minded Mr. Wilton calling him lil' feller. He was a nice old man and Mickey knew that he meant no offense, so he took none.

"I hope yer bein' careful, n' not goin' aroun' by yerself, especially at night, what with all these disappearances goin' on."

"Disappearances?" A look of concern replaced the grin on Mickey's face as his heart did a tiny flip-flop in his chest.

"Don't get out much do you? Yep, seems like we've got a problem on our hands. Guess it ain't some big city maniac passing through like everyone thought. Folks 'r gettin' mighty spooked. Too many people vanishing into thin air, leavin' lots a' blood but no bodies. Not a one. Weird ain't it? Nuff to give ya the heebliejeeblies. So you be careful lil' feller, hear?"

"Gee, that's terrible. Yes, Mr. Wilton, I'll be careful" promised Mickey. And with that, Mickey urged his legs to carry the rest of him toward the rows of Postal boxes at the rear of the store, while he fumbled the key out of his pocket.

The bus ride home was a blur, as Mickey tried to decide how he was going to broach the subject of the disappearing townsfolk to Erin. He knew he had to say something, since she had a right to know what was happening. He was more aware than anyone of just how much Erin valued her anonymity, and he was afraid for her.

What if the cops started snooping? What if the state cops came to town and got to nosing around? What about the F.B.I.? What if the family came under suspicion? What if, what if, what if?

He told himself he was panicking, getting carried away for nothing. There was absolutely no reason on God's green earth why the family would be linked to the missing people of Hester.

"Of course not. I'm just being silly," he admonished himself, eyebrows drawn together.

Erin and the digits had always kept a low profile, and it had served them well up until now, so why worry? By the time he arrived back home, Mickey had convinced himself that he, Erin, and the others were above suspicion, and as he closed the front door behind himself, the smile returned to his face.

"Erin, I'm home!" called Mickey as he approached her bedroom.

"Enter, darling!" trilled Erin eagerly.

Erin gasped and her jaw dropped when she lifted the lid off the little black velvet jeweler's box.

"It's the most beautiful thing I've ever seen!"

Rudy had outdone himself. The ring he had crafted was by far his best work yet. It was a massive solid gold lion's head, with its mouth open, as if preparing to let out a roar. The mane was so intricate, Erin could actually see each individual hair, rippling in the wind. But the eyes—the eyes were incredible. They were made up of three different, tiny, precious and semi-precious stones—diamonds, emeralds, and amber—so as to produce a three dimensional effect, and it worked. For not only did the big golden cat seem to be looking right at her, as the eyes twinkled and glittered, catching the light, she could swear that he was almost breathing. It was *her* lion—the big male from Sarah's painting—and Erin couldn't have been more delighted.

That night in her dreams, he came for her again. Together they roamed the countryside, drunk with freedom and power.

And her friend told her stories. Erin received mind pictures from him as they stalked and roamed, and mostly the stories were happy.

But some were decidedly not.

Besides the visions of unlimited vistas of African plains, stretching as far as the eye could see, there were disturbing ones. Erin had mental images of flames . . . fire.

She could smell acrid, choking smoke, and hear screaming. During these frightening scenes, her emotions also were affected, and were all a-jumble with terror, confusion, and pain. All of Erin's senses were assaulted as the huge cat tried to tell her something . . . wanted her to *know* something. The images were, thankfully brief, lasting only a few seconds, but powerful. And so real that she could actually see, hear, feel, and taste the sensations.

The relief was enormous when the visions retreated to the nether regions of her mind, and she could concentrate again on her night hunts with her companions, but, troubling though it was, Erin felt she was approaching an understanding.

# Chapter 20

## They Don't Come Home At Night . . .

A cold chill of foreboding ran up Mickey's spine when he heard the raps at the kitchen door, for it was a rare occurrence. The twins hardly ever approached the big house, and he knew it could only be them, for the rest of the family came and went as they pleased. His fears were confirmed when he heard Patrick's voice.

"Mickey, we need to talk to you," called Erin's brother.

He and Isolde exchanged a worried look before he ran to the door to answer the insistent knocking.

"Yes Patrick, what is it?" asked Mickey.

"Follow me."

Mickey had to practically run to keep up with the twin who had already wheeled around and was barreling back down the path toward the cottage.

*"Now what?"* he mumbled, uneasy.

Sarah was standing in the middle of the living room/gallery when the two arrived, and was actually ringing her hands, the perfect picture of dismay.

"Hi Sarah, what's the problem?" asked Mickey, trying to sound upbeat, as the uneasiness in his mind grew more intense by the second.

Patrick spoke up. "The animals, that's the problem. Some of

them aren't coming back."

"What do you mean, they aren't com . . ." began Mickey as he scanned the room. "Oh, my God . . ."

It was true. The frames appeared to be emptier than they had been the last time he'd seen them. A thought hit him like a brick hurled by an angry rioter. "The python . . .?"

"Gone."

The frame depicting the Amazon rain forest, with its tangled roots, huge tropical plants, and dense vegetation, had always contained a thirty-foot python, draped and coiled over the thick, dead branches of an ancient tree. And now the zoological wonder was absent.

"And that's not all," exclaimed Sarah, as Mickey tore his attention from the painting where the gargantuan snake used to be.

The lion pride now seemed to be half of what it was—the large male being the most conspicuous in its absence. The same went for the herds. The numbers of elephants, giraffes, rhinoceros', and many others, all seemed to have dwindled, to be cut almost in half.

The creatures that remained, seemed to Mickey, to almost be holding their breaths, and they were watching him. He was sure of it. For as hundreds of eyes, maybe thousands, stared at him, *locked onto him*; he felt the hair at the back of his neck prickle and stand right up on end. Mickey felt mesmerized, hypnotized, until with a monumental effort he tore his eyes away and, scrubbing the back of his neck with the palm of his hand, yelled "Erin!" Bolting from the room, he flew out the door, and pistoned down the steps.

Without stopping to knock, Mickey threw open Erin's bedroom door and came to a screeching halt beside her huge bed, where he began to shake her ferociously, for her eyes were closed.

"Erin, wake up, wake up!" shouted the distressed dwarf, adrenaline racing through his system like a runaway car that had lost its brakes at the Indy 500.

"Mickey, listen!" It was Isolde, who had appeared at his side, her eyes the size of dinner plates.

He stopped his frantic shaking for a second, both hands on one of Erin's soft, massive shoulders, to cock an ear towards the sounds drifting in from the edges of his peripheral hearing. And when he turned his full attention to the source of Isolde's agitation, he could hear it.

Sirens. Lots of sirens . . . and gunshots!

And they all seemed to be coming from the general direction of the downtown shopping district of Hester.

# Chapter 21

## DAY ONE

At Mom 'N Pop's Grocery, on the main street which led into town, Iris Phister and Bonnie Haug were enjoying their weekly jaunt into town to lay in a few groceries, and catch up on local gossip. If the truth were told, they did a lot more talking than shopping, but that was the fun of it. On one afternoon a week, they would solve all the problems of the world in general, and those of their friends and acquaintances in particular.

From Mom N' Pop's they would head for Freda's Café for lunch and a glass of wine. This last part they kept to themselves as their own little secret, as they had been doing for the last twenty years or so, and all told, it made for an immensely satisfying and pleasant afternoon.

They complimented each other perfectly because where Iris was fair, Bonnie was dark, and where Iris was short and pleasingly plump, Bonnie was tall and thin. It was a friendship that had begun many years before, on the chalk hopscotch grid in grade school, and had never wavered since. The bond had not only withstood the test of time itself, but also the human roller coaster ride of careers, marriages, births, and deaths, as well as everything else in between.

Retirement now sat well on their shoulders, Iris having spent her life as a nurse and Bonnie a legal secretary *"for the only attorney in these parts worth a tinker's damn, Mr. Bennett C. Calhoun, God rest his soul,"* according to Bonnie, and the two were thoroughly enjoying it.

Perhaps if either of the ladies had an inkling that this was to be their last day together, they would have had Freda bring a whole bottle of wine to the table instead of just their usual two glasses.

Also in the grocery store that day were Cindy Lovett, and her boyfriend since junior high, Bobby Boyle. At least one day a month, Cindy and Bobby played hooky.

They were much more interested in each other and their respective anatomies, than they were in reading, writing, and arithmetic, and today they were stoned on some really good ganja. Bobby had swiped it from his parent's oh-so-clever stash in their bedroom laundry hamper. After sharing a joint and making out for a while, the two young lovers got the munchies, and decided to head over to Mom N' Pop's for snacks.

Completely wrapped up in each other, they strolled through the aisles hand in hand, alternately giggling and kissing. The mom-half of Mom N' Pops watched them for a moment, giving her gray head a slight toss, and with a disdainful sniff turned her attention back to the cash register. *"Damn kids. They better not steal anything."*

She was, arguably, the better half of Vera and Bert Cleary, or "Mom" to her friends. Bert "Pop" Cleary had died of a massive heart attack twelve years earlier, leaving "Mom" to man the ship alone. The Cleary's had been the proprietors of the town grocery since the end of the Second World War, or going on fifty-two years, give or take. In that time, the pair had seen good times and lean—the worst of it during the seventies when the word "mall" became a permanent staple of the North American language and psyche.

The big food chains that always attached themselves to shopping malls, like barnacles on the underbellies of boats, had almost done them in. But they had clung to the safety bars of the roller coaster ride of recessions and booms and ridden it out, and the store was now an institution for the locals, as almost anything becomes if it survives long enough.

The main business district, and the heartbeat of Hester, with its stores, shops, and offices, including Mom N' Pop's, were lined up along both sides of Morgan Street, as if clinging together for support. Seven blocks long, it petered out slowly at both ends like a fraying piece of knitting.

The further one traveled past the respectability and correctness of those seven blocks either north or south, the shabbier and more tattered grew the fray. The neat and tidy, regularly sand-blasted brick buildings gave way gradually, but inexorably, to more widely spaced structures that had seen better days. The same could be said for the inhabitants of said structures.

There was old Mr. Slowicki, who owned a piece of property bordered on either side by knee-high dried-up brown weeds. Likewise, was his front yard, which really could only be called a "yard" by the most extreme stretch of the imagination when considering the advanced state of neglect it projected.

This ugly and overgrown frontage sloped slightly upward toward a house that had, at one time many years ago, been a pretty family home, but now resembled a haunted house. The story went that Mr. Slowicki bought the property in the fifties, when he and his young bride had arrived from Poland to start their new lives in America:

They had high hopes and bright shiny visions of the future in this land of opportunity, and Mr. Slowicki built their dream house with his own bare hands and a lot of love.

Mrs. Slowicki, meanwhile, set about planting her flowers. She had a green thumb, and the grounds around the home reflected it, so colorful and breathtaking was the display. Paying particular attention to the front yard, the young wife spent many an hour agonizing over the placement of each bulb, seed, and cutting. The resulting splendor was a sight to behold, and a favorite Sunday afternoon diversion for the locals would not be complete without a cruise past the Slowicki farm to view the garden in full bloom.

Mr. Slowicki's world came crashing down around him, however, two years later, in the mid-sixties. First came the joy at the announcement that his wife was pregnant. But devastation followed joy eight months later, when Mrs. Slowicki hemorrhaged and died in childbirth. The child survived a few hours, until it too had succumbed.

Mr. Slowicki never recovered from the loss, and grew increasingly antisocial, old before his time, and more and more peculiar with the passing years. It was a common sight in the summertime to observe the old man out in front of the once white-painted but now gray and weathered hovel, the windows broken and never replaced. The roof sagged like an old swayback horse, and in spots had given up and fallen in as if it just didn't give a damn anymore.

On those days, Mr. Slowicki would be out in front, hoe or shovel in hand among the weeds, pantomiming the act of gardening, and mumbling to himself. His attire consisted of an ancient pair of men's cotton once-upon-a-time white underwear, now many shades of gray, held up below the sagging skin of his aging belly by who knew what force of will on their part. The elastic had obviously given up the will to live decades before, just as their owner had. The seat of the decrepit garment hung down almost to the backs of Mr. Slowicki's knees, and swayed back and forth in time to the useless motions he made with whatever imaginary garden tool he had chosen that day.

A short distance from the Slowicki house lay his old barn, now in ruins on the ground, a pile of rotting kindling.

The adjoining stretch of land, once alive with cattle grazing on the green grasses, and drinking from a large, natural pond, was now a jumbled tangle of brambles, wild bushes, creeping vines, and groundcover.

About a mile down the road from Mr. Slowicki, the sound of birds calling and crickets chirping was replaced by the familiar noises of human habitation. The roadhouse was named "Rowdy's," and the name described the clientele perfectly. On any given day, the graveled parking lot contained several battered pick-up trucks, one or two shiny new Buicks, BMW's, or Cadillacs, (local businessmen on long liquid lunches, thanks to their expense accounts and drinking problems), and a uniform lineup of Harley Davidson hogs, leaning on their kickstands and gleaming in the sun, all shiny paint and chrome. The latter belonged to the local version of a motorcycle club called Satan's Sabres, a motley collection of tough guys from all over the county looking for camaraderie, strength in numbers, and that "family" feeling that few of them had ever received from their own homes while they were growing up.

Rowdies was a fringe place full of fringe people. The patrons could always count on dim lighting, loud music, (courtesy of Rowdy Callahan, the owner), and three pool tables, no waiting.

Among the regulars was a girl named Mercy Lovett.

She was the older sister of Cindy Lovett, Bobby Boyle's beloved, and belonged to no one in particular. By the age of eighteen she could shoot pool like a pro, swear like a trucker, and drink any of the Sabres under the table. Mercy happened to be patronizing Rowdy's on the same afternoon that Cindy and Bobby were toking, smooching, cutting school, and making a *"munchie run"* to Mom 'N Pop's Grocery.

Just as the lovebirds had finished choosing just what brand of salt, fat, and chemicals they had a craving for, and were heading for the cash register hand-in-hand to pay for it, all hell seemed to break loose. The plate glass windows that covered the entire front of the store, and were plastered with hand-written signs announcing the terrific bargains to be had by lucky shoppers that day, suddenly came crashing inward. The glittering shards sprayed ten feet in all directions.

Cindy let out a high-pitched squeal as Bobby dropped their bags of goodies. He threw his arm protectively around her, and dragged her backwards down the aisle from which they had just finished strolling. He didn't stop moving until they were backed up against the dairy products cooler, where they stood staring and shaking, rooted to the spot while they watched the terrifying scenario unfold before them.

Perhaps it was the marijuana they had smoked that gave them the feeling that they were watching a movie, or maybe the scene was so unbelievable that their brains simply couldn't process the information, but Cindy and Bobby turned to stone. Bug-eyed, staring, stone.

Although unseen, something *big* had come crashing through the windows of Mom 'N Pop's; something fucking *huge!* And it ran right over top of Iris Phister on its way into the store.

It *squished* poor Iris into pig mash. Blood and guts flew everywhere, and mixed in with the glistening, needle-sharp, airborne spears of glass.

Bonnie Haug, who just a second before had been exiting the grocery store, while chattering up a storm with her friend Iris, had became a human pincushion. The last visual thing that registered with the one eye not pierced by a flying glass projectile, was the sight of Iris, or what was left of her, bursting into a red geyser on the floor. Her arms and legs were jerking and twitching, as they skittered away from what had been Iris's ample mid-section just moments before.

The monstrous thing plowed through the remains of the two ladies as if they were ectoplasm, and descended on Vera (Mom) Cleary before she knew what hit her. As the teenagers gaped in incomprehension from the back of the store, Vera was yanked off her feet and catapulted into the air. It happened so fast, and with such force, that her ten-year-old baffed-out hush puppies were left behind, standing side by side beneath the cash register as if her feet were still in them. Her screams began as she was shot up into the space above where she had been standing only seconds before, but were cut off abruptly when the thing started to shake her back and forth like a rag doll in a rambunctious puppy's mouth. Because it squeezed Vera as it shook, her ribs snapped like dry twigs, puncturing lungs and heart with a tremendous series of loud cracks. Then her spine broke in two, and Vera Cleary *was* a rag doll, all floppy and busted, blood spewing out of her mouth with every shake.

As suddenly as it had begun, the joggling stalled for just a moment and Vera's lifeless body seemed to fade backward in mid-air, like a quarterback in a football game was setting up for a long throw, and was using her for the pigskin.

Then the bloody rag doll was hurled through the store, right down the middle of the produce aisle. Vera's flight ended abruptly when she crashed into a neatly stacked display of Florida oranges.

Amid a waterfall of cascading citrus fruit, Vera Cleary came to rest.

By this time, Cindy was in a state of catatonia, and Bobby was about to join her, but for the sound he heard next. For as traumatized as he was, recognition forced itself into his besieged, (and now stony cold sober) brain, and when the big elephant trumpeted its victory, Bobby found his legs, grabbed his paralyzed girlfriend, and ran like he'd never run before.

# Chapter 22

## Isolde Keeps a Secret

As the sirens wailed on their way to Mom 'N Pop's, and Mickey tried desperately to wake Erin, realization hit Isolde like a punch in the gut.

"She's out there! With them!"

Mickey straightened up and he and Isolde stared fearfully into each other's eyes.

"Do you hear that? Do you hear it?"

"Yes Mickey, I hear it. It sounds real bad. What are we going to do?"

"Nothing."

And Isolde decided on the spot not to tell Mickey of her pregnancy. Not yet.

# Chapter 23

## Erin and Friend Go Sightseeing

What joy! What freedom! Erin and her mate, the big male lion, had been venturing out more and more, and not just at night any more, but in the daytime too. Leaving her enormous housebound body behind while she went exploring was delicious beyond belief. And they were getting bolder, and more adventurous all the time.

The pair were trotting down the main street of town, sniffing and enjoying all of the fascinating smells around them when the rampaging elephant burst through the front of Mom 'N Pop's. The sights and sounds of the resulting carnage were irresistible, so they stopped in the middle of the street to watch, transfixed.

Only when they heard the sounds of approaching sirens did they break into a trot and continue on their way, heading for the edge of town. Loping away from the ear-piercing noise, they passed unseen. Mr. Wilton was just coming out of his Postal Station to see what all the commotion was about when they ran by him without stopping, and then raced past Doc Blumberg's office, the dry-cleaner's, and Freda's Café.

To see the two big cats, if they could in fact be seen, would be like watching a couple of oversized kittens gamboling and playing tag with each other, while they romped unhindered and unfettered, true to their natures and wildness, beautiful to behold.

As they left the café and civilization behind them, the sidewalks ended, and Morgan Road showed fewer signs of human habitation. The lions slowed then, and began to investigate more closely the familiar scents of wild creatures, their burrows and their dung. Occasionally wandering off the sides of the road to curiously inspect a fallen tree or a thick stand of shrubs, Mr. Slowicki's long neglected property came into view up on its hill. A motion caught their eye at the same time. It was Mr. Slowicki himself, in his ever-present sagging underwear, talking to himself in the language of his homeland, and making the usual faux raking motions with his invisible garden tool.

Side by side, Erin and her tawny partner assumed a stalking stance. In the unclipped high grass lining the side of the road in front of Mr. Slowicki's front yard, the lions crouched down until their bellies almost touched the ground, and began to creep silently toward their prey.

***

The Hester Police Department had five sworn officers, and Chief Orin Higgins had been a member for a very long time. Born and raised in Hester, he had joined the force at the age of twenty-one, and worked his way up through the ranks, from patrolman, to Sergeant, to Captain, and finally Chief. Orin was sixty years old, and he could have retired almost twenty years before with full benefits, but he loved the work too much to quit. He never married and had no children, so the department became his family, and he treated it as such. The Chief was a big man, standing nearly six-foot-four, and in his youth had cut quite a striking figure in his uniform with his sandy-colored hair, green eyes, aquiline nose, and strong masculine jaw. Now, however, the years and two broken noses had started to take their toll on his looks, but not in bad way. His once thick and shiny locks had receded like the tides over time, and turned almost completely white. The paunch that now threatened to spill over his belt, combined with the second chin that blurred his once-firm jaw line made him seem even more imposing. And his noble nose now had a decidedly leftward lean to it, thanks to a powerful roundhouse thrown by Abel Swensen in the seventies, while Orin tried to break up a drunken dispute between Abel and his wife Gerta.

The beak took another beating in the late eighties when Mrs. Purdy's German Shepard "Wowser" got out of her yard one day, and ran amok in the Bolen's chicken coop down the road. At the time, Orin was still a Captain and as such, in a small town like Hester he was still sometimes called upon to intercede in more minor matters than he would be when he was eventually elected Chief of Police. The Bolen incident had really been quite comical to watch when it happened:

Captain Higgins chased the merry mutt around the coop, panicky hens squawking, their feathers flying as if someone had ripped open a feather pillow and tossed the contents into the wind. Without warning, the resident rooster came charging full tilt at the intruders. Wowser stopped dead in his tracks, staring in surprise at the enraged bird hurtling toward him like a scud missile, claws out and wings flapping. Unfortunately for the Captain, he was right on the dog's tail, with his arms spread, prepared to lunge. And he would have had him too, except for the momentum he had built up during the chase, which prevented him from being able to stop in time.

He tripped over Wowser, who halted right in front of him, and dog and cop both went rolling ass over teakettle. Orin hit the ground hard, face first. Hence the second of two busted noses that everyone in town would forever after claim gave his face character.

That is, of course, after they got through laughing while telling the story for the one-millionth time. The tale was still a favorite at Freda's, at Wing Fong's, and anywhere else that people gathered to eat, drink, and swap stories.

But Chief Orin Higgins was a man born with a natural good humor, and the ability to laugh at himself, so he took the chiding in the spirit with which it was intended, and even joined in on occasion. This trait in particular made him much beloved and respected among the citizens he was sworn to protect and serve.

Next in the pecking order, and in sharp contrast to Chief

Higgins, came Captain Ronald Morlin. Ronald was a by-the-book kind of cop, and as uninspired as they come. He was severely imaginationally challenged, and as such, possessed no sense of humor to speak of. He was tall, but spare and lean, due to his strict dietary adherence to the four basic food groups, and his full daily requirement of vitamins and minerals, as dictated by the National Institute of Health. Chief Higgins relied on Ron to always do the right thing, or at least to always know what the right thing was. Sometimes though, Orin had to intervene when Ron took certain edicts to the extreme. Like the time he wanted to charge Able Swensen for being intoxicated in a public place one night. Driving home at midnight after finishing his shift, Ron observed Able staggering and swaying along the side of the road after a few too many at Rowdies, heading home to Gerta.

Able took exception to being accosted in this manner by Ron, and started getting verbally abusive when the Captain tried to cuff him. Ron called the station, and the Chief rode out to their location to mediate. After pacifying Captain Morlin, Orin drove Able home himself, cracking off a few good jokes to defuse his temper, and hopefully divert him from taking the incident out on Gerta. It worked.

As well as Chief Orin Higgins, and Captain Ronald Morlin, the Hester Police Force boasted one Sergeant, two full-time Patrolmen, and a civilian dispatcher named Sybil Hatchett.

Sybil was a familiar sight around town, and considered by almost everyone to be an odd duck: She was widowed at the age of twenty in 1967, when her husband of six months was killed in Viet Nam. Sybil never recovered from the loss, and was never quite the same again. She went to work for the Hester Police Department a year later. At work she knew her stuff, and took great pride in the fact that she was never late, never absent, and knew everything about everybody in the entire town. But on her off hours, she could often be observed standing at attention in front of the small war memorial set smack in the middle of the little park off of Monroe Street, with her hand raised to her forehead in a full military salute. When not at the park, Sybil would wander up and down the streets of Hester mumbling to herself, and never looking anyone straight in the eye. She wore the same outfit to work every day—a navy knee-length skirt with matching blazer, and a white blouse— probably figuring she looked quite cop-like and professional, which she did. But her off duty attire was somewhat different. She wore brightly colored muumuu's and caftans, and straw hats of every size and color, adorned with an eclectic assortment of plastic fruit and flowers. No one could have said what her hair actually looked like, (a subject of great and exhaustive debate at Meg's Hair and Beauty Salon), because when her husband died she pulled it straight back, tied it into as tight a bun as was humanly possible, and wore it that way for the next thirty years. Being a small woman, from a distance Sybil gave the impression with her big hats and dresses, that there wasn't really a person in them at all, and she resembled a large Japanese kite wafting along the sidewalk.

Sergeant Benny Bertram, and Ed Spears and Jesse Logan, the two Hester Police Department Patrolmen, completed the Hester force:

Benny was a smallish man, rather on the timid side, who had the title of Sergeant thrust upon him simply by virtue of his seniority, rather than because of any outstanding, or distinguished police work. He lived alone with his mother. The two had moved to Hester from New York City after his father, a New York City Police Officer, was slain in the line of duty years earlier by a corner drug dealer with a handgun, a meth habit, and an itchy trigger finger. After the funeral, Mrs. Bertram made two promises to herself. One: she and her young son were leaving this madhouse with its big city crime, and finding a safe place to live. And two: she was determined that Benny would follow in his father's footsteps, become a Police Officer, and make her proud, because it was what her husband would have wanted. She kept both promises.

As for Eddie Spears and Jesse Logan, they were inseparable. The two were rarely seen apart, either on duty or off. Jesse was a native Hesterian, and met Eddie for the first time at Hester High School, when Eddie, his younger sister Dawna, and his parents moved to the town from Palo Alto, California. The boys hit it off right from the start. Both were handsome, big for their age, had a penchant for football, and loved practical jokes. In school they stacked each other's lockers, and tied each other's football cleats together. There was artificial barf, itching powder in jock straps, and forged notes from pretty cheerleaders professing undying love. The jokesters giggled their way through high school together, but when gags, exams, and proms were over, Eddie and Jesse unanimously decided that they wanted to be policemen. So after taking a year off to tour California together, they passed their civil service examinations, and completed their training programs at the Law Enforcement Academy.

Now they were full-fledged Police Officers, shared a Patrol car, and they couldn't be happier. During their first year of duty, Jesse and Eddie's sister Dawna fell in love and got married, making the young cops true brothers. Dawna Logan was naturally pretty in a shampoo commercial kind of way, and truly loved her husband. She was not interested in a career, and whenever she read Cosmopolitan Magazine, she sometimes had twinges of inferiority about it, but all she really had ever wanted to be was a wife and mother, and married to a good man, and that she was. In fact, on the day that found her husband and father-to-be, Jesse Logan, and his partner Eddie Spears racing in their patrol car to a 911 call at Mom 'N Pop's Grocery Store in downtown Hester, Dawna was four months pregnant.

# Chapter 24

## Isolde Pays a Visit

Isolde was in a quandary, and didn't know what to do about it. She was desperate to tell Mickey that they were going to be parents, but knew that he was so worried about Erin and the seemingly reckless way that she was behaving, that now was not a good time.

She thought back over the past five years, and how happy had been, and felt terror at the very idea of any kind of change in their lives. The sirens were signaling something, of that she was certain, and it wasn't anything good. Mickey was privy to everything that Erin did, and sometimes at night, when he and Isolde were curled up together in the bedroom that they shared, he gently tried to tell her things. He said there were things that she ought to know, but Isolde would distract him with nuzzling and snuggling, and pretty soon Mickey would forget about everything but the love he felt for this woman in bed beside him.

Now for the first time, Isolde fervently wished that she had let him talk more, because now she needed to know. She was going to have a baby. *A baby!* she marveled. And it needed to be protected at all costs. Isolde realized that if she didn't know what she was up against, she couldn't protect herself or her loved ones.

So, thinking, *for-warned is for-armed,* Isolde made up her

mind to find out everything she could about just exactly what it was that was going on around her. She started a mental checklist.

*Okay, I know the animals in Sarah's paintings come to life somehow. I know they sometimes prowl at night. And I know that Erin has begun to leave her body and join them. I have to find out more.*

And then Isolde said the word to herself for the first time. *Cannibal. Erin is a cannibal.* The word felt ugly in her mind and she wanted to reject it. But she knew she couldn't. The time had come to face reality, to look at something and call it what it really was, without shrinking away from the truth, no matter how loathsome or repulsive. Cannibal. *Oh God!*

And then she had to admit to herself that Mickey, the man she so dearly loved, was a part of it. *NO!* Screamed her mind. *Yes. I have to save my family.* And Isolde made a resolution to do just that.

When Mickey had recovered his faculties somewhat, he gave Isolde a long, loving hug. He held her tight, as if clinging to a piece of floating debris after a shipwreck in the middle of the ocean.

And when he finally let go, and looked into her eyes, Isolde knew he had regained control, because the shell-shocked expression he had worn which had so scared her when he entered the kitchen had been replaced by a determined calm. She breathed an inward sigh of relief because he was little Charlie Bronson again; shaky, but himself. *Thank you Angels,* thought Isolde, for Mickey was her rock.

"I'm going to check on Erin again," he said.

"Okay honey," replied Isolde. "I'll go out to the garden while you're gone. I need a couple of carrots for dinner."

As Mickey left the kitchen, Isolde put the salad in the refrigerator, turned off the oven with the two Rock Cornish Game Hens in it, (dinner was ruined anyway), and headed for the back door. She figured the place to initiate her investigation would have to be Patrick and Sarah's house. It seemed to be the logical point at which to begin, since she knew that things had started to go strangely sometime after Beau had begun spending so much time there. So, with a swarm of fluttering and dive-bombing butterflies in her stomach, off she went.

All was quiet around the twin's domain. There were no observable signs of life, since the small house had no windows, except for the little square one in the front door under the carved gingerbread overhang, and a tiny curtain was always kept drawn over it. In spite of the appearance of tranquility which surrounded the cottage, Isolde tread as silently as she could for fear of being discovered snooping, and she wasn't sure why. She only knew that the twins didn't like her. Didn't like anyone much for that matter, and they especially did not enjoy being visited unannounced. But *the hell with them,* she thought, and unconsciously rubbed her hand protectively on her tummy as she crept.

When she had almost reached the front door, she segued off to the side, ducking into the high bushes that proliferated around the sides of the house. *Being small has its advantages,* she mused to herself, as she worked her way into the foliage.

Now Isolde was behind the greenery and standing right up against the side wall. The butterflies in her stomach went crazy, and became a twirling, juggling, and tumbling three-ring circus. Her jaw dropped, as her eyes opened wide to comprehend what she was seeing. For the house had a picture on it, a painted picture, and it looked far too old for Sarah to have rendered it. The house was made of wood so old that it resembled gray barn board. And it had obviously been hand-painted at some time, by some*one*, very long ago. Because even though the paint was extremely weathered and faded, chipped and peeling, there was no mistaking the image. It was a lion. A big male African lion with a shaggy mane and huge incisors. And although the painting was done in an exaggerated, and rather naïve style, the creature was intended to be depicted as ferocious, which it was. Looking further up toward the roof of the structure, Isolde had to crane her neck, since the crown of her head almost, but not quite, reached the top of the large, spoked wheels that sprouted out of all four corners of the building. *No, not a building. Wagon. It's a wagon!*

As she leaned back and tilted her head, the beaming sun made

Isolde squint as she tried to make out what was painted above the lion's head. Even with the sun in her eyes, and major deterioration of what had once been brightly colored paint, she could tell that there were words there. Not much was left, thanks to the elements and the probable age of the wagon, but the characters were done in some long-discarded style. *Victorian,* thought Isolde, although she was no expert in calligraphy. Most of each letter had been partially obliterated, but she could distinguish some of them. There was a B and a partial A. And an N. And another partial letter, a U? And an M. And what appeared to be an R. Isolde read the letters aloud, thoughtfully.

So wrapped up was Isolde with the puzzle before her, that she practically jumped out of her Keds at the sound of the voice which came from right behind her.

"Looking for something?" It was Patrick. Isolde had been so involved with examining her discovery that she didn't hear him sneaking up on her.

"Um . . . N . . . No . . . um . . . I . . . uh . . . Yes . . . uh . . ." Quick recovery, "Oh, hi Patrick! Gee, you scared me! I, uh, I came out to the garden for some carrots, and uh thought I saw something moving. You know, in the bushes, so I came to check it out because I thought it might be Mrs. Stringer's cat, Susie. You know Mrs. Stringer from next door." *I'm babbling!* "I heard her calling Susie a little while back, and figured that her cat must be lost, so when I heard the rustling in the bushes, well, I thought it might be her, so . . . you know . . . that's what I was doing. In the bushes. Looking for Susie." *Whew!*

"Uh-Huh" replied Patrick, not looking the least bit convinced. "Well, you needn't waste your time. Mrs. Stringer found Susie."

"She did? Oh, okay then. Good. It must have been a squirrel or something. Sorry if I disturbed you, Patrick."

"No problem. You'd better come out of there before you get stung by a bee."

"Sure, alright. I have to get back to the house and finish making dinner anyway."

"Say, want to come in for a minute? I'll tell Sarah we've got company." A tiny shudder rippled through Isolde at this exchange. It wasn't Patrick's words. They sounded perfectly normal. It was the way he was looking at her. His eyes were slightly narrowed, and his chin was raised as if he were looking down on her (although they were almost the same height) suspicion dripping off of him like rainwater. And even though her hackles were now raised, and the air around seemed suddenly to be infused with a very creepy, almost dangerous feeling, Isolde found herself accepting the offer. "Sure, sounds good. But just for a few minutes. You know, dinner and all." *What am I saying!*

"Good" Patrick said as he wheeled and disappeared back the way he had come, pushing aside full leafy branches as if he were battling his way through the Amazon jungle. He looked back over his shoulder to make sure that she followed, and Isolde found her feet moving on their own.

As she trailed Patrick out of the thick foliage, their conversation flash-forwarded through her mind. *Come to think of it, I haven't seen a squirrel, or any other kind of animal around here in* ages. *No birds, no stray cats, no chipmunks. Hmm.*

When Isolde caught up, Patrick was already standing in the doorway, smiling a weird smile. As she climbed the three wooden steps that led to the open door, Isolde felt like her legs were made of lead. They didn't want to go. *Why don't I listen to them?* she asked herself, as she plastered a playing-dumb kind of smile on her own face.

Patrick swung the door wide to allow her in, and she glimpsed Sarah standing behind him.

"Well, well, well, to what do we owe the honor?" piped up Sarah.

*Was that sarcasm?* wondered Isolde, her stomach suddenly queasy.

Patrick answered his sister, "Isolde was looking for old Mrs. Stringer's cat."

"Ah."

"No, no, I thought I saw something in your bushes, that's all. And I thought that Susie was lost, so I went in to check, but Patrick says that Mrs. Stringer found her so . . ."

*Why are they looking at me so funny?*

As Patrick busied himself with shutting and locking the door, (*locking?*) Sarah moved forward while raising her hand, a tiny, phony smile creeping over her face, and grasped her by the elbow, steering her forward.

"Well, as long as you're here, come in and have a cup of tea. We see you so seldom. Let's catch up," cooed Sarah, just like an old girlfriend she hadn't seen in a while. But Sarah was not her friend, and never had been.

*Catch up on what? We don't even know each other. Not really.*

But since Isolde could not think of a graceful way out of this incredibly uncomfortable situation, she decided to use the opportunity to find out what she could, and allowed Sarah to lead her by the arm into the miniscule kitchen.

She was struck, as she always was in the few times she had seen them, by how much the twins resembled Erin. Their eyes were identical. The most beautiful shade of sea-green she had ever seen. They also had the same pale skin, and glossy, black hair. Very attractive. But. And the butterflies were disco dancing now. *But,* there was something in those lovely eyes, and it wasn't pretty.

"Why Isolde, you're shaking!" Sarah exclaimed as she seated her at the table. "Are you all right?"

"I'm fine, really. Maybe I'm coming down with something," lied Isolde.

"Well then, a nice cup of herbal tea will do you some good."

"Thank you."

Isolde knew very little of the family history, but thought that she could guess where the vague feelings of hostility came from. Mickey had told her that Erin and the twins' parents were ashamed of them when they were born, and rejected them more than nurtured them. She felt a pang of pity for these two beautiful little people, since she herself was well acquainted with rejection, and the pain it can cause. But she thought they were luckier than she, in that they had each other for company and consolation.

Sarah placed a cup of steaming tea in front of Isolde, and as she sipped, she began to relax. Patrick joined them at the table, and the three spent half an hour chatting about absolutely nothing.

"Oh yes, the vegetable garden has really outdone itself this year."

"Must be the nice spring we had; all that rain."

"Yes, but not *too* much."

"And did you know that the Norton's across the street have moved out?"

"For sale sign's been up for the longest time." And so on, until Isolde was ready to scream. By this time, she thought that maybe she had let her imagination run away with her, maybe the twins didn't deserve the sinister qualities that she was so quick to pin on them. Perhaps, being pregnant, her hormones were playing tricks on her. She began to think that she hadn't been fair to them. Sitting here drinking tea and talking, they could be anyone in the world.

And that's when she heard it.

*CAAA! WEEOO! WEEOO!*

What was *that!* The sound took her by such surprise, that Isolde spilled her tea (her second), and dumped her chair over backwards when she jumped up.

"That? Oh, that was nothing. Here, sit back down, finish your tea." But Isolde had no intention of finishing her tea, this conversation, or anything else in this house. She started backing toward the front door, babbling an apology. "No, sorry, thanks, it's been fun, but um, I've gotta go, dinner's burning . . ."

Halfway through the living room, as she spun around ready to bolt, a movement caught her eye, off to the right. A huge multicolored Macaw was just closing its beak. A painted Macaw, in a picture frame, surrounded by enormous jungle leaves. And then she really did scream.

"Eeeek!" Patrick had twisted the deadbolt latch behind her when she arrived, locking her in, and now she fumbled furiously to open it. The bird continued its bone-chilling screech, adding to her horror as she desperately groped all three locking mechanisms on the door until she found the right one. Finally, with a cry of relief she did, and out the door she ran, like her hair was on fire.

*Normal people, what was I thinking? I know about the animals! Oh my God! What was in that tea?* And, as she ran, she heard wild laughter behind her.

# Chapter 25

## The Morehouse's Tale

After leaving Isolde in the kitchen, Mickey hurried down the hallway to Erin's bedroom. Slipping in, he rushed to her bedside and bent over her. Her eyelids were fluttering, but she was still gone. That did it; he had to do something. He was too nervous to just sit around and wait, and he had to find Erin somehow. Then he remembered the sirens he had heard earlier in the day, and knew that he had to go see for himself what had happened. *Was there a connection?* So he grabbed his jacket off of the coat rack by the front door, and left the house.

When he arrived downtown, it was obvious that something catastrophic had befallen Mom 'N Pop's. The main street was blocked on both sides by Police Patrol Cars, and people were milling around everywhere. Mickey gaped at the destruction.

The whole front of the store was demolished, as if a Sherman tank had decided to go through, instead of around it. And from his vantage point behind the Police barricade, he could see there was blood everywhere. It was drying now, and turning brown, but even a blind man could tell what it was. And whatever had plowed through the front of the store had gone berserk in the aisles before creating its own exit door out of the back wall.

Groceries were everywhere. There was barely an aisle left

standing, and the interior was an indistinguishable mish-mash of food. From cantaloupes to marshmallows, from milk and orange juice to potato chips, mountains of smashed edibles and drinkables covered everything.

Mickey sidled up to a cluster of people, some of whom he recognized from his weekly trips to town.

"Hi Mr. Morehouse." Mr. And Mrs. Morehouse were standing with their arms around each other, and she was weeping silently into her husband's shoulder. The Morehouse's were a retired couple, in their seventies, and had settled in Hester ten years before, thinking it a nice, peaceful place in which to spend their golden years. They had been on the sidewalk two stores down from Mom 'N Pops, having just left Doc Blumberg's office. Mrs. Morehouse visited the Doc's office once a month for a vitamin B12 shot.

"Hello, Mickey".

"What happened here?"

"It was the most incredible thing I've ever seen," replied Mr. Morehouse. "We had just left Doc Blumberg's office, when we heard the crash. At first I thought a bomb had gone off, and then the whole front of the grocery store just imploded! Glass was flying everywhere, and I ran into the drycleaner's to call 911. Then my wife and I ran across the street. We saw Bonnie Haug and Iris Phister leaving, but just for a second, because all of a sudden Iris was smashed to the floor by some kind of concussion or something. And Bonnie was thrown backwards by the blast or whatever it was, and she was covered in glass and blood."

At this, Mrs. Morehouse went into a fresh burst of tears. Iris and Bonnie had been members of her bi-weekly bridge club, and the sight of her two friends being slaughtered, and their guts splattered all over the place was too much for her.

"There, there." Mr. Morehouse pulled her tighter to him, and comfortingly patted her arm. He had served in the Korean War as a medic, and was much more inured to the sight of bodies being blown apart than was his wife.

"Then came the craziest thing I ever saw. Mom Cleary was grabbed by something I couldn't see, and got tossed up in the air and hurled through the store." Mickey was staring up at him with a look of disbelief, as if Mr. Morehouse was telling him that aliens had just landed on Monroe Street, and were serving up ice cream. "Yes, I said hurled, like when I toss a Frisbee to Scout."

"How horrible," breathed Mickey.

"Well son, I'll tell you, it *was* horrible, and there's more!" Mr. Morehouse was really warming up now.

"After Mom got thrown, the whole place just blew apart! It was like something you'd see on a show about those guys that follow tornadoes. What do they call 'em, storm chasers. There was a whirlwind in that store, I swear, except it was invisible. Just then, while the place was being smashed to smithereens, two kids came running out, a boy and a girl. Well, the boy was running and he had the girl by the arm. She was basically flying behind him like a flag in the wind, because I don't think, from the looks of her, that she was capable of running on her own. Anyhow they made it out, and he was screaming something about an elephant! Well, I didn't see or hear any elephant, but something sure as hell *huge* attacked the place. It all happened so fast, in the space of a couple of minutes, and the cops arrived just as the kids hit the sidewalk. Two cops went in with guns drawn, you know, careful like, but by then the whatever had busted its way out the back of the store. They got a couple of rounds off as the back wall exploded, but you can't shoot at air and expect to hit anything, so they called for the meat wagon, and an ambulance. Another cop tended to the kids. The boy was pretty much incoherent then, except for repeating over and over, 'the elephant, the elephant.' But the girl, I could tell she was completely traumatized. Saw it lots in the war. Ambulance took them both away. Then when they got the go-ahead from the cops, the meat wagon took away Bonnie and Mom, and what was left of Iris, and roped the whole area off with crime scene tape. Damnedest thing *I* ever saw, and believe you me, I've seen a lot."

"My God." Mickey was stunned, and in the grip of a sense of foreboding like nothing he had ever experienced before. Then Officer Jesse Logan took control.

"Okay folks, nothing more to see here now. Please, go back to your homes, nothing more to see." He dispersed the crowd professionally and authoritatively, and they wandered off singly, or in small groups, some in shock, and some of them weeping. And Mickey, along with his secret, left too.

# Chapter 26

## Mr. Slowicki Tends His Garden

Erin and friend were unimpressed with the chaos that was transpiring downtown, but stopped to observe briefly anyway. Then they left Morgan Street behind, and headed for the edge of town. They had other, more interesting things on their minds. Things like Mr. Slowicki. Side by side, they crept up through the tall grass by the roadside, to the man in the gray, baggy undies.

It felt familiar to Erin, like she had done this before many times. It felt natural and good. Her massive partner, all muscle and sinewy was communicating with her with his mind. She was receiving images of vast, endless hunting grounds, with miles of tall grasses as far as the eye could see. And dotted sporadically in the distance were moving, grazing, and undulating herds of food. The trick was to spy a weak one. To single out one alone and unprotected, or disabled.

And they had one in their sights.

Mr. Slowicki was unaware of the killing machines moving in on him. Once during his solitary mumbling and hoeing, he raised his head and sniffed, when the slight summer breeze brought a faint odor to his nostrils. It broke into his befuddled mind long enough to freeze him in mid-hoe, but only for a moment, and then was gone when the breeze shifted.

The lions were halfway up the front yard then, but froze in place when he did, ancient instincts and razor sharp senses alert to the slightest nuance of detection. But then the prey went back to what it was doing, and they broke their statue-like poses, creeping closer. Then they were ten feet away, then five.

Following many thousands of years of predator programming, they crouched lower to the ground, lips curling back, and saliva beginning to drip off of huge, dagger-like fangs.

In his last moment of life, and with the first lucid understanding Mr. Slowicki had had in many years, he heard the heart-stopping roar of the King of beasts as it pounced. And as the male laid open his abdomen with one gigantic swipe from a paw as big as a catcher's mitt fitted with razor-like claws, Mr. Slowicki watched his intestines spill out with awe, onto his weedy, long-dead garden. And then he died.

Erin waited, as a good female should, while her mate fed. And when he was sated, his furry face and little beard dripping saliva and blood, it was her turn. While her mate tore off a leg and dragged it away, to be hidden in a tree and enjoyed later, Erin tore into Mr. Slowicki with vigor.

When she had eaten all she wanted, she found that she was alone, her mate having taken his prize and heading back to the safety of his lair. So, feeling drowsy from the days excitement, as well as the satisfaction of a full stomach, Erin went home.

# Chapter 27

## Mickey Goes Home

As Mickey arrived at his front door, he felt dazed. He was well aware that Sarah's animals were spending more and more time out of their frames, and encroaching upon the civilization around them, but the full extent of their wanderings, and the dramatic implications of the horrific events in Hester were now hitting home.

He was scared.

# Chapter 28

## Mickey Gets Mad

Erin awoke from her nap feeling great. No, more than just great, she felt fabulous. Like she had just returned from the most wonderful, restful vacation of her life. And she stretched and yawned, wondering vaguely why she wasn't hungry, because she was always ravenous when she woke up. *Oh well.* Then the phone rang, and it was back to business.

"Hello?" She used her sweetest voice today, like tinkling bells.

"Hi, my name's Mel. Is this Erin?"

"Why, yes Mel, sweetie. What can I do for you today?"

"Um, I got your number from the phone book, and I was hoping that you were in. It's just turning twilight, my favorite part of the day, and I'm lying out under a big shady tree in my back yard. Um, I was thinking that maybe it's almost bedtime, and that um, maybe you were getting ready for bed. . . ."

*Hmm, New client*

"Why Mel, you must be psychic! As a matter of fact you caught me right in the middle of taking off my clothes. I was just pulling off my sweater when the phone rang. Only I had a bit of a problem. You see I have masses of long blond hair, all curly-like, and when I pull my sweater over my head it gets all swept up, and then tumbles right back down over me." Groan. "Right now I'm

116

just unhooking my bra, little lacy thing with a tiny hook in front? Oops, there it goes! He he. The ends of my hair are tickling my nipples and making them tingle. Can you see my problem, Mel?"

"Uuuunn . . ."

"But my breasts are so full and round that I have to massage them to try to stop the tingling, but the more I touch them the harder my nipples get, and then I have to touch them too, but just with my fingertips. And it feels so gooooood! Would you like to help me? Would you like to kiss them Mel? If I try hard enough, I can feel your tongue, ever so soft, and your sucking ever so gently."

Mel was breathing shallow now, and fast. "Then what . . ."

"Oh Mel, I have to move my hands down, now I'm taking off my panties, there, I'll just slip them right down my leg, lil' lacy nothing kind of thing. Oh oh, I touched myself, just brushed my hand against myself, so sensitive down there . . . ahhhh . . . oh . . . oh . . . oooooh . . ."

She finished old Mel off with a great flourish.

"Bye bye sweetie."

"Buh B-Buh-bye . . . thank you." Click. *Another day, another dollar* thought Erin with a smile, as Mickey entered the room.

"Why Mickey darling, what's wrong? You look like you've seen a ghost or something. Are you all right?" Erin still bore the expression of a contented house cat. Nothing could ruffle her today.

"Erin, we have to talk. I'm worried."

"What about, Mickey darling?" Erin was all innocence and light, and those eyes boring into him.

"Well, uh, I just came from town, and uh, well, I'm worried about you," he blurted.

"Darling, you just let me worry about me, okay? I love you for caring, but I'm fine, really." Then as Mickey stared into the incredible sea-green eyes, the steeliness just behind them began to assert itself, and he knew he was treading on thin ice.

"Well, just wanted you to know, that's all . . ." he trailed off lamely.

"Lovely darling, now please send Isolde in would you? I need a hair wash and a sponge bath."

"Sure, Erin, anything you say."

And so, as usual, Mickey went off to fulfill Erin's request and headed for the kitchen to find Isolde, his mind and his heart in turmoil.

When Mickey entered the kitchen, Isolde came flying at him like a kamikaze pilot, throwing her arms around him and hanging on for dear life.

"Oh, Mickey thank God you're home!"

He embraced the distraught little love of his life, wondering what had sent her into such a tizzy. "Honey, I'm here! What is it?"

Isolde told him what had happened when she was caught snooping by Patrick, and the subsequent tea drinking episode.

"You're never to go back there again! Do you understand? Never!" ordered Mickey as he held her. And the worry lines in his forehead were so pronounced that he looked like he had aged twenty years since the morning. Charlie Bronson as a senior citizen.

"Where's Beau?" he demanded.

"H-he went into town this morning before breakfast and I haven't seen him since. Why?" Isolde's snuffling was winding down.

"Never mind, no big deal. Erin wants a bath, so you'd better go. But remember what I told you, okay?"

"Okay Mickey. Never never."

"Alright then, off you go." And he looked tenderly into Isolde's eyes as he wiped the last trace of wetness off of her cheek with his thumb, before he released her.

As he watched her go, he was angry. Angry at Erin for refusing to discuss his concerns. Angry at the twins for getting them all into this predicament in the first place. And most of all, angry at Beau. *What's the little prick up to now? He should have been here to protect Isolde. He's supposed to be the tough guy. Hah! Where is he when you really need him? Wait'll I find him, boy oh boy, is he ever going to get an earful!*

# Chapter 29

## Doc Takes Out The Trash

At the same time that Mickey was raging internally at Beau, Doc Blumberg was locking up for the night. He lived in a small but cozy apartment behind his medical office, and it was almost full dark when he returned from the hospital. *Poor kids* he was thinking to himself. *Wonder what the hell happened over there. In all my years . . . never seen anything like it.* Since Cindy Lovett was his patient. *Hell I delivered her!* Doc had received an emergency call from the hospital that she had been brought in, and was in a bad way. He had found her so totally traumatized that there wasn't really much he could do, except to sit with her for awhile, try to calm her hysterical parents, leave orders for round the clock observation, and a sedative prescription just in case. *I'll go in and see how she's doing first thing in the morning,* he promised himself.

Doc was pre-occupied, and his brow was furrowed with concern, bushy white eyebrows drawn together, when he took the trash out back to deposit it in the can for pickup in the morning.

Then he heard it. W*hoosh . . . whoosh . . . whoosh . . . ssss . . . Now what?*

"Heyo! Anyone there? Hello?" Dropping the trash bag in the can, he stopped to listen for a minute, head cocked to one side; the side without the hearing aide. The sound didn't come again. *Must*

119

*be getting old . . . hearing things. Gotta get the apparatus checked one of these days,* he thought, and started back for the house.

*Whoosh . . . whoosh . . . sss . . . Wait a minute, there it is again. Now I'm sure I heard that.*

"Hello! I said, is anyone there?"

No answer.

Doc's heart did a nervous little loop-de-loop, and he started walking faster.

"Ooomph!" *Shit!* Doc tripped over something in the dark, and went down like a sack of potatoes. *Damn! Don't remember leaving anything in the damn path.* He felt around, trying to gain some purchase so that he could lift himself up, and his hand sunk up to the wrist in something squishy and moist, *Yuuuk! And what a stink!*

The elderly Doctor distractedly hoped he hadn't broken a hip, as he heaved himself painfully up from the grass where he had landed with a thud, wiping his hand on his pants. Then . . . *sssssssss . . .*

The sound was right behind him now.

*"Oh my God, gotta get in the house!"* He was upright, legs wobbly but working, and took a step. Whuumph! Before Doc's foot was fully flat on the path, it was yanked out from under him and hoisted up, the rest of his body following. Then using his leg like a baseball bat, something swung him through the air, and slammed him against the side of his house, *THWACK!* Again, and again, and again. But old Doc Blumberg only felt the first one.

The next morning, little Katie Wilson who lived next door came skipping out of her back door, as she did every morning on her way to school. Her family's backyard was separated from Doc's by a white two-foot high picket fence, and she couldn't miss seeing the regurgitated body of Violet Stringer where it lay in the middle of Doc's back pathway, although Katie could not have known what, or rather, who it was.

All she knew was that it had obviously once been human, judging from the jagged bones sticking out, and the strings of hair. It was an unrecognizable blob of tissue and bone, sucked dry of internal organs, blood and flesh, and then the indigestible parts thrown back up in the form of a compacted, hideous oozing thing.

The little girl stopped mid-skip, staring, while some sort of comprehension dawned. And as she turned to run screaming back into her house, she caught a glimpse of the clapboards on the back of Doc's house, smeared and splashed with blood and gray stuff.

Katie's mom called the police. The coroner was able to identify Violet Stringer from dental records, but Doc was nowhere to be found, although parts of his brain were recovered from the back wall of his home.

# Chapter 30

## Confrontation

The next morning, Beau came marching into the kitchen bright and early with an even cockier smile on his face than usual while Mickey and Isolde were having their breakfast, the improbable orange ponytail bouncing.

"Good morning, peasants!"

Mickey was on him like an enraged hornet whose nest had just been violated. "Where the hell have *you* been?" Demanded Mickey.

"Whoa! Doesn't anyone say good morning around here anymore? And it's none of your business."

"Like hell it's not my business! I'm in charge around here, and don't you forget it!"

"Yeah? Well, that's what you think."

"It's what I know! And yesterday those two buddies of yours out back scared Isolde half to death!" Mickey was livid, and fed up with Beau's arrogance.

"Well, she shouldn't have been out there in the first place. That'll teach her!" And with that Beau turned his back on Mickey and Isolde, and stomped out of the room.

The pair looked at each other, dumbfounded. Then Mickey said simply, "Something's got to be done about him."

Isolde sat quietly during the entire exchange. Things were deteriorating. She was a gentle soul, and avoided confrontation whenever possible, so the obvious and growing animosity between Beau and Mickey was beginning to bother her a great deal. And those weirdo twins!

She knew that Beau was spending more and more time out back with them, and their animal paintings, and she could tell that there was more going on here than just three pals getting together for a cuppa joe.

Beau had always frightened her a little, but now there was a feeling almost of malevolence about him. Something sinister that she couldn't put her finger on, and she didn't think that Mickey should be taunting him. Isolde knew what he was capable of. They all did. Beau was Erin's executioner, and he performed his duties with zeal. She thought he enjoyed his role too much, and she was worried about Mickey. She spoke up for the first time.

"Mickey, please don't worry about Beau right now. I have something very important to tell you."

Mickey had picked up his fork again, still simmering, and was staring at his scrambled eggs.

"Honey, look at me."

Isolde broke his reverie, and Mickey put his fork back down, realizing that he had lost his appetite. He turned to her. "What is it?"

Taking a deep breath, Isolde spit it out. "I'm going to have a baby."

Suddenly she had Mickey's full attention. "*What?*"

"I said 'I'm going to have a baby.'" Breakfast and Beau forgotten, Mickey grabbed Isolde up and squeezed her to him. "A baby! You're, I mean, we're pregnant!?"

"Yes honey, we're going to be parents."

Mickey was ecstatic. "When! How! I mean why didn't you tell me! How long have you known!" He took her by the shoulders and held her at arms length, searching the pretty face that he loved, a million questions and a million emotions bubbling up inside of him.

"I found out for sure last week, and I wanted to tell you, but you were so upset . . ."

# Chapter 31

## Dreams Of Fire

Erin was dreaming again.

She had been having the same dream periodically ever since the age of fifteen, when she first had heard the tremendous cacophony of animal sounds. With the passing years, they had been intensifying, and new elements were included in them all the time.

At first, it had been the sounds and the odors. In the beginning, she wasn't able to determine what it all meant. She couldn't tell *why* the dream creatures were raising their voices . . . to what purpose. Somehow she knew that she was being told something, that she was supposed to be aware of something, but she didn't know what that something was.

Over time, Erin became sure that the cries were of fright rather than just joyful noise. That they were screaming in pain and anguish.

Eventually, on top of the natural earthy scent of wild live bodies covered with hair, or fur, she detected the unmistakable smell of smoke. Then the animals started to come to her as individuals, and not just a vague impression of a group of suffering, living things. And she knew they were suffering, of that she had become certain. And that was when the big male lion had first appeared to her out of the nebulous mist of the nighttime dreamscape.

He approached out of the smoke and haze, looking regal and fierce, and gazed straight into her eyes. It was he who was trying to relay some very important information, and it was he, representing all of the others, the agonized others, who was asking for help. He looked at her with beautiful, intelligent, emerald eyes.

She couldn't turn away.

And amid the chaos of emotions which surrounded him like a thick, writhing fog, and the painfully heart-wrenching sorrow of the helpless screams, the magnificent lion showed her pictures. Mental images came at her like arrows shot from a crossbow. She saw fire, raging and merciless.

Then out of the horrendous conflagration, through the smoke and the heat, animals appeared. Animals in unbelievable torment. The screaming came from them. They were terrified, and trapped. She saw cages, row upon row, containing dozens of species. There were massive bears, brown, black, and grizzlies, throwing themselves against the bars of their prisons. A python, thirty feet long, twisted and contorted on the red-hot concrete floor, being roasted alive. Busting through the bars of its cage, a huge Bengal tiger escaped to safety, only to be shot dead as it ran in terror. Apes of all descriptions, chimps, baboons, and monkeys were perishing in the flames, burning alive. Dolphins, Beluga whales, and any manner of exotic fish boiled in their shallow water tanks.

The lion did not show Erin everything at once, as it was too devastating. But over time, as each year passed, he gradually revealed missing pieces of the puzzle. In each dream a little more.

Erin wept in her sleep when the dreams came. The suffering was unbearable, and she began to actually feel their pain, and their outrage, and confusion. Erin was beginning to become one of them, and that is what the lion wanted. The zebras and the parrots, the elephants and rhinoceros, were moving into her mind.

But in the morning when she awoke, she had no clear picture of what the images were trying to tell her. They wanted help, but what kind? Were they real, or just imaginary dream figments? Finally, when the lion knew that she was ready, he took her with him. At first it scared her to leave her huge, bedridden body behind, and she only stayed out a little while, not sure if she was dreaming it. The memory of the first time was still very vivid, like watching a movie over which she had no control.

Erin remembered it like it was yesterday. At first there was a rustling sensation through her limbs, like a sudden gust of wind rustles a pile of raked up leaves on a fall day. Then an invisible hand began to pull, pull, and she was rising up out of herself. Only as she rose higher and higher, she could look back and see her physical self still lying sprawled in her king size bed, eyes closed as if sleeping.

She was as light as the air, a cloud, a mist. And the lion beckoned to her to follow him, so she did. The first few nights, she followed along behind him, trying to accept the onslaught of new sensations coming at her. Every sense seemed heightened—hearing, smell, taste, touch, and sight. She found that she could see in the dark, and she could hear the Hester River, even though she knew that it was far away, well past the edge of town.

And she knew that even had she been able to get up and walk in her physical body, instead of being trapped in her bed as she was, her ears could never have picked up the sound of the river as it flowed past the town. Could never have heard it as she did now, skipping over the rocks that formed little rapids here and there, and babbling so pleasantly with the current.

Sometimes the lion showed her images of himself, in another time. A time when he wasn't free to roam at will, or even be with his own kind.

He was in a box, a wooden one that was constantly moving. It was hot and closed, and there was no water to drink, no grass to lie down in, and no food to eat except rotting scraps tossed in by the human things.

And sometimes the box stopped moving, and he would be dragged out by a chain around his neck, and whipped and poked with sticks. At these times, there would be many human things, making lots of noises and clapping their hands together while he was poked and whipped and prodded. He wanted to be free, to once again roam the savanna with his pride; to find his own food, and feel the sunshine over his head and the grass under his feet. And he died wanting it, his raging spirit desperate for revenge.

# Chapter 32

## No Turning Back

As time went on, Erin knew that she was becoming more lion than human, and she didn't care. She had never been so happy. In her human form she had never been accepted by her fellow human beings. They had laughed at her, tormented and abused her throughout her life, and she was able to understand perfectly the pain, humiliation, and loneliness expressed by her friend when he told her about the menagerie caravan in which he had been forced to ride. Erin never knew that such unconditional respect and acceptance existed, of the kind she received from the lion, such loyalty, so she gave herself over to the gradual transformation without hesitation.

After their first human kill together, she knew there would be no turning back. Erin had acquired a taste for human flesh and she liked it. That was when the idea came to her. In her human form she had access to a steady supply, and the ability (with Beau's help, as well as the twins) to secure it. To the lioness Erin, the human Erin, or the *body* of the human Erin, was from now on, only a tool to be used—a means to an end.

# Chapter 33

## Rowdy's Roadhouse

Rowdy's Roadhouse had a bad reputation.

It was not Rowdy Callahan's intention that this be so when he opened for business in the mid-seventies, but in the nineties it was a fact of life. When his father passed away in 1975, he left Rowdy the sole beneficiary of his insurance policy. Wanting to make the money count, and ensure a future for himself, Rowdy opened the bar.

His real given name was Donald Quentin Callahan, named after his father Donald, and his grandfather Quentin. He earned the name Rowdy in high school, because he was well known for never backing down from a fight, and was even better known for starting more than a few himself.

The decor of Rowdy's could best be described as early barn dance, and the atmosphere was *"anything goes."* It matched his personality perfectly, not to mention that of his clientele. Some of Rowdy's best and most loyal customers were a local Motorcycle Club called Satan's Sabres. People not in the know about such things referred to them as a bike gang, but the members insisted that they were a club united by a love for riding motorcycles, Harley-Davidsons in particular. They were a disparate group culled from all corners of the county who had found each other, as people with similar interests and philosophies. The majority were from broken homes and dysfunctional families—homes with alcoholic parents, and some had abusive upbringings. Some were farm boys with a wild streak that their fathers couldn't control, and some were just plain bullies. But they all had certain things in common that drew them together, and engendered a fierce loyalty to each other, and to their ideology. The first and most pronounced was a disrespect and acute mistrust of society in general, and authority in particular. The second was a hatred for police, and all forms of law enforcement. And the third was a love of riding. They cherished their Harleys. They were big, loud, powerful machines that always made an impression on folks who watched them being ridden by in a pack by the Sabre's, be it awe, fear, disdain, or envy. They found a visceral pleasure in roaring down the road together, and a oneness and sense of belonging that most had never experienced in their lives before. They called themselves brothers and considered themselves a family. To assert their individuality within the confines of the group, they customized their machines according to their own personal tastes and tendencies, and maintained them with tender loving care. The bikes were painted in a dazzling and vibrant array of colors, and some were blinding in the sun with the amount of chrome applied to almost any part that would stand still.

The Sabre's had a clubhouse of sorts two miles down County Road 9; it was a ramshackle old farmhouse with a big gate, a jukebox, and three bedrooms outfitted with nothing but filthy mattresses on the floor, but Rowdy's was the hangout of choice, and they felt right at home. There was always an assortment of women available, looking for whatever they were missing in their lives, and willing to do just about anything, in the hopes of finding the mysterious "*whatever*."

The girls who frequented Rowdy's Roadhouse knew the score, knew the risks, and were more than willing to take them. Although sometimes the naïve ones, looking for a little excitement to shake up their small town existence, got more than they bargained for, and the Sabres would find themselves having to deal with either the law, or an irate father.

But for the most part, everyone minded their own business, and the unspoken rule was generally "live and let live." The one thing you could say for sure about Rowdy's place was that it was never boring, and it was about to become just about as *unboring* as a place could get.

# Chapter 34

## Family Outing

The rhinos were out.

There were two adults, a male and a female, with a young one about six months old, shambling down the road leading out of town. The trio had trotted right down the main street of Hester, occasionally veering off to the right or left, and casually crushing anything in their path, oblivious. The damage included little Ashley Thomas's tricycle, carelessly dropped on her family's lawn when her mom called her in for lunch, as well as the mailbox in front of Mr. Wilton's Postal Station, which was left looking like a crumpled up, discarded cigarette package tossed to the sidewalk. Mrs. Morehouse's prized dahlias and chrysanthemums fared no better, and were trampled into mulch, as the rhinos unconcernedly meandered along, brushing aside everything in their way. Parked cars were pushed into each other, and one Volkswagen Beetle was overturned. Fortunately, there wasn't a lot of traffic moving that day, because of the grocery store debacle the day before. But the drivers still brave enough to venture out were mysteriously involved in a series of fender benders, resulting in blaring car horns, and several verbal altercations in the middle of the street, with much fist shaking and foul language.

The trail of chaos the rhinos were leaving in their wake went practically unnoticed by the tank-like creatures, who just weren't interested. Being herbivores, the humans made no impression on them, except as minor obstacles to be brushed aside, or trampled under, or plowed through. A rhinoceros is not by nature mean-tempered, but it can become belligerent if confronted or threatened. This did not occur downtown however, as the only threatening came from the citizens of Hester themselves, toward each other.

The lumbering group left the downtown core, and continued along the road leading to the outskirts of Hester.

Rhinoceros's have very poor eyesight, and inevitably they came shambling alongside Rowdy's, where they became intrigued by the midday sun glinting and twinkling off of the shiny Harleys parked out in front.

Mercy Lovett already had the first beer of the day in her, as she did most days about this time. Her parents had given up hope of their eldest daughter ever finishing school, or becoming a secretary or teacher, and now figured the most that they could hope for was that she wouldn't end up in jail, or worse yet, in the morgue.

Bewildered by what they had done wrong as parents, they now pinned their hopes on their remaining child, Cindy. At least she was still in school and making passable grades, but today Mr. And Mrs. Lovett were posted by her bedside in Hester Community Hospital, where she lay sedated and unaware of their presence, due to her witnessing of the elephant attack in the grocery store the previous day. They had spent the night in Cindy's room, on cots supplied by the hospital staff, and were waiting for Doc Blumberg to show up as he had promised he would.

Mid-morning, however, Officer Ed Spears appeared to inform them that there had been a terrible accident involving the Doc, and that he wouldn't be coming any time soon. Darcy and Catherine Lovett glanced at each other, the lines of worry carved deep into their faces. *What's going on* their eyes asked, and then, looking back down at their daughter, they each took one of her limp, unresponsive hands in theirs, and continued their frightened vigil.

# Chapter 35

## Party Animals

Mercy liked to be at Rowdy's when the Sabres were in attendance, because no matter what time of day or night it happened to be, it always turned into a party. Today five of the guys were already in the bar, playing pool and hanging out.

Martin Thompson, or 'Shiv', was the boss: He had grown up on a pig farm in rural Hester County, helping his father slaughter and butcher hogs from the time he was five years old. At least that's what he did by day when he was not in school, where his attendance was sporadic at best. By night he was usually slapped around by his father in lieu of a bedtime story. His older brother, Larry had run off to join the army when he was sixteen, being big for his age (as all the Thompsons were), leaving Shiv as the sole recipient of his father's fits of unprovoked rage. Shiv had no mother, because at the age of three, Lloyd Thompson, in one of his frequent and violent rampages, had smacked her so hard at the dinner table one night, that her chair flew over backward.

She was rendered unconscious when she bashed her head on a sharp corner of the kitchen counter. Not wanting to call an ambulance, or drive her into town for medical attention for fear of being found out, Lloyd picked his wife up, and deposited her on the living room sofa. In the morning she was dead.

Little Martin saw none of this since he had been sent to bed without any dinner for some infraction or other, and at daybreak, when Lloyd went out to tend to the hogs, he hauled a bundle out with him, slung over his shoulder like a sack of pig mash. Peeling off his wife's clothing, which he torched in the burn barrel behind the barn, he tossed his wife into the pigpen. Pigs will be carnivorous if given the opportunity, and Lloyd Thompson's were no exception. Instead of mash and pigweed, the porcine eating machines devoured Mrs. Thompson, all except for her head and bones which were relegated to the burn barrel, reduced to ash and chips. Lloyd mixed them in with the fertilizer that was spread over the furrows turned by the plow, in preparation for the coming years' corn planting.

In the morning, when little Martin asked after his mama, Lloyd told him that she had "run off" during the night, and that it was the two of them from now on, so he'd better get used to it. Every time someone asked after her, he gave the same answer, and no one was surprised, knowing what a bastard Lloyd was. So Martin grew up nurturing a simmering hatred that exploded whenever he was challenged. Like his older brother, Martin was a big boy. At sixteen, he was over six-foot- two, and one solid muscle thanks to his years of heavy labor on the farm. Also like his brother, he too left home, but not to join the army. At least not the army Larry chose. When he went, he stole his father's life savings, which he knew was kept in a secret place in the pig barn, since Lloyd did not trust banks, and he bought his first motorcycle. It was a big Indian, and for a while he toured the state, sleeping wherever he wanted, eventually meeting up with some local boys on bikes, and the Satan's Sabres were born.

Martin was big, smart, and fearless, and by virtue of these qualities, he was made president of the club. Robert "Bull" Henry was the main muscle in the group. Although not known for his intelligence, Bull could always be counted on for his fighting ability. He could back anyone down with a glare, and those who were stupid enough, or drunk enough not to be intimidated, ended up black and blue. He was Shiv's right hand, and was as loyal as a Rottweiler.

Gary "Stink" Potter got his name from the lingering cloud that always seemed to surround him. He was the smallest of all of his cronies, but as mean as a cornered rattlesnake, and possessed an aversion to soap and water. The guys in the club were the only ones allowed to call him Stink, and on an occasion when some drunken fool, thought that he could get familiar, he would see Stink turn into a small but deadly threshing machine right before his eyes.

Juan "Speedy" Gonzales acquired his moniker not just from the famous cartoon character, and the obvious name connection, but from the way he rode his bike. He only knew two speeds, fast and faster. He never took to the road at anything but breakneck speed, and had the road rash scars to prove it, not to mention an assortment of broken bones over the years:

His family had moved to Medford, Oregon from Los Angeles when Juan was ten, trying to create a normal life for their son, away from the street gangs and corruption of South Central Los Angeles. But Juan (or Johnny) as he was called, found Medford unbearably dull and inhospitable, and longed to leave. His folks ran a repair business for small appliances, and one day a rich kid from the other side of the tracks came puffing in pushing an old Harley-Davidson. The rich kid asked for a glass of water, while Juan slowly walked around and around the bike, a look of wonder on his face.

"Is that yours?" asked Juan awestruck.

"Yeah, I guess," replied the kid. "My father had it out in one of the garages, left over from the war. He said I could have it if I got it out of there. But I don't want it. You want it?"

"You serious?"

"Dead. Just get me a glass of water and it's yours."

"Hey man, you got it!" So Juan's dad helped him resurrect it to full rumbling glory, and Juan was in love. And he had his ticket out of Oregon.

Kissing his mom and dad, and his sisters good-bye, Juan set out on a cross country trek to find a place to belong. Doing odd jobs along the way to feed himself, Juan eventually found himself in New York State. He marveled at the fact that he had crossed an entire country alone, and when he arrived at the boundary of Hester County, he sat down by the banks of the Hester River to have a smoke and ponder the wondrous fact. His bike was parked on the shoulder of the road between the gravel and the water, when he heard the familiar, unmistakable sound of Harleys approaching. They stopped.

Getting off of his rock, he climbed the slight incline that dipped down from the road and found three rather large guys inspecting his wheels.

Before long, they were swapping pleasantries, and then stories, and when an invitation was issued to join them, Juan knew he was home.

Melvin "Ratchet" Soames was the mechanic in the club. Notwithstanding the fact that Melvin's family owned a gas station and garage in town, and he had grown up watching his father and uncles work on vehicles, Melvin was born with a gift. He could fix anything, without manuals or instructions. And his favorite thing to fix was a motorcycle. He could bring them back from the dead, and enjoy every minute of it. He was the nicest one of the group, and kids and dogs liked him. Generally when a fight broke out, or his "brothers" were threatened, he was "in" like a dirty shirt, but he didn't look for trouble as some did, or blow his stack easily.

Aside from Shiv, Bull, Stink, Speedy, and Ratchet, there were other peripheral members. But most didn't have as much time to casually fritter away as did the principle members. Some held down full-time jobs, while others had wives and kids. They were more or less weekend warriors, so when the rhinos wandered into Rowdy's on the afternoon in question, there were five Satan's Sabres there to welcome the deadly armored tanks that were nonchalantly trotting across the parking lot and heading straight for them.

Also there that day was Mercy Lovett, an old barfly named Mavis Whitfield, and a motley collection of locals, from town and country, with nothing better to do.

The rhino trio left the road, crossed the ditch, and ambled across the graveled expanse of Rowdy's parking lot, curious about the row of glinting objects parked in a row out front. The talk inside the bar was all about the bizarre events and strange disappearances that had been taking place in Hester, and seemed to be increasing in number.

While her sister Cindy languished in Hester Hospital in a vegetative state, Mercy was killing another afternoon in Rowdy's with her friends. When she got the news the day before that Cindy and her boyfriend Bobby had been in some kind of accident, she had rushed to her side. But on arrival, she had found her parents already there, ensconced on either side of the traumatized teenager.

They glanced up when she entered the hospital room, with tearstained, grief-stricken faces. Anxiously Mercy asked what was going on, but the shock had rendered them mute, and both simply turned back to watching their youngest daughter for signs of life.

Mercy interpreted the reaction to her arrival as a signal that her presence wasn't welcome, so she wheeled around and bolted from the room, heading for the place where she always felt accepted . . . Rowdy's.

Now Mercy had her soothers—a beer bottle in one hand and a pool cue in the other. Shiv was standing behind her with his arm around her waist, waiting for her to take a shot.

Ratchet was planted on a barstool, nursing a beer and tinkering with a carburetor. Rowdy found no fault with this and supplied all the rags that Ratchet needed as he worked. His hands were covered with black grease and oil, as usual, but his concentration wasn't complete today. "Hey Mercy, how's your sister doing?" he called, still frowning down at the bike part in his hands.

"Yeah, what happened there?" asked Stink. He and Speedy were having a hand of poker at a corner table by the juke box, which was pounding out a Bruce Springsteen song, *Born In The USA!*

"Don't know. I went to the hospital to find out, but my asshole parents didn't want me around their little *darling,* so I left. But I saw the grocery store smashed to rat shit, and man, what a mess. Must have been some explosion."

She set her bottle of beer down on a nearby table, aimed, and took her shot. She missed. "Shit!"

"I heard it wasn't an explosion. But something fucking big

trashed the place. Heard three old broads bought the farm. Real blood bath." Bull spoke up for the first time. He was posted in his usual spot at the end of the bar, with his back to the wall so that he could observe everyone coming and going from the place, and no one could surprise him from behind.

"Well I heard something about an elephant," said Stink.

"An elephant! What have you been smoking? Ha ha ha," laughed
Speedy.

"Yeah, Stink, next you'll be telling us that aliens landed in your back yard and abducted your dog! Ha ha." Ratchet was getting in on the banter.

"Oh yeah Ratch? Well, you *are* an alien, and fuck you guys. What do you think a' that? "

"I think you better lay off the doobs for a while Stink, you're hallucinating. And fuck you too," commented Speedy good naturedly. "Now what're ya gonna do, pass or play? Waiting for Christmas or what?"

"Fuck you. I'll pass."

"Well at least they're not trying to finger us anymore," said Shiv. It was true.

When the first disappearances began, the police had started questioning the usual suspects. And the Sabres were naturally at the top of the list. But they could find no connection between the victims, let alone evidence that would tie them to any of the Sabres. They found no bodies, no motives, and no weapons, so reluctantly they'd had to begin looking in other directions, fishing for something upon which to start their investigation. As well, the animal experts, game wardens, and hunting parties had come up empty-handed. Pools of blood, that's all they had for the longest time, until now. Now they had a meatball made out of an old lady, brains painting the side of a house, the rest of the owner missing, a demolished grocery store, and several squished people. Not to mention the inexplicable destruction to public and private property, like cars, mailboxes, garbage cans, lawns, and the like.

But Shiv's only concern was that his club was out from under the cloud of suspicion, at least for now. When you thought about it though, it was getting pretty weird around this town. *Better make sure the guys stay on their* guard.

"Animals." Ratchet was sitting at the bar with his carburetor, two seats down from Mavis Whitfield.

Most of the time she mumbled to herself in a steady, monotonous litany, between sips of course. And no one paid any attention to her, because she had been sitting on the same barstool and chattering to herself day after day, for so many years, that she was pretty much invisible. At Rowdy's she was just a crazy old drunk.

"Snake'll do that. Swallow you whole and spit you up. Yuh. Animals. Kill you, drag you off. Animals. Gets mad, Elephant'll tear up a place. Yuh. Animals. Yuh."

Something in her rambling caught Ratch's attention. He and Rowdy, who was maneuvering a bar cloth up and down the scarred surface of the counter, were the only ones in the bar who could hear her above the music, now the Stones' *Honky Tonk Woman*.

"What're you going on about now, Mavis?" Asked Ratch, semi-interested, but mostly amused.

"Animals."

"Aw, don't pay any mind to her Ratch, she's nuts," said Rowdy.

"Hey I'm bored okay?" replied Ratch. "What about animals Mavis?"

"My great granny. Was ten years old, first time it happened, back in '65,'" said Mavis. "Terrible thing. Flames. Fire. Animals screaming. Trapped." Mavis' eyes were wide now, but staring vacantly into her glass of gin, as if seeing something there . . . pictures.

"First time what happened Mavis? 1965?" Ratchet put his project down on the counter now, all but forgotten, and swiveled his barstool toward her.

"*1865*. Fire. Great granny told my granny and she told me. Animals, hundreds of 'em. Burnin' up. Yuh. Burnin' up in the flames and screaming, horrible screaming." She mumbled something unintelligible.

"What? What fire? What animals?" asked Ratch, all ears.

"Happened again in 1868. Horrible thing. Fire. Winter. Freezing, couldn't put it out. Animals screaming to get let out. Elephants, tigers, lions, monkeys, birds, all screaming. Heard 'em in her sleep the rest of her life. Yuh."

"Yeah, I heard something about it long way back." One of the farmers with a drinking problem spoke up now. The juke box had run through its last selection, and had been allowed to go silent.

"About what?" asked Mercy.

"In the 1800's or so. New York City. Museum owned by Barnum, burned to the ground. Twice. Lot a' animals killed, stuck in them cages in the basement."

"Gross," said Mercy.

"Bummer," agreed Stink automatically, uninterested. "Let's play cards."

Suddenly, from outside the bar came a tremendous crash.

"The bikes!" yelled Shiv, who sprinted for the front door like someone had lit a firecracker under him.

"What the fuck!" bellowed Bull, who heaved himself off of his barstool, and was hot on his boss's heels. Shiv flung open the big wooden door just in time to see the five Harleys crash to the ground, one upon the other, like big metal dominoes.

*"HEY!"* he hollered, outraged. *"WHAT . . . Uuuumph*! Shiv was thrown backwards with such force that he bashed into Bull, who was right behind him, and the two went sprawling.

"SHIV!" screeched Mercy as she ran to where he landed with a resounding thump, blood gushing from a baseball sized wound in his stomach. The force of the collision sent all two hundred and fifty pounds of Bull soaring backwards, where he crashed into the jukebox, sending Stink and Speedy's table, drinks, and cards flying.

The card players were on their feet, ready for action, withdrawing hidden knives from secret pockets, and assuming offensive stances.

Bull slid down the front of the jukebox and was trying to raise himself from the floor, the wind knocked out of him.

Then from behind Mercy, where she was kneeling beside the unmoving Shiv, the pool table that she had been playing a game at moments before, upended.

"Holy shit!" yelled one of the farmers. "Let's get the hell out of here!" and he was on his feet.

His buddy, more hammered than he was, was slower on the draw, and comprehension escaped him, as he gaped around the bar bug-eyed. Ratchet made a dive for Mercy, while Rowdy jumped onto the top of the bar with a baseball bat in his hand, kept underneath the bar for emergencies. Retrieving it from under the counter, he hefted it threateningly, poised to do battle.

Stink stared in stuporous wonder as right beside him, Speedy was hoisted into the air, as if by an invisible front-end loader, and hurled through the bar like a javelin thrown in an Olympic event.

Interrupted mid-flight when he crashed into the rows of liquor bottles and glasses on shelves behind the bar, he dropped like a cast iron safe heaved off of a tenth floor balcony, amid a glittering shower of glass and liquid.

Discretion being the better part of valor, the first farmer made a bee-line for the men's toilet, only feet away, but his pickled friend was not so lucky.

Frozen to his chair by incomprehension and at least seven straight shots of whiskey, he was mowed down where he sat, as if a Mac truck had mistaken him for asphalt.

Bull got shakily to his feet, and with a roar of rage, picked up a table and started swinging at nothing.

With a mighty toss of its horned head, the big male rhinoceros smashed Bull and the table against the wall, where it left him looking like a giant squashed fly.

Perched up on the bar, unwilling to give up everything that he had worked so hard for, Rowdy clutched his bat, crouched a little with bent knees to get his balance, and started swinging at the unseen foe.

Ratchet was on the floor with Mercy, where she was sobbing over Shiv's body. Oblivious to everything else going on around her, Mercy clung to Shiv with an iron grip, until Ratch literally tore her off of him.

Pinning her flailing arms to her sides and forcing her to hunker down in front of him, he hurriedly half-walked and half-dragged her toward the front door, which was now just so much firewood.

The last thing they heard as they made it out of the opening, were two screams of pain, one human, and one decidedly not.

Swinging wildly, Rowdy suddenly connected with something solid, and hard. The first scream came from the baby rhino when the bat came into contact with its snout. This brought the wrath of the female down on Rowdy, who hung in mid-air for a second as the bar was ripped out from beneath him.

Pinwheeling with his arms, the bat went airborne, and then Rowdy landed in a heap on top of what had once been his favorite thing in the world—his bar. Mavis Whitfield sat unmoving and unconcerned through the surreal battle raging all around her, until the bar counter toppled, taking her down with it.

"Animals," she muttered, as the long brass railing which ran the entire length of the bar, landed heavily across her throat, and Mavis joined her granny.

Stink was the only one to witness whatever it was that had launched the attack, departing the bar. When he watched Speedy sail overhead and into the wall of glass, like a big bird, he realized that his buck knife was useless, although he still had it in a death-grip, and crouched down behind the fallen jukebox, waiting for his turn, his exit cut off. *Thank God* he thought to himself, when he saw Ratch and Mercy make it out the opening where the front door used to be.

Then, miraculously, it was over.

With a mighty cracking and tearing of wood and drywall, the back wall of Rowdy's Roadhouse was torn wide open, and the killer power was gone, leaving destruction, bodies, and silence in its wake.

Stink appeared outside just as Ratch heard the loud, dramatic sound of the "things" exiting out the back of Rowdy's.

"Hey man, give me a hand would ya?" said Ratch. He had his hands full trying to right his fallen bike, and keep Mercy from rushing back into the bar, at the same time.

"Sure Ratch. Come here Mercy." Stink grabbed the struggling girl around the waist and held on to her while Ratch got his bike back on its kickstand, doing a quick mental check to make sure it wasn't too badly damaged.

"Hold on to her, I'm going in to see about the guys, and then we're getting the fuck out of here. Gotta get to the cops."

Stink stared at Ratch as if he had suddenly grown two heads. He'd always thought that the day one of the Sabres suggested going to the cops would have to be the end of the world or something. *"Maybe it is the end of the world,"* he thought.

"Okay, I got her."

Mercy was calming down a little, but still kept repeating Shiv's name. "Oh God, Shiv, oh shit, Shiv."

Stink gripped her shoulders and made her face him. "Mercy, Shiv's dead. And when Ratch comes back, we're outta here, got it?"

Looking angry, scared, and defiant all at the same time, Mercy said "Okay, okay, alright!" But she wasn't happy about giving in.

Ratch reappeared then, looking slightly green, and towing someone behind him. It was the drunk farmer who had beat a hasty retreat into the bathroom when the melee broke out. Ratch had him by the scruff of the neck, and was propelling him toward the bikes. The man was shaking so hard that his false teeth were chattering like mariachis, and there was a dark stain down one leg of his green work pants.

Mercy and Stink watched Ratch drag the terrified man over to where they were standing.

"Found him in the john, but everyone else is toast. How's your bike? Good. I'll take this guy and you take Mercy. Fire up your scoot and let's get the fuck outta here!"

# Chapter 36

## Monkey Business

Dawna Logan was in a good mood and in her favorite place: the kitchen of her and Jesse's recently purchased ranch style home.

Pregnancy agreed with her, and she hummed to herself, a tiny, pretty smile on her face. *It just doesn't get any better than this,* she thought, as she did every day of her life. *A wonderful husband, a nice home, and baby makes three. How lucky can one girl get?*

The young wife thought she was imagining things when she felt the hem of her skirt being lifted up and then dropped. *What's this? Just a breeze silly,* she reprimanded herself. It was June, and a lovely one at that, so Dawna had all the windows open to air out the house, and allow in the scent of the late spring flowers she had planted. *What was that?*

She felt a sudden and unexpected jab of fear in her mid-section at a sound from the living room that didn't fit. Neither the television or stereo was on, and she was alone in the house. Then there was a crash, then another. *Oh God, someone's in the house!* Now the "breeze" was lifting up her skirt again, as well as her blond ponytail.

"Ouch!" Something was yanking on her hair. In an instant, it was like she was being grabbed everywhere all at once.

"Ow, ouch, ooh, ow, stop it!"

Dawna whirled and twirled, beginning to panic, but she couldn't see anything.

She danced and jumped around the kitchen trying to get away from the *hands?*

They felt like hands, pinching and poking and pulling, at her clothes, her hair, her skin. Now the level of noise in the living room was accelerating from the odd crash of objects breaking, to what sounded like an all out war being waged with her bric-a-brac, nick-nacks, collectibles and framed photographs.

What Dawna didn't know, and what her husband didn't tell her for fear of upsetting her, was that Hester seemed to be under siege. From the time the rhinos finished redecorating Rowdy's Roadhouse, the animal attacks had begun to escalate at an alarming rate, and Dawna Logan, wife of Officer Jesse Logan, and mom-to-be was about to find out, the hard way.

The monkeys had found a play toy, and they were having a great time. And they were all over her.

The more she screamed, the more they played. There were little monkey-hands everywhere. Her clothes were shredded right off of her body, and she could feel her hair being pulled out of her head in clumps, as little rivers of blood began to pour down her face. She gasped for air as little arms gained a stranglehold around her throat.

*"Phone"* she gasped, *"Have to phone Jess.....eeeeeeeee!"*

The hands had fingernails, and now they were gouging out hunks of flesh. They ripped and tore at Dawna, gouging out her eyes and flinging them at each other, as she sank to the Mexican tile floor in a heap. Dawna's last conscious thought was for her baby.

\*\*\*

Officer Jesse Logan had other things on his mind as he and his partner, Officer Ed Spears were rushing out of the station to answer an urgent call, unaware that at that very moment, Mrs. Logan was being torn to shreds.

Sybil Hatchett had received a desperate call from a hysterical

Mrs. Myers, pleading with her to send someone *quickly!*

From what she could make out, Sybil ascertained that Mrs. Myers beloved Bassett Hound, Walter, was being eaten alive right before her eyes by something, and she could hear the poor dog squealing and yelping helplessly in the background.

The phone hadn't stopped ringing all morning, and Sybil had to call upon all of her years of experience just to keep up with the volume. As Jesse and Ed were running out the door, Sybil heard the roar of motorcycles pulling up to the curb out front, as well as loud voices, and some pretty spicy language.

Satan's Sabres and the Hester Police Department had never had anything but a suspicious and adversarial relationship, and *never* had they pulled up to the Police Station before, so the sight of the two Harleys and their riders was a strange development in an already increasingly bizarre day.

Ratch was the first to dismount his bike, practically dumping the farmer riding behind him onto the ground in his haste. Ed and Jesse stopped in their tracks to see the biker bearing down on them like a freight train.

"You guys better get out to Rowdy's now; there's a bunch of dead people out there!" The words "dead people" immediately homed the two young officer's attention right in on Ratch. He was angry and agitated.

"Alright calm down, and tell us what's going on," said Ed.

"It was fucking horrible, man," added Stink, who had now settled his own bike on its kickstand and joined the group. "Something came in and demolished the place, and killed everyone in there! Do something!"

"Shiv's dead! And Bull! You gotta go out there!" cried Mercy, who was shaking and hugging herself as if she would blow apart any minute. The farmer who had ridden in on the back of Ratch's motorcycle had now sunk to the curb in a stupor and was staring off into space with expressionless eyes, and a trickle of drool hanging off of his slack lower lip.

"Okay, you guys wait here. The chief should be here any minute and you can make a statement. We'll go check it out," ordered Jesse.

"Fuck you, man," said Ratch. "I gotta check on my guys!" And with that, he and Stink stomped back over to their Harley's, fired them up, and took off down the street as if the devil himself was after them, ignoring the threats of the officers.

*Dawna.* Jesse said, "I have to go home."

"Whaddaya mean go home?" asked Ed, incredulous. "We've got to get out to Rowdy's!"

"I've got a bad feeling, Ed. I've got to go home . . . make sure Dawna's alright."

Ed trusted his partners' instincts. *She's my sister.* "Okay we'll stop there on the way." A feeling of doom was beginning to worm its way into the pit of Ed Spears' stomach. The creeping sensation increased as the men in their squad car pulled into the Logan's driveway.

"Dawna!" Jesse called his wife's name as he sprinted onto the front porch. His heart was pounding as his trembling hand tried to insert his key into the lock. *Please let my intuition be wrong,* he pleaded to himself.

Jesse burst through the door with Ed right behind him. "Dawna! Dawna, where are . . . where . . . wha? . . ."

The place was a total shambles. Completely destroyed. Jesse's throat constricted in fear, and his voice went up two octaves as he raced through the landfill that used to be his living room.

"DAWNA!" As he reached the kitchen, he took the grisly scene in at a glance, and dropped to his knees beside his ravaged wife.

"God NOOOO!!!" Jesse took her shredded body in his arms, but he knew that she was dead, and he rocked her body, screaming out her name. Her four-month-old unborn fetus was now a squishy blob of red and blue tissue splattered on the kitchen floor and still attached to Dawna's uterus by the umbilical cord.

Ed dove onto his knees on the other side of the blood-soaked woman and her husband, where he desperately felt for a pulse, automatically but pointlessly falling back on his now useless first aid training. But he knew it was hopeless.

"Let's get her to the hospital, Jesse!" They were both crying now and someone had to take charge. "Jesse!"

Jesse snapped out of it, tenderly picked Dawna and his tiny, dead child up in his arms. As they hurried out to the squad car, he placed it back into Dawna's raw, gaping, bleeding belly.

Turning on his lights and siren, Ed backed out of the Logan's driveway with a screech of burning rubber, and tore off down the street in the direction of Hester Hospital, Jesse cradling Dawna and weeping in the back seat.

Ed had to drive in a madcap, swerving fashion to avoid the many abandoned vehicles, fender benders, and wrecks that created an obstacle course all the way to the hospital. Not to mention the upended garbage cans, mailboxes, street signs and tree branches that littered the once neat and tidy streets of Hester. *Why didn't I notice this on the way out to Jesse's house? It's like a herd of elephants just tramped through here! Elephants. Bobby Boyle said an elephant trashed the grocery. I've got to talk to him . . . figure this out.*

Then he noticed the people.

The normally sleepy town of Hester was alive with people. They were running to and fro, criss-crossing the street, and milling about their yards and those of their neighbors.

Some were crying, others were shouting, and it was pandemonium. Before he had even brought the vehicle to a complete stop in front of the hospital, Jesse threw open the back door and hit the pavement running, with his dead wife in his arms. Ed was right behind him.

He slammed the transmission into park, and bolted for the electric eye doors of the emergency entrance. The scene that greeted him was unbelievable.

He had never imagined that so many people could be crammed into the small emergency room that was meant to serve a quiet farming community. Hester Hospital was really more of a large clinic, rather than anything resembling 'ER,' and had always been adequate for the community that it served. But today it was a swirling mass of wounded and hysterical people, and the small staff was obviously having trouble trying to cope with the sheer numbers of injured.

Nancy Bennett was the head nurse on duty, and she was

performing triage as best she could, separating the most serious cases from those that could afford to wait their turn. She had been up all night, and it looked like there was no end in sight for her as the place was a madhouse. Hair askew, and uniform blood-spattered, she valiantly did what she could for the citizens of the town in which she had grown up.

She was settling an elderly couple on the floor in a corner of the waiting room, which was the only available space left to put anyone, when Jesse came bursting in.

"Nancy! My wife!"

"Jesse!"

"She's pregnant!" sobbed Jesse.

Tearing herself away from the hands grabbing at her uniform from all directions, and the begging voices of the throng of bleeding people, she rushed over to Jesse and Dawna.

One look told the experienced nurse that both Dawna and her baby were dead. "Come." Jesse followed. "Bring her in here." Twelve years as an emergency room nurse had taught her economy in words and actions.

No treatment rooms were available, so Nancy led Jesse and Ed into the nurse's lounge, where she gestured to Jesse to lay Dawn's body down on a vinyl-covered couch. "Leave her with me Jesse, I'll take good care of her," she said kindly. Jesse searched her exhausted face, and read between the lines. There was of course no hope there, but her compassion was evident, and it helped. Tears running down his face, while Ed stood back and watched, Jesse smoothed the bloody hairs away from raw, ground hamburger that had been his young wife's lovely face. He felt his heart break in two as he leaned down to kiss her, with a whispered, "I love you."

"C'mon Jesse. There's nothing more you can do here," said Ed gently, his gray eyes red-rimmed and puffy, his handsome face resolute. Nodding, Jesse stood, letting a finger trail lovingly down the carnage where Dawna's cheek should have been. Then taking one long shuddery breath, he pulled himself to his full height, squared his shoulders, and exhaled, calling on every ounce of strength he possessed. "Okay, let's go."

Once outside, the two partners stood for a second and looked into each other's eyes. The haunted expression of one was a mirror image of the other, and no words were needed. Drawing strength from their friendship, they turned and headed for the squad car. Ed turned the key.

"Ready?" asked Ed.

Jesse nodded.

# Chapter 37

## Down On The Farm

Chief Orin Higgins had been conspicuous in his absence since the evening before the elephant attack at Mom 'N Pops:

Around dinnertime, Sybil Hatchett had received a call from one of the corn farmers out on Route 17 about an invasion of his fields. Orin had hopped into his police vehicle and gone to see what the trouble was. When he got about two miles out of town, driving out on Route17, Orin could see that he didn't need an agent from the Department of Agricultural to tell him that something was very wrong. Normally at this time of year there should have been large expanses of young, green corn plants about twelve inches high, for as far as the eye could see. Now the crops were trampled into the ground. Flattened and shredded, there was barely a shoot left standing. *What the hell?* He approached the entrance to Serge Benoit's farm, and turned into the long gravel driveway that led to the large red brick farmhouse.

Before he was even parked in the roundabout driveway in front of the house, Serge came bounding out of the house and grabbed the handle of his car door. He was talking a mile a minute, and practically spitting in the Chief's face in his excitement.

"Whoa, whoa, Serge. Let's take it from the top. Now try to

calm down and tell me what happened."

Mr. Benoit made a monumental effort to take a deep breath, and slow his speech.

"My corn, it's smashed. I came in from the fields for lunch, and then I heard the dogs barking up a storm. When I ran out with my shotgun, this is what I found. He raised his arms and waved them expansively in all directions. "When I ran out to where my dogs were, I found Bessie on the ground, squashed like a piano had dropped on her, and Dooner had a broken leg! I thought maybe old Polasky's Brahmas had broken out of their pen and stampeded through my fields, so I ran with my shotgun, but there was nothing! Nothing!"

"Let's go take a look."

The cop and farmer set out for the devastated cornfield. They came upon the dead dog, Bessie, first. What was left of her had once been a Shetland Sheepdog cross, intelligent and protective. Now she resembled the corn, only bloodier. "Where's Dooner?" asked Orin as he bent down on one knee to examine the damage.

"I brought him into the house. My wife's tending to him while we wait for the vet."

"This poor dog's been crushed."

"This is what I'm telling you!" said Serge, getting excited again.

"Settle down Serge, I'm just trying to get a picture of what could have done this. Did you check to see if the Brahmas were loose?"

"Of *course* I did! I told you, they're not!"

"Hmm. There aren't any prints. No hoof prints, nothing."

Then they heard it.

At first it was in the distance, but the sound of thousands of thundering hooves was closing the gap fast.

And then they could hear the mooing. Hundreds of bovine voices raised to a level that would rival any herd of cows in turmoil on the face of the earth. But they didn't sound like any cows that Serge or Orin had ever heard before.

It had a wild, untamed quality to it . . . some unfamiliar species. And they were coming this way.

"I can't see anything!"

"Me either! Oh my God, run!"

It was too late.

The wildebeest herd cut the two men down like they were dandelions in the path of a giant lawnmower.

Later when Mrs. Benoit came out in search of her husband, she found his shattered body along with that of the police chief and Bessie; she had a heart attack on the spot, bringing the body count to four.

# Chapter 38

## Ed and Jesse Visit Rowdy's

After leaving Dawna's body at the hospital, knowing that in Nancy Bennett's capable hands, Dawna and her baby would be treated with respect and dignity, Ed Spears and Jesse Logan drove out to Rowdy's Roadhouse in stunned silence.

As they pulled into the parking lot, they observed three Harley-Davidsons lying on their sides, and two pickup trucks parked out front. There was also a splintered, gaping hole where the front door used to be.

Suddenly all business, they unholstered their weapons and took the safeties off, while they cautiously approached the entrance. Jesse had a moment of deja vu as he surveyed the devastation. It was obvious from the hole in the back wall, through which the sunlight now poured in, that whatever had done this was gone.

They moved from body to body checking for signs of life, but knowing they would find none.

As he bent over Shiv's inert form and examined the wound, Ed said, "I've seen this before, or something like it, although this is way bigger. It's a gore wound."

"A gore wound?"

"Yeah. My father took me to a rodeo once, when we visited

my uncle and cousins in Texas. I was ten years old at the time, and one of the bull riders was gored by the thing. I was standing nearby when the clowns carried him out of the ring, and the wound looked like this, only much smaller. This is a gore wound alright."

"Hey!"

Just as he finished speaking, Ed caught sight of something just out of the corner of his eye. It flashed past the ragged opening at the back of the bar, which the exit of the rhinos had created. But it went by very past, just a quick wink of color, and then it was gone. For a second, Ed thought he was seeing things, but he was on his feet and loping across the debris-strewn floor like a gazelle.

"Where are you going?!"

"There's somebody out there!"

With the agility of an athlete, Jesse sprang up and gave chase. Guns drawn and ready, the partners dove through the hole in the wall. Backs to each other, and thirty-eights at the ready, held in both hands and pointing up, the two scanned the scrubby, overgrown back field of Rowdy's for movement.

"There he is! Hey . . . hey you . . . freeze! Police!" A bright spot of red was barreling through the tall grass, low to the ground.

"Wait. It's a kid!"

"A kid!" They lowered their guns and squinted their eyes, trying to get a better look at the running figure.

"That's no kid! I think it's one of those midgets from Dalton Street. See the red hair?" Beau's carrot colored ponytail was bouncing as he ran, just visible above the weeds.

"He's not a midget. Hey! I said freeze!" But Beau was just a speck now, in his red shirt, and disappearing fast.

"There he goes. What do mean he's not a midget?"

"He's a dwarf . . . there's a difference," said Ed as he watched Beau vanish from sight.

"Not as far as I'm concerned. And what do you think he was doing here?"

"Don't know. One thing's for sure, though. He couldn't have caused this mess."

# Chapter 39

## Isolde Gets The Rest Of The Story

Mickey arrived home from town looking more Bronson-esque than ever, after his chat with Mr. Morehouse, and went straight to the kitchen.

"Isolde, we have to talk. Come here, honey." After leading Isolde to a kitchen chair, and settling her in it, Mickey pulled one up for himself, where he could speak to her face to face.

He told her about the events of the morning, and the destruction of Mom N' Pop's Grocery. He explained to her all about Erin's out of body travels, and what she was becoming. And he described the goings-on in the little house that belonged to the twins.

"Isolde, the animals in the paintings are alive."

"Alive!"

"Yes. Alive. That's why the bird scared you. It's alive. I've known all along, but I didn't want to frighten you. I also never imagined that it would come to this. I thought it was harmless."

"Harmless!" Isolde's blue eyes were filled with wonder. "But how . . . ?"

"How, I don't know. But after I saw what an elephant did to the store, I went to the library. I found a book. A book that told a horrible story."

He continued, a stunned expression on his face. "In the 1860's, Phineas Taylor Barnum owned a museum and menagerie on the corner of Broadway and Ann Streets in New York City. In July of 1865 it burned to the ground. Most of the human exhibits escaped, but the animals perished in the flames.

"Human exhibits?"

"Yes. You know, what he called his freaks. The giantess, the bearded lady, the Siamese twins, and people like us."

"Oh God."

"Well, Barnum rebuilt the museum, and three years later, in March of 1868, it burned to the ground again. And again, hundreds of animals died. Now they've come back. I don't know how, but they've come back through Sarah's paintings." Isolde said nothing, but sat and listened, feeling numb.

"After that, he created the three ring circus, and a traveling menagerie."

"Oh Mickey, Patrick, and Sarah's house . . . it has wheels."

"Wheels?"

"Yes, wheels. I saw them when I sneaked into the bushes alongside. And there's a picture of a lion on the side. Mickey, it's not a house at all, it's a wagon."

"A wagon?"

An awful thought occurred to Isolde. "But some of those things are vicious, and dangerous. And if they're getting out . . ."

"Exactly. I'm losing control here Isolde, and we've got a baby to think about now."

Isolde's hand went automatically to her belly, and she looked down at it, not speaking.

After a long minute, she placed her hand on his arm and looked into his eyes. "What do you want me to do?"

"I think we'd better be prepared for the worst. It's just a matter of time before everything blows up in our faces. Before someone comes knocking on our door. But first there are some things I have to do. I need to find out what Beau has been up to. He's been acting even more suspicious than usual, and I just know that he's way more involved in all of this than I thought."

"Honey, please be careful."

"I will. But keep this to yourself. Don't let Beau know that I told you anything. Promise?"

"I promise."

"Good. Now I'm going to see about Erin."

"Alright honey."

# Chapter 40

## Once Bitten, Twice Shy

Erin was still gone.

Mickey didn't even try shaking her anymore, because he knew it did no good. She was out running with the lions, and would return when she was good and ready. It was all coming apart. Their home wasn't the same anymore. *Damn.* He had to come up with a plan. A contingency plan. What if Erin never came back? What would they do, where would they go? And what if they were found out? All those dead people. He had to protect Isolde and the baby.

He stood there chewing his lower lip, looking upon the mountain of flesh that was Erin, yet wasn't anymore, not really.

Mickey stood at Erin's bedside for a long time. He loved her so much, and he *owed* her his life. He had never known what happiness was until Erin took him in, but now he knew in his heart that he was at a crossroads, and there were decisions to be made. The lives of the woman he loved, and that of his unborn child depended on him, and he wouldn't let them down, no matter what. *Time to get some information out of Beau, even if I have to beat it out of him.*

Beau had always made it clear in no uncertain terms that his room was off limits, but Mickey didn't care anymore. It was time for him to get up anyway. Beau had been keeping strange hours for some time, and had taken to sleeping at odd hours of the day and night. No one knew where he went or what he did, and up until now, no one really cared. It was a lot nicer around the house with him gone so much anyway. But now Mickey had a gut feeling that Beau's weird schedule had something to do with the twins and the paintings, and he was determined to find out, for the sake of his family.

Not bothering to knock, Mickey entered Beau's bedroom. He was sleeping. *Now there's a surprise,* he thought.

"Hey Beau, wake up. I want to talk." Beau didn't stir.

Mickey gave him a tweak on the shoulder. "Beau, I said wake up."

*"Oh no, not him too!"*

Beauregard had left his body.

Mickey backed out of Beau's room and shut the door. *So Beau's out there too. What is he, a bear, a leopard, a snake?* Whatever Beau was becoming, Mickey just knew it wouldn't be benign.

In his human form, he was dangerous enough, but knowing Beau as he did, it was a sure bet that the little monster would gleefully choose a form that would do as much damage as possible. *Now what?* His last recourse was to go to the twins, as Isolde had tried to do, and find out just exactly how much trouble they were in.

"That's it. I'll go to the source.*"*

As he knocked on the twin's door, Mickey was no longer surprised to hear the jungle sounds coming from within. When Patrick let him in, he looked none too friendly.

"What do *you* want?" Suddenly he felt something rush past him, several somethings, and he felt a nip at his ankle.

"Ow!" A low growl, and then they were gone. "What was that?" Mickey asked as he peered down at his torn pant leg.

"That was your destiny" replied Patrick, and broke into a cackle. He was joined by Sarah, and the sound of their laughter was almost maniacal.

*Destiny?* "What are you talking about?"

The laughter ceased suddenly, and the smiles dropped off of their faces as if wiped off by a washrag.

"We never wanted you here. Or your little girlfriend either. We got along just fine until you came along," snapped Patrick.

"Yeah, and at least up until now, you two were only a nuisance. Now you're a threat, and we can't allow that," piped up Sarah with a steely glint in her Erin-like eyes.

"A threat to what! What have we ever done to you?"

"Sarah's animals need freedom. They have a right, a desire to be free, and we've given them that."

"A right to kill people? And terrorize them? Who do you think you *are!* How dare you!"

"Oh, don't act so fucking sanctimonious! You're in this up to your neck. And what do you think you've been doing for Erin all this time . . . arranging tea parties?"

"I do whatever Erin asks me to do. I owe her. But the killing I leave to the ones who seem to enjoy it so much. Your buddy, Beauregard for one, and you two and these . . . these *abominations* of yours!" Mickey was losing his temper, something he didn't want to do. Especially here. As he raised his voice in anger, he became increasingly aware of his surroundings.

There was now an audible rustling and shuffling going on around him. Nervously shifting his feet from one to the other, he sneaked quick glances around the room, while trying to maintain a show of bravado. The twins sensed his growing anxiety, and exchanged small knowing smiles, their eyes narrowing. Just as Isolde had said, he noticed that the python was not in its tree branch.

His eyes were flicking from frame to frame, and he was startled when they met the glare of a huge Bengal tiger, almost hidden in tall grass, but looking right at him. It licked its chops. Mickey shivered involuntarily, and tore his eyes away, expecting to be devoured any minute. But he stood his ground.

Turning back toward Patrick and Sarah, he aimed what he thought was his most venomous expression at them. "You call these things off!" he demanded. "Or I'll . . ."

"You'll what?" Sneered Patrick.

"I'll . . . I'll . . . you'll see . . ." Mickey trailed off lamely.

"Ha ha ha ha!!" Now they were both laughing uproariously, almost doubled over in their mirth. *Scritch Scritch . . .*

Something was at the door. Sarah went to open it, still hiccupping and sniggering. She opened the door wide.

"Aaah! Owww! Ouch! Get away, get away!" The somethings were back. Whatever had rushed past and nipped at him when he arrived were back, and they surrounded him. Only this time they were all nipping and biting, coming at him from all angles.

"Oww! Get them *OFF* me!" At that, Patrick made a gesture with his arm, and the attack stopped as quickly as it had begun. The snarling, yipping pack obeyed Patrick's command, and leapt into a nearby picture frame, where they became visible.

*Hyenas! They're hyenas!* he thought, flabbergasted.

Mickey was left panting and out of breath, while his legs felt like they had turned to mush. He reached for the corner of a table to steady himself while he took some deep breaths, and tried to compose himself after the harrowing experience. It was his worst nightmare come true, being overrun by a pack of wild dogs.

"Get the message?" asked Sarah coldly.

"Bastards!" cursed Mickey.

\*\*\*

Upon returning to the big house, Mickey went straight to Beau's bedroom. He was still unwakeable. Throughout the morning, he checked on him again several times, always finding him comatose. He was surprised to discover, when he checked on him after lunch, however, that he was gone. *He must have snuck out when I wasn't looking.* Mickey had no way of knowing that Beau had gone to admire the rhino's handiwork at Rowdy's Roadhouse, and it was indeed Beau that Ed and Jesse had spotted in the tall grass behind the bar.

What Mickey didn't know was that the little psycho had become so adept at changing his form from human to snake, and back again, that he was able to do it almost at will. He could now leave the house in his body or outside of it, depending on his mood.

That evening, as Isolde and Mickey sat glumly eating their dinner, Beau entered the kitchen looking a little the worse for wear. His clothes were disheveled, and had burrs and pieces of sticks and grass all over them. And his orange hair, which was usually slicked back and secured with an elastic band, had errant strands hanging out in loops and tangles.

"Where have you been?" demanded Mickey.

"Around."

"Yeah, I'll bet!"

"Hey, I don't need this crap. I'm going to my room. I need a nap."

"Well, I intend to find out where you've been disappearing to, you can bet your scrawny little ass I will!" But the threat fell on deaf ears, because Beau had already left the room.

# Chapter 41

## Into Africa

"Better call the meat wagon. And let's get to the station and talk to the Chief." Ed and Jesse were rounding the corner of Rowdy's on the way back to their patrol car in the parking lot out front. By unspoken agreement, they chose not to pass through the bloodbath in the bar.

"Speaking of the Chief, I wonder where he's been. Nobody's seen him," said Jesse.

"Sybil said she sent him on a call out on Route 17 last night, and she hasn't heard from him since. And he wasn't at work this morning. It's odd that he hasn't radioed in."

"Hmm. Wonder what that was all about. Well, maybe he had some personal business to take care of." Ed felt a stirring of uneasiness in his chest. "Although with all this craziness going on, you'd think he'd be here to help. We sure need him. Do you believe that hospital fiasco?" They were climbing into the patrol car, and he glanced at Jesse's face as he asked the question. When he saw the ripple of pain that washed over his friend, that suddenly made him look twenty years older, he wished he'd kept his mouth shut. "Sorry Jesse."

"I'm okay." His facial expression belied his words, but he was a cop, a trained professional. He had a town in crisis to deal with, and a lot of dead bodies on his hands, and so he focused on his work.

But it was difficult to focus on anything other than the death of his beautiful wife and his unborn child. Jesse and Dawna had truly loved each other, and were deliriously happy about the impending birth of their baby in five months. *I will avenge them.* He was a man on a mission now. It wasn't just the anonymous faces of the citizens of a small town that he was obligated to protect anymore.

Now it was personal.

As he and his partner drove away from the remains of Rowdy's Roadhouse, his blender-blade thoughts swirled and whirred around and around in his mind trying to mix the bizarre ingredients that made up the haunting of Hester into a cohesive recipe that he could digest and make sense of.

He began trying to connect the apparently random elements of the destruction and pandemonium that had begun in earnest that morning and were now escalating completely out of control all around him.

As Ed maneuvered the patrol car out of the parking lot and back out onto the main road, he reached for the radio.

"Sybil, this is three nancy zulu, come in. Over." The radio was dead. "Headquarters, this is three nancy zulu, come in. Over." He clicked the button on the hand held radio a couple of times. "This is three nancy zulu, come in. Over." Nothing. "Shit!"

"What is it?" Ed's exclamation broke into Jesse's thoughts.

"The damn radio's dead."

"That's weird."

"What the hell . . . now what?" About a mile from the scene of the rhino attack, the car started to hiccup, and then died.

"What happened? Out of gas or something?" Jesse was looking at the instrument panel.

Of course we're not out of gas! It just quit." Ed was losing his temper.

"Stinking county budget! If they'd maintain these fucking things properly, this wouldn't happen. Alright, let's have a look, it's probably something simple." The cops got out of the car and popped the hood. They walked around to the front of the vehicle and stuck their heads in to examine the engine.

"See anything?" asked Jesse.

"No."

They jiggled and joggled wires and hoses to see if something had come loose.

"Shit, shit, shit!" Ed and Jesse exchanged exasperated looks, and resignedly straightened up, not quite sure what to do now.

Jesse stuck his hands in his front pockets and let out a long, frustrated breath, as Ed ran his fingers through his blond marine-style crew cut. Both automatically began scanning the location for signs of habitation. A house with a phone would do nicely right about now. Or a passing car they could flag down. But there was nothing, and they knew it. It was two miles from Rowdy's to town and they were stuck halfway. The only house between the two points was Mr. Slowicki's place, and twin grimaces said they both knew it. The thought of approaching the crazy old guy's property was not exactly appealing, but desperate measures . . . etc.

"Let's get this thing over on the shoulder. We'll have to hoof it." Not willing to give up without a fight, Ed tried the ignition one more time, but it was useless. The engine didn't even try to turn over. So he put the transmission into neutral and each of them placed their hands on the doorframes. Assuming the age-old pushing position, they put their backs into it. Once the car was rolled onto the shoulder of the road, they secured and locked it, and stepped out in front of it to scan the road ahead.

"Ed . . ."

"Are you seeing what I'm seeing?"

"What *is* this?" Jesse had a frown of confusion on his face.

The landscape had changed. Was changing. Right before their eyes. A minute ago the surroundings had been boring and familiar. Scenery so recognizable that it went unnoticed because they had passed by it hundreds of times before. But now the road had all but disappeared, and was narrowing down to what looked like a cow path. The vegetation was different too. Gone was the scrub pine and tangled brush that took up most of the untended and unused county property for miles along both sides of Dalton Road.

Ed rubbed his eyes, blinked, and looked again, but his vision wasn't deceiving him. To the left was an African savanna; tall waving grasses stretching for miles. Occasional Acacia trees supported what looked like large, prickly nests high in the branches. To the right was a rain forest complete with a canopy; a continuous layer of thick, green, impenetrable tree crowns. Ed and Jesse could feel the humidity settling upon them like a warm, moist blanket that had been removed from a clothes dryer while still damp. Beneath the canopy, was an understory, made up of the crowns of small trees, and saplings of the giants. The forest floor was relatively open, due to the absence of grasses or shrubs, and was interspersed with the rotting stumps of fallen giants, and occasionally dense clumps of bushes and ferns. They gaped, open-mouthed at the impossible transformation. Gone were any signs of civilization. The road had vanished, and so had their patrol car. They had been thrust into another world, and another time. Here was a place where twentieth century man did not exist.

"I don't think we're in Kansas anymore Toto," said Ed.

Jesse didn't laugh. The surreal vision surrounding them was becoming clearer and more distinct by the second, and now the apparition was accompanied by sound. From high up in the lattice of the canopy came the squawks and chitterings of what could only be primates. Monkeys, chimpanzees, and apes.

"Let's go."

"What do you mean let's go?"

"We'll follow this path, where the road used to be. It's going in the same direction, we'll follow it. We must be hallucinating or something."

"Hallucinating? From what!"

"I don't know! Maybe the walls in the bar had asbestos in them or something. How should I know? Let's just get out of here!" Ed was already heading down the path.

"Well, wait for me. Jesus. I don't believe this." Jesse followed Ed, shaking his head.

"Pssssst! Psssst!"

"What was that?!" Ed signaled for Jesse, who was walking right behind him, to stop, and drew his gun.

"Psst. Over here!" It was a voice, a female voice, coming from a huge clump of giant, leafy primeval-looking ferns.

"Who's there?"

"It's me. Mercy."

"Mercy? Come out of there. What are *you* doing here?"

Mercy Lovett emerged from her hiding place behind the lush greenery. "Boy, am I glad to see you guys. I was coming back to take care of Shiv. I couldn't bear to leave him like that, but Ratch made me go. Once they took off, I started walking. It's only two miles. But everything started changing as soon as I left the outskirts of town, and now I don't know where I am." Mercy was talking very fast, her eyes were opened very wide, and she looked completely bewildered. And scared. "What the fuck's going on?"

"No idea. But we're in this together, so come with us. This path should lead us back to town."

"If there *is* a town," Jesse intoned quietly, a suggestion of dread creeping over his face.

Ed and Mercy just looked at him.

"Wait, there's more," Mercy said, tearing her eyes away from Jesse after a long moment, and turning back to Ed.

"More?"

"Yeah. I heard something. In the underbrush. It was moving around and kind of snorting, and it sounded enormous. Now give me a gun."

"Give you a gun! You gotta be kidding."

"Oh yeah, I always kid around when my life is in danger, and some ferocious *fucking* beast is tracking me! Now give me a gun, I said!"

"Like hell! And besides, we've only got two."

"Bullshit! I know you guys carry throwaways. Now give me one or I'll start screaming and attract that thing's attention!"

"NO!"

"Okay then, Aaahh," Mercy opened her mouth, threw her head back, and let out the beginning of a really good one. Like a flash, Jesse clapped his hand over her mouth, and the scream came out like, "Mmmmph."

Then they all heard it.

Branches snapped and deadfall crackled as something large

began to move about in the brush. "Okay, okay, here!" Ed reached into his boot and produced a small, chromed derringer. He picked up one of Mercy's hands and slapped the small weapon into it.

"You know how to use one of these?" Ed asked as Mercy stared at her palm for a second.

"Pfffft! What do you think? Of course I know how to use one. Shiv taught me."

"That figures. Alright let's go. And keep your voices down. We have no idea what we're up against here, if anything."

"Fine."

The path was narrow, so they had to walk single file. Ed took the lead, while Mercy walked in the middle, and Jesse brought up the rear. At first, there were jungle noises: tropical birds calling to their mates, large insects whirring and chirping, and the monkeys frolicking and screeching to one another up in the high canopy.

*I feel like we're in a movie,* thought Mercy, as they forged ahead through the foliage that slapped at them here and there where it had grown over the path. Then suddenly, everything went silent. The birds stopped cawing, and the bugs stopped rubbing their legs together. It was like all life had come to a grinding halt, and was holding its collective breath.

*"Grrrrrrrr."*

"Get down!" whispered Ed through gritted teeth. "Listen!"

They crouched in the path, guns drawn, and listened.

"Grrrrr." It sounded closer, not ten feet away, if normal acoustics could be trusted in this un-normal place.

"Into those bushes . . . now!" ordered Jesse. Mercy was frozen to the spot. Jesse grabbed a handful of the back of her shirt, and the three dove into the fronds of a giant fern just in the nick of time. Something burst out of the bushes onto the path where they had been walking not five seconds before, growling and snarling.

Ed began firing his weapon in that direction, although he couldn't see what he was shooting at. The bushes from which the attack had come, parted again, and the thing was gone. They could hear it crashing through the forest in a frenzied retreat. They crouched in shocked silence for a minute, looking at each other in stunned incomprehension, as reality reared its ugly head.

They were being stalked . . . hunted.

As the echo of the gunfire faded, the jungle dwellers once again took up their chorus where they had left off, before the approach of the ghostly predator.

"What was it?" Mercy spoke first.

"Sounded like some kind of big cat. An invisible one. But the gunshots must have scared it off." Then more to himself than to the others he muttered, "I can't believe I just said that" shaking his head in disbelief."

"Thank God. Looks like we're going to need the guns after all. So we'd better save ammo. Only shoot when absolutely necessary, and only as *many* as necessary. Got it?"

Mercy nodded.

Jesse said, "Got it."

"Okay, let's move. And try not to draw attention to ourselves." Carefully they withdrew from behind their cover of ferns, and once again started down the jungle path, Ed again in the lead.

They all began casting wary glances back over their shoulders now, and scanning the savanna on one side, and the rain forest on the other, determined not to be caught off guard again. Life could be heard all around them, wild and untamed, and there was no doubt that real animals inhabited the environment, but they were invisible to the eye. The human eye at least. The problem was, and a problem that was on the minds of all three, was that *they* were not invisible, and stuck out like nudists at a high-society ball.

Ed had been mentally trying to gage how far from town they were now, if, as Jesse had said, there *was* a town to go to.

*This is insane!* he thought, still having trouble believing his own senses.

But so far, the landscape seemed endless, and showed no sign of an end of the road, a light at the end of the tunnel, a town at the end of the path. Nothing but jungle on one side, and the savanna on the other.

Then Eddie Spears was flat on his face.

He had tripped over something in the path, and went down with a bone-crunching thud onto the hard-packed dirt walkway.

They could see nothing in the way, and Jesse and Mercy rushed to help him up. *Sssssssshhhhh Swish swish.*

"Get him up!" yelled Jesse as he and Mercy struggled to haul Ed off of the pathway and onto his feet. Ed was trying to regain his footing, but the breath had been knocked out of him, and his nose was broken, making it hard to breathe through the blood filling his nostrils and coursing down his throat.

And something had a hold of him.

Ed felt the first constriction just as Jesse and Mercy together gave a mighty yank, tossing all three backwards onto their butts. *Ssssss swish swish.*

"Yeeeeks! It's coming!" Screamed Mercy. Ed forgot about his gushing nose as he joined the other two in their frantic attempt to escape the snake. They resembled the participants in a giant spider race as they scrambled backwards on all fours.

Jesse gained his feet first and made a lunging grab for the other two. He had a shirt collar in each hand and was already making a break for it in the other direction with Ed and Mercy in tow, when Mercy let out a high-pitched wail of pain. By this time Ed was also upright, and he and Jesse each snatched up one of her arms.

Mercy was now the rope in a desperate tug of war. The python had sunk its fangs into the toes of her right foot and was hanging on. With the two cops pulling on her arms, she was hoisted off of the ground, stretched as taut as a new clothesline.

"Owwwwww!" Blood spurted out of the wounds where the fangs had dug in.

"Pull, Jesse, pull!" Ed screamed.

"I'm pulling!"

"On three! One, two, three!" With a tremendous backward thrust, the three once again went sprawling, and Jesse had his gun out without missing a beat. He fired two shots in the direction of the snake, and elicited an ear-splitting squeal for his effort. The giant serpent turned and slithered away into the rain forest. They could see the trail it made as it bent the vegetation over which it traveled.

Mercy was sobbing and holding her gushing foot. When they

were sure the snake had slithered away, Ed and Jesse stooped down to survey the damage. Two of Mercy's toes were gone. Torn off by the snakes fangs when they ripped her foot out of its mouth.

"Quick, give me your belt!" said Jesse, as he held her bleeding foot in the air, and applied pressure with his hands to stanch the flow. Ed hurriedly pulled his belt out of its loops and handed it to Jesse to use as a tourniquet, while trying to stuff his police paraphernalia into his pockets. The holster he tossed aside as no longer necessary, but kept anything that he thought could be used as a weapon, or life-saving device.

# Chapter 42

## Crunch In The Woods

Just before Ed and Jesse took off for Rowdy's Roadhouse, Ratch and Stink had departed the Hester Police Station on their Harleys with roaring engines, and a feeling of dread in their chests.

Ratch was reeling from the memories of the horror at Rowdy's, and the *way* his friends had died. But he was no stranger to gore, thanks to old Lloyd, and his childhood teachings. Still, it was one thing to hang a pig up by its feet and slit its throat. It was quite another to witness the slaughter of people whom he had considered his *true* family. People that he had pledged to devote his life to, and who devoted theirs to him. People who were always there through trauma and triumph, good times and bad. Ratch had believed that they were invulnerable in battle. But how could you fight something that you couldn't see? Ratch was a realist, however, and believed anything was possible in this life, and he didn't dwell on the how, what or why the killings had happened. He accepted that it had, with no questions asked, and concentrated now on what was left of his club.

With Shiv and Bull gone, he was now the boss, by attrition. It was a responsibility he took seriously, and felt, as he rode his bike with vengeance in his heart, that a battle was going to be fought, and he refused to lose it. He was grateful for the company of Stink, riding hard beside him. He was a tough little bastard, and never shrank from a fight, no matter how big or deadly the opponent.

It was easier to navigate in and around the parking lot that Morgan Street had become, on two wheels. They zig-zagged back and forth, avoiding the debris left by the rhinos as they barreled through town. Once they left the small business district behind, the road cleared and they cranked the bikes up to nearly a hundred miles an hour. The farmland and fields sped by in a blur, with the big engines rumbling in their ears, and vibrating with raw power between their thighs.

It took about fifteen minutes of hard riding at top speed to reach the piece of unkempt property on the outskirts of Hester that the Sabres owned, on which sat a dilapidated old building that served as their clubhouse. Initially Ratch noticed nothing, so intent was he on reaching his friends. Images of Rowdy's, and the splattered bodies of Shiv, Bull, and Speedy filled his head, and at first he paid no attention to the trampled crops, or the utter lack of movement upon the landscape as it flashed by him. Only slowly did he become aware that something was amiss.

Confused, he thought that they'd somehow taken a wrong turn and were on a strange road. But he realized in an instant that this was impossible. Only one road led out of town, and they were on it. This route was as familiar as the short path he took in the mornings from his bedroom to the john across the hall to take a piss.

As they slowed the bikes to begin the approach to the winding gravel drive leading to the house, there seemed to be a sudden drop in the temperature. Then everything started to happen fast.

Gearing down to make the turn into the driveway, the chill in the air became apparent. The warm June breeze that had been blowing Ratch's long loose hair straight back on the wild ride from town felt more frigid by the minute. And as he convinced the big thrumming engine of the Harley to slow down, he saw his breath escape his mouth in plumes of mist, and dissipate in the cold. He glanced at Stink riding beside him, and saw that he felt it too.

It was like they were literally riding from one season right into another. Stink, with his warm breath also swirling around and away from him, looked back. His usually surly countenance portrayed confusion, and a quizzical aspect that was a new one to Ratch. By unspoken agreement, they slowed even more as they made their way toward the rickety house at the end of the driveway. Cautious and alert, they approached the familiar structure that suddenly wasn't so familiar anymore.

A spooky, hazy mist was now floating close to the ground, and enveloping the lower portion of the property, giving everything a surreal, haunted feeling. And the cold. The bikers were shivering now with it, their bare arms covered with goose bumps, for they were wearing their regular summer uniforms of tank tops and sleeveless leather vests with the club logo of the Satan's Sabres colorfully embroidered on the back.

Majestic snow-capped mountain peaks were rising out of the low-lying, moisture-laden mist in the distance now, and huge old-growth pine trees dotted the landscape. It appeared that the Pacific Northwest in all its untouched, ageless glory, Bigfoot country, had somehow been magically spirited from thousands of miles away, and had come to claim this scenic, tranquil section of New York State, and the quiet little town of Hester  for itself.

Stink's bike was the first to stutter. As it began to choke and hesitate, Stink looked down at the engine in dismay. Then Ratch felt his own motorcycle begin to cough. The two limped along, mentally urging the machines to keep going; don't stop now. They were snailing along now, side by side, when the engines failed altogether. But the bikes weren't just failing, they were *dissolving,* right out from underneath them. Ratch and Stink could actually *feel* them melting away. In seconds the riders were standing on the narrow path, which a moment ago had been a gravel drive, with their arms and legs spread apart as if their hands gripped handlebars, and their feet were still on footpegs.

*What the fuck . . .?* Stink was staring, incredulous, at the space between his legs where a gas tank had been only seconds before.

"Shhhh, listen." Ratch lowered his arms from the no-longer-there handlebars, and held a finger up to Stink to be quiet. Stink listened. Ratch was the boss now. Stink raised his head, shaking his tousled black hair out of his eyes, to look in the direction that Ratch was riveted to.

It was the clubhouse. *Used* to be the clubhouse. But it was only an apparition now, and disappearing fast in the mist. The majestic, towering pine forest around them grew more dense as they drew closer together and looked around. An unnatural hush had replaced the summer sounds of birds and bees. A blanket of snow covered the ground, and muffled their accelerated frosty, plumed breath as it sailed out into the crisp, cold air.

Instinctively, Ratch and Stink slowly reached inside their clothing for their weapons, their eyes never leaving the dark recesses between the thick pines around them. When they had armed themselves with the razor-sharp knives that they always carried for self-defense, they wordlessly met each other's eyes.

The grim and determined expression on Stink's face told Ratch that he was prepared to face anything, and that the bewilderment of minutes before, of watching their bikes and clubhouse vanish, was already in the past. Along with fearlessness, adaptability was one of Stink's valuable assets, and Ratch gained confidence just having him there.

With a toss of his head, he indicated the path ahead, and they began to move. An eerie sensation of being watched made them forget about the cold. Every sense was on the alert for danger, and Ratch was almost vibrating with the tension in the silent, frozen, ominous air around him. As they proceeded along the path, they found themselves trying to focus their vision into the dark places that they passed, to sharpen it, so as not to be ambushed by whatever it was that was watching. But they couldn't have predicted that the attack would come from above.

*SCREE! SCREE!*

"AHG!" Suddenly Stink was flailing his arms and wildly slashing the air over his head with his six-inch blade, as his unruly mop of tangled black hair seemed to rise up of its own accord. His feet were almost off the ground as something tangled itself in his hair and tried to lift him. In an instant, Ratch joined him, blade flashing. Trickles of blood now began to flow down Stink's forehead as the massive eagle sunk its talons into his scalp. Stink resembled a macabre marionette bouncing on the strings of a puppeteer as he fought ferociously to keep his feet on the ground, and disentangle himself from the grip of the huge, ghostly, screeching bird. As the battle raged, Ratch kept up the slashing motions above Stink's head, yelling, "Get OFF him, you FUCKER!" But to no avail.

He kept it up, however, his mind searching frantically for any other weapon he could use. Cramming his free hand into the pockets of his jeans, he felt his Zippo lighter and yanked it out. In one motion, he pulled it out, flipped the lid back, lit it, and began waving it over Stink's thrashing, now streaming head. Then with one last *SCREE!* the bird let go. The sudden release of tension sent Stink sprawling in the snow on the path, now dotted with spreading blobs of red, like a cherry sno-cone. Momentarily stunned, he gave his head a shake, sending droplets of blood flying.

"Holy Fuck!"

"Are you all right?!" Ratch scanned the sky as he bent to help his friend up off of the ground.

"Yeah, yeah, I'm all right. Jesus!" Stink was wobbly as Ratch heaved him up to a standing position. Once on his feet, he ran his hand over his face and stared at the blood that came away in it. "Just like Rowdy's."

"Yeah. Just like Rowdy's."

"What happened there man! How'd you get rid of it?!" Stink was wincing a little now, as he gingerly felt the gouges in his scalp.

Ratch lowered his voice, almost to a whisper, mindful that there were probably, *no not probably, definitely,* eyes on them. "I used my lighter."

"Your lighter? Holy shit! Are you sure that's what did it? It sure wasn't afraid of our blades!"

"No I'm not sure. But it stopped didn't it?"

"Yeah. Whatever IT was. Fuck." Stink was now wiping his bloody hands off on his jeans. Stinks' head snapped up, and he stopped mid-wipe when he heard it. In the winter quiet, the snapping twig sounded like a gunshot. "Shit, something's coming."

"Let's get outta here." A terrified scream rent the air.

"RUN!"

As they bolted down the path, their leather soled motorcycle boots slipping and sliding in the snow, the scream came again. And it sounded familiar.

"Wait!" Ratch skidded to a halt, and held his arm out to stop Stink. They listened.

"It's Crunch! Crunch is out there!"

"It *IS* Crunch!" Their own fear forgotten, they began to holler. "Crunch! Hey Crunch!"

Crunch's real name was Trevor Crossley, and he was a long-standing member of the Sabres. He had earned his nickname because of the many accidents that he had been involved in on his motorcycle over the years, and miraculously survived, to ride again. From beyond the tree line at the edge of the path, Ratch and Stink heard a faint voice.

"Ratch!" It was definitely Crunch's voice. Pained and scared, but his voice nonetheless.

"Don't come in here! Bears!"

Ratch had an idea. "Stink, find some dry branches."

"Crunch! We're coming in!"

The voice was a little stronger now. "No! Don't come in! I'm telling you, there's bears!"

"Hang on Crunch!" As Stink hurriedly looked for the driest branches he could find, it didn't even occur to him to question Ratch. He knew he was a natural at problem solving, and could always figure a way out of a fix, so he gathered sticks and branches. Meanwhile, Ratch whipped off his vest, tore the black, sleeveless muscle shirt off that he was wearing underneath, and replaced the vest. Tearing sounds filled the silence as Ratch began to rip the shirt into strips.

"Okay, that's enough." He picked out a short branch from the small pile that Stink had gathered, with some good heft to it, and started winding strips of cotton around one end, instructing Stink to do the same.

"Okay, ready?"

"Ready."

"Let's go." Ratch had the tree branch in one hand, his lighter in the other, and took the lead. Stink followed with his own rag-wrapped club, and ever-present knife clutched tightly. Armed as well as they could be under the circumstances, the two left the dubious safety of the path, and plunged into the dark unknown territory of the pine forest, where their friend was obviously in trouble. It was like entering another world. The loss of light was immediate and unnerving. The dense pines towered above them, the needled branches nearly reaching the ground in spots, and so numerous and dense that their pupils dilated trying to adjust to the low light.

As they got closer to where the sound of Crunch's voice had seemed to originate, disorientation set in. The view of the path behind them was quickly swallowed up by the trees, and their nerve endings prickled like tiny bugs under the skin. Now they could hear not just one twig snapping, but whole branches cracking. And it wasn't just the weight of the snow making them bend and break. Something was moving about through the trees ahead. Something big.

As they crept along, Ratch lost his bearings, and used a stage whisper to try and locate Crunch.

"Crunch, where are you?" He listened. The sound of something . . . *bears?* The crashing about in the lower branches of the pines grew louder, but Crunch didn't answer.

"Crunch, can you hear me?"

Then "GRROWWWWW . . ."

"Oh, Fuck! Here we g . . .!" Ratch was thrown off his feet and sent rolling and hurtling through the snow, the club flying out of his hand and landing in a drift ten feet away.

"GRRROWWW . . ." The bear batted him again just as he came to rest at the foot of a huge pine.

It was playing with him.

As he went tumbling again, he screamed out to Stink, "My lighter! Grab my lighter!"

With the precision of Baryshnikov, Ratch gaged the distance from Stink in mid-roll, and gave it a mighty fling toward him. He had lost his club when the assault began, but fortunately the lighter was gripped so tightly in his fist that he still had it, even as he rolled and tumbled under the bear's gigantic paws. Stink saw the glint of silver fly through the air toward him, and made a dive for it. The weight sent it deep into a snow bank, and Stink set upon it like a mad thing, and began frantically digging. Trying to keep his eyes on Ratch, who would get flung, then scramble away, only to be flung again, he dug furiously and hit pay dirt. The lighter!

"Ratch! I got it!"

"L . . . Light . . . th . . . light . . . UnnGH . . ."

"Hang on Ratch! Hang on!" Ratch was able to get enough out, even with the air knocked out of him, and multiple red gashes appearing on his body, for Stink to know what to do. He lit the rags.

First a tiny lick of fire, and then the whole end of the club burst into flames. Then screaming like a banshee, Stink charged the invisible attacker with all the hatred within his wiry body, swinging wildly at where he thought the bear was, trying to distract it away from Ratch. He was losing. The bear seemed not to notice, but kept on batting his new toy around. Suddenly there was another banshee beside him, with a club in his hand.

"LIGHT ME!" It was Crunch, appearing out of nowhere gripping Ratch's lost club.

He reached it out to Stink and lit it from the flames. Now they were both swinging and screaming like baseball players gone mad.

As they waded in crazily between Ratch and the bear, the torches finally made an impression, and Ratch was scrambling to safety, bleeding but alive. With a roar that literally shook the trees around them, the bear took off through the forest at breakneck speed, judging from the tremendous cracking and snapping of branches, and its labored panting getting further and further away.

"Ratch!" Crunch and Stink charged over to where Ratch lay in a bloody heap. Sticking their still-burning torches upright in the snow, in case the bear came back, they hunched over him.

"He's still breathing!"

"Ratch, can you hear me! Ratch!"

"Unnn. Oww. G . . . Gone . . .?"

Stink almost fainted with relief. "Yeah, Ratch. It's gone. Can you sit up?"

With Crunch on one side holding him, and Stink on the other, they helped him to a sitting position, and waited while he caught his breath.

"Are you all right? Is anything broken?"

"Crunch? Wh . . . where did y . . . you come from? Ow. Fuck!"

"I was in a tree when I heard you guys. Fuckin' bear treed me. Sheesh! That's when I called out. But it heard you too, so I shut up. Then when I climbed down, I saw it nail you, Ratch. So I snuck over and we scared it away. That was a great idea, those torches."

"Yeah, no shit," said Stink. "Think you can walk, Ratch?"

"Think so. Ow. Yeah, I can walk." And Ratch was on his feet. The three stood looking at each other for a minute, all thinking pretty much the same thing. *Are we all that's left? Who else is out there?* As the adrenaline began to recede back to a more normal level, the cold once again pierced their flesh, and the shivering set in. "Fucking cold out here."

"Out here where? Where are we?"

"No idea. Bikes are gone. Clubhouse is gone. I'm the only one who made it out," said Crunch. "Where's the other guys?"

Stink and Ratch looked at each other, then back at Crunch. That's when they noticed that he too was bleeding. His clothes were in tatters, and there were several long gashes across his midsection, wrapped crudely with strips of leather and cloth. His eyes followed theirs, and he looked down at himself.

"Now you can see why I was up the tree." A tiny ghost of a smile appeared on his lips as he spoke, but then vanished as quickly as it had come, when he remembered the chaos at the clubhouse. His eyes were haunted as he looked back up at Ratch and Stink, and Ratch spoke.

"Well, let's build a fire and warm up while we figure out what to do. No point in freezing to death."

"Good idea."

With the three pitching in, it took about ten minutes to gather up enough dry sticks and branches to build up a roaring fire. Once they had gotten a large blaze going, they pulled up a fallen tree trunk to sit on, and began to warm up. Bruised and bleeding, Ratch, Stink, and Crunch sat in silence for a few minutes, examining their wounds, and catching their breath.

Ratch broke the silence. "We've gotta figure out how to get out of this."

"Well, one things for sure. They don't like fire."

"They who? What do you think that was Crunch?" asked Stink.

"It was a grizzly bear, I'm sure of it."

"A grizzly bear? How do you know that? We couldn't see it."

"I was at the clubhouse, and it got in. I was there with Jimmy and Buck, working on Buck's bike out behind the house. I went in to get a couple of beers, when I heard a scream. I heard Buck yelling Jimmy's name, so I went running. When I ran around the side of the house Buck was being bashed around, with blood flying everywhere. I tripped on something slippery, and fell on my ass. Jimmy's head was lying right beside me, and I almost stepped right on it!"

"Jesus."

"But I couldn't see anything! Not anything! So I made a run for the house to get a gun, and it chased me! I could hear it growling right behind me, so I got in and slammed the door, but it crashed right through it as if it was nothing. When I heard that I turned, and that's when it slashed me." Crunch looked down at his bandaged mid-section. "I didn't wait around to get *my* head torn off, so I dove behind the bar and pulled up the trap door to our stash spot in the floor, and jumped in. It was mad too, because it didn't see where I got to, so it started to just demolish the place. I could hear it right above me, growling and bashing the place apart, so I waited. I don't know how long I was down there, but finally I guess it gave up, and left. When I was pretty sure it was gone, I opened the hatch and got out. Man, you should have seen the mess. The only thing I know of that's big enough to cause that kind of damage is a grizzly, I'm sure of it. Everything was real quiet, you could hear a pin drop, so I wanted to see how Buck was. I knew Jimmy was dead, because I saw his head. God, what a mess."

Crunch went silent for a minute, and a shudder ran through his body as he relived the horror of staring into the eyes of his decapitated friend. Then he took a deep, wavery breath and continued. Ratch and Stink said nothing, just stared at him, their eyes wide with fear and revulsion.

"There was nothing I could do. I think every bone in Buck's body must have been broken. One of his legs was twisted around his neck . . . eechhh . . . That's when everything started to change. I noticed it getting cold, and the house started disappearing. I couldn't believe it! Right in front of my eyes, the house and bikes and everything was like, *transparent!* I could see right *through* it! And then the whole property vanished altogether. This mist started rising, and all these pine trees appeared, out of nowhere. That's when I heard the bear coming back, I could hear it snuffling and snorting. So I ran. Then it started to chase me, so that's how I ended up in the tree. Man, you never saw anybody climb so fast! I got pretty high up until I thought I was out of reach, and started ripping my clothes and tying them around me to stop the bleeding. That's another reason why I know it was a grizzly bear. Nothing else I know of could have made claw marks like that. I was still up in the tree when I heard you guys call me, and, well . . . you know the rest. Now what do we do?"

# Chapter 43

## Deadly Shadow

Mercy sat wincing on the jungle path.

Jesse used Ed's heavy leather belt as a tourniquet to try and stop the bleeding from her right foot, while Ed tore his shirt into bandages. Once they had the foot tightly wrapped, they removed the belt and carefully lowered the leg. Mercy had lost the two smallest toes on the foot to the python, and was in a lot of pain. But the fact that she was alive at all was a testament to the strength of the two young officers.

Keeping eyes and ears tuned to the jungle around them, Ed and Jesse crouched down on either side of the girl in case any adjustments had to be made to the patch-up job they had performed on her foot.

"How does that feel?"

"How do you *think* it feels? Ow." Mercy was more than a little ornery.

"You're welcome."

"Screw you. Ow."

"Alright . . . alright . . . if you two are finished exchanging pleasantries, I think we ought to decide what to do from here. Mercy, do you think you'll be able to walk?"

"To get out of this shit hole? Are you kidding? Just watch me!" She placed both palms on the ground, and began hauling herself up from her sitting position. She got halfway up, but fell back down with a thump when her wounded foot touched the ground. "Shit!"

The officers were on their feet now, and both stood looking down at the belligerent girl.

"Well that answers my question," said Ed. "You'll have to use a crutch."

Mercy looked disgusted, but said nothing.

"Stay put while we find something to make a crutch out of," ordered Jesse as he and Ed fanned out along either side of her, to look for a suitable piece of wood.

"Real funny. Where'em I gonna go?"

They ignored her.

The next ten minutes were spent picking up and discarding branches and sticks, until Jesse found one that looked about right.

"Here Mercy, try this."

"Fine. Give me a hand."

Ed and Jesse bent down, and each put an arm around her waist to lift her. While she kept her right knee bent stork-style, Jesse placed the makeshift appliance under her armpit.

"Good. Now we're going to let go, and I want you to try leaning on it." The stick had a fork at one end, and after Jesse snapped a piece off of the two ends, it roughly resembled a crutch, crude but serviceable.

"Hey, it works!" Mercy was putting her full weight on it now. "But it kind of hurts my armpit."

"Let's wrap this around it then." Ed bent down to remove his shoe and sock.

"P.U."

"Never mind. Here, lift up." He wound a sock around the "Y," and replaced his shoe on his foot.

"That's better. Let's roll." It didn't take Mercy long to get the hang of walking with a crutch, although Ed and Jesse had to both take the lead now, to clear vines and other obstacles from her path. Even so, it was slow going. Jesse was the first to notice that the light was changing. Or rather, the *dark* was changing. In a tropical rain forest, the sun can rarely penetrate the thick canopy high overhead, so the forest floor remains dim and shadowy. But now, it suddenly seemed to get even darker. Mercy was completely preoccupied with trying to move forward in spite of the awkwardness, and the intense throbbing in her foot. Ed was intent on trying to discern any nuance of sound or movement in the jungle around them, so they wouldn't be caught off guard, in the event of another attack by God knew what. Jesse stopped walking just ahead of Ed, and put his hand out, while peering up toward the green, fluttering, ceiling-like canopy. "Does it seem to be getting darker?"

"Actually, I think you're right. It *does* seem darker."

SPLAT! A blob of water hit Ed right in the eye, as his face was upturned to examine the dimness. "Hey!" Then, two more. "Oh great. Just what we need."

"What?" Mercy halted her jerky progress now, and was looking at him impatiently.

"It's raining." Splat, splat. The fat drops were landing on Jesse now.

"So what? Big strong copper afraid he's gonna melt? No big deal, let's keep going," said Mercy, just as the skies opened up.

Off balance to begin with, Mercy was driven to her knees by the deluge, and dropped her walking stick. In an instant, the three of them were being beaten down by a sheet of water so thick, it was as if the monkeys up in the trees were pelting them with water balloons. Ed was yelling something, but the deafening sound of the sudden downpour drowned him out. He had to make do with sign language, and didn't have to do it twice. He motioned to a gargantuan fern with fronds the size of umbrellas, indicating that they should take cover under it. He reached for Mercy, as Jesse ran to retrieve her "crutch," skidding the last couple of feet on his butt.

In the space of a few minutes, the jungle path had turned into a skating rink of slippery, slimy mud. As Ed got a grip on Mercy, and began dragging her toward the relative protection of the fern, his feet flew out from under him twice. With only one leg, Mercy had no choice but to go sprawling in the mud bath with him, each time letting out a wail loud enough to rival the thunderous pounding of the cloudburst.

Once they had made it to the fern, and got themselves positioned underneath it, Ed and Mercy watched Jesse's clumsy approach with amusement. Considering the circumstances that they now found themselves in, Ed felt startled when he discovered an urge to laugh. Glancing over at Mercy, he saw that she too, in spite of what must have been excruciating pain, also had a smile on her lips, and the first twinkle in her eye he had seen since this whole bizarre escapade began.

Jesse looked absolutely furious, as he dove under the fern with them, and this brought forth a true belly laugh from Ed. The rain was so loud that Ed's guffaws couldn't be heard, even though his mouth was wide open, and he was almost doubled over with mirth. Forgetting her lost toes, Mercy looked from Ed's open-mouthed glee to Jesse, who was now covered in squishy muck from head to foot, and went into a fit of uncontrollable giggles. Being laughed at made him even madder than he already was, and he slammed his fist down onto the mushy ground beside him. He slapped the walking stick down next to Mercy, who found this hilarious, and reached out to pull one of the wide fern leaves toward him, thinking to tear it off for use as a face wipe. He froze. As his hand stopped in mid-air, and his stomach did a complete three hundred and sixty degree flip flop. . . . Eyes.

His jaw dropped open as he stared, petrified, into the streaming gloom. He could have sworn, just for a second, that a pair of glittering yellow eyes were looking back at him.

Without taking his gaze off of the spot, he reached behind him and slapped at Ed, and then Mercy, to try and get their attention. Still grinning, and hitching a little as their merriment subsided, they both turned to him. He was pointing at something, and the look on his mud-smeared face said that they had better pay attention. Then as quickly as it had started, the rain quit, as if someone had turned off the tap. Ed was immediately serious. He had been Jesse's partner long enough to know that his friend was definitely reacting to *something*. "What is it Jesse?" He was startled by how loud his voice sounded in the aftermath of the drumming rain.

"Shhhh, I thought I saw something."

"What?"

"Eyes." The last vestige of amusement dripped off of Mercy's face like the rain from the fern leaves.

"Where?"

"Right there, where I'm pointing. I *swear* I saw two eyes looking right at me." They were whispering now, and in spite of herself and her show of sarcastic bravado, Mercy started to tremble.

In a hushed tone, Ed said, "But so far the animals have been invisible."

"Yeah. So far." All three were on alert now, as they strained to see into the murky foliage. The only sound was the drip, drip, drip of water droplets falling to the ground, as they rolled from the leaves around them. They waited. Jesse reached for Mercy's stick as stealthily as he could, while not turning his gaze away from the place where he had spotted the . . . *eyes?* They sat, like statues, for five minutes. Ten. Jesse began to think that maybe his eyes had been playing tricks on him. *A trick of the rain glinting off of a leaf perhaps.*

Then, *"RRROOOWWW . . ."* A part of the shadows detached itself, and leapt straight at them. It had two glowing, yellow eyes.

The black jaguar was huge, and was on Jesse in an instant. With a horrifying scream, it body-slammed him to the ground, and with a great gnashing of its deadly teeth, went for his throat.

Jesse fought for his life.

Ed could hear Mercy shrieking in the background, as he jumped on the big cat's back. Jesse was holding the snarling beast at bay with one hand, trying to keep the vicious-looking daggers away from his jugular vein, while he took aim with Mercy's stick.

Ed was plastered to the infuriated cat's back, and was pummeling it from behind with both fists. Anger and fear for Jesse drove him to use all the strength and fury that was in him. But his blows seemed to just bounce off of the creature like rice thrown at a wedding. The beast was powerful and strong.

But even though his punches were connecting with very real-feeling muscle and bone, Ed realized, impossibly, that he could see right through it, like a piece of gauze. He could see Jesse underneath it, struggling to hold its jaws away, only inches from his face. *No wonder I couldn't see it in the shadows, it IS a shadow!* He thought in terror. But it was a shadow with just as much substance as Ed himself.

Likewise, Jesse saw Ed on the nightmarish thing's back, trying to tear it off of him. Then just when he felt his arm giving out, and thought he couldn't hold the cat off one minute longer, he brought up the hand with the stick in it, and jammed it into the jaguars mouth. As it choked and gagged on the stick, Jesse saw his opportunity, and rolled out from underneath.

Jesse was momentarily out of harms way, and the jaguar was now in a frenzy trying to remove Mercy's walking stick from its gnashing jaws. Ed took his cue.

He dove sideways from its back, and just as the police academy had taught him, he rolled right into a firing stance, with one knee on the ground, and went for the handgun in his pocket. But just as he took aim, the apparition winked out of existence, like a star in the nighttime sky. Just a *pfft* sound, and it was gone, leaving a tiny puff of smoke to dissipate in the damp, humid air.

Still crouched in the shooters position, he stared unbelieving. Jesse's mouth hung open while he too stared, his breath coming in uneven, raggedy gasps from the exertion of battling the jungle cat. Mercy was the first to recover.

Leaning back a safe distance away, on both elbows, her throat raw from screaming, she spoke in an awed, raspy whisper. "I don't believe this. Where'd it go?" Ed and Jesse didn't have an answer to the question. They were both panting and puffing, and taking in large gulps of air, while their heart rates decelerated to less dangerous levels.

"Who cares where it went, so long as it's gone. Whew, that was close. You okay Ed?"

"I'm okay. You?"

"I'll live." Ed stood up slowly, and lowered his weapon, taking his finger off of the trigger.

They wouldn't have been so relieved if they knew that the whole scene with the jaguar had been witnessed by another pair of eyes. Big brown ones. And no one saw the orange ponytail slipping silently through the sodden foliage.

Beau's control over his ability to change forms was getting stronger with each passing hour, and he knew that he wasn't the only one. For he too had been able to see the filmy essence of the jaguar, as it ambushed Jesse. He knew that when it disappeared in a puff of smoke, it had returned to its picture frame in Patrick and Sarah's house. He had the ability to do the same, but when he took on the incarnation of the python, he preferred to be out and about. He was quickly getting very adept at switching back and forth, and enjoyed it immensely. Especially when he could take someone by surprise, as he had done to Mercy on the game trail. His only regret was that he had only gotten her toes.

After that little disappointment, he had slithered along and followed them, and then watched as they fought off the cat. It had made for an entertaining afternoon, but now he decided he'd better get home and see what those two saps, Mickey and Isolde were up to.

He snickered to himself as he pondered the confusion of the citizens of Hester. And their fear gave him joy.

# Chapter 44

## The Candlemans Go Fishing

Morris and Shirley Candleman had gone fishing early in the morning, as they did on many mornings when the weather was agreeable, since they had retired two years before.

And their faithful Golden Retriever, Solly, always went with them. It was one of his favorite things to do in the whole world. Just before dawn, Morris would get the tackle boxes and gear ready, while Shirley made a lunch and stowed it in the cooler. Solly would dart from one to the other, wagging his bushy blond tail furiously in barely contained excitement, as if every time were the first instead of the hundred and first.

The first bump on the bottom of their thirteen-foot aluminum rowboat jolted Morris awake. After the first couple of hours on the placid water of the Hester River, the three generally settled into a companionable doze while the sun came up. But now Solly was standing with his front paws on the railing of the craft and barking at the water dramatically as if a team of housecats were performing a synchronized swimming routine just out of his reach.

"Solly, what is it boy?"

"Morris? What happened?" Shirley's voice was sleepy, and she blinked as she looked from Solly to her husband.

"Don't know. Must have hit a log or something. Solly! What

do you see?" Morris was scanning the water on the side of the boat where the dog was, and leaned over looking for a stray piece of driftwood or a large fish gliding by just below the surface.

The next thump threw him and Solly overboard with a big splash. Shirley screamed and clutched the rim of the rowboat on her side. It was rocking back and forth in the wake of whatever had dumped man and dog into the river. Solly was the first to surface, and he came up dog paddling just feet away, turning toward where Morris had gone in headfirst. Then Morris popped up, spluttering and cursing.

"Morris! Are you all right?" The relief in Shirley's voice quickly faded into a frantic panic. "There's something under the boat! Swim Morry, swim! Here Solly! We've got to get back to shore!" Morris swam the few feet back to the boat, and began to clamber in, with Shirley's help. Then they both grabbed hold of Solly, and heaved him over the side and into the bottom of the boat, where they landed with him on top of them. Morris lay there for a minute and caught his breath. Solly jumped up and shook himself, spraying water everywhere, and immediately went back to barking over the side of the boat.

"Grab an oar, Shirl! Let's paddle our asses out of here!"

"You got it!"

As the Candlemans began to row to shore, they both noticed something strange.

"Morry, this is weird. We must have drifted further than usual this morning. I don't recall a spot in the river that was ever this wide before."

"I'm glad you see it too. Thought I was going senile there for a minute. Where the hell are we? Never seen trees like that before on this river. Solly, sit boy! You're rocking the boat!"

"Me either! Why, they look almost tropical, but that can't be. Maybe some rich guy down river hired one of those fancy gardeners or something."

"Could be. But it sure doesn't look familiar. I thought I knew every inch of this shoreline. Hm. You know, actually, I don't recognize anything. Row Shirl."

"I'm rowing, I'm rowing for crying out loud! I'm not Arnold

Schwartzenegger you know!"

"Okay, sorry. Don't get your knickers in a knot. Solly, what the *hell* are you barking at?"

"Don't pick on him. He's barking at whatever bumped into us. God Morry, you're turning into a real old crank."

"Well, excuuuuse me! I'm soaking wet and rather uncomfortable, if you don't mind. And I'd like to get home and change."

"Well, we're getting close. Just row, we're almost there."

They were twenty feet from shore when the prow of the small boat was lifted from underneath, straight up into the air, and balanced there for a few seconds, like the space shuttle aiming for the moon. Now all three were tossed into the river in a jumble of arms, legs, and fur.

The hippos were playing.

Morris surfaced and treaded water while he frantically searched for his wife.

"Shirley! Shirley, where are y . . ." The frothing water boiled around him, and he was staring down the throat of a huge hippopotamus. Its mouth was wide open not three feet from him, and the sight of the tusks were enough to send him into shock. The crazy thing was that he could see right through it. *But that was no ghost that tipped us over,* he thought crazily. His eyes never left the animal as he treaded backwards in the water to put distance between him and those ferocious jaws.

"Shirley!"

"Morris! I'm over here!" Shirley had bobbed to the surface now, and she coughed up river water.

"Thank God! Shirl!"

Then Shirley too saw the hippos.

"Shirl, swim! Swim for it!"

But Shirley was transfixed by the sight suspended in the water by her life jacket, mouth open and bobbing like a cork.

*She's going to die!*

Suddenly, Solly appeared behind Shirley, and paddling like mad, snatched the back of her life jacket in his mouth.

"Solly! That's it! Good boy!" Morris managed to swim up alongside Solly and Shirl, and with her between them, they pulled her through the water.

Then the massive creature, down whose cavernous throat Morris had gaped, let out a tremendous bellow and began swimming after them.

The other hippos were batting the rowboat around with their snouts like a bathtub toy, and Morris tried to shake Shirley out of her stupor while he desperately tried to swim to shore with one arm. Just as she began to come around, the first animal dove under the water and came up directly underneath the three of them, breaking Solly and Morris's hold on Shirley and scattering them in three different directions. They flopped back into the river with tremendous splashes. *We're never getting out of this alive,* thought Morris desperately. Just then he thought he heard something above the roiling racket.

"Hey!"

Morris had bobbed back up to the surface again, and shook the water out of his eyes to get a better look. "Help! Help!"

They were close to shore now, and Morris thought he could see a person standing there, frantically waving his arms.

"Over here!" It was Bobby Boyle. After sitting with Cindy Lovett's parents by her bedside for a while, and watching her for signs of life, he had left the hospital to discover that he was in a different world.

What had once been Morgan Street was now transformed into an Amazonian environment. He found himself alone, in a rain forest where the heat and humidity were stifling. And it was alive with sound. All around him there were thousands of birds calling, monkeys cackling, and insects buzzing, chirping and whirring.

He stared around in awe at the tangled jungle that had replaced the main street of Hester. Where the hospital had stood, now was a dim and tangled rain forest. He knew that the Hester River, a familiar landmark, ran along behind the hospital. And because he didn't know what else to do, he headed for it. He didn't have far to go. As he approached the riverbank, Bobby heard splashing and shouting. Then he saw that there were people in trouble. He could also see the hippos, and took in the seriousness of the situation immediately. Distractedly Bobby realized that he was not surprised by the improbable tableau unfolding before him, and put it aside in his mind, so he could concentrate on what had to be done to help these poor people in the water. He quickly scrutinized his surroundings, and spied the tangled and overgrown vines that were growing everywhere.

He chose a strong one, and hacked off a long section with the penknife that he always kept in the back pocket of his jeans. Dragging it to the river's edge, he could see that there were three people struggling in the chaos being created by the hippos, as they rebelled against the invasion into their domain. *No, it's not three people, it's two people and a dog!*

Shirley had recovered her senses now, and had joined in with Morris's chorus of "Help! Help! We can't make it!" Shirley was a strong woman for her age, but she knew she was almost out of strength and half drowned.

Apparently, and fortunately for the Candlemans, the hippos had deduced that the human intruders were not a threat after all, and were now just playing with them. As the animals alternately surfaced and submerged, the couple and the dog were being bounced around in the swells created by the huge bodies all around them.

Shirley now had her wits about her again, although one of her arms seemed to be useless, and dangled in the water at a funny angle. Still, she, Morris and Solly were able to join up again, forming into a linked group, once again endeavoring to reach the shore and safety.

"Here! Grab this!" Bobby had the vine coiled up now and was preparing to toss it to Morris to grab on to. He was swinging the heavy coils back and forth to gather momentum for the toss.

"Okay, throw it!" yelled Morris.

"Ready? Here it comes!"

The first throw fell short by several feet.

"Shit! Hang on. I'll try again. Now get ready!" The second time it worked. The end of the vine landed in the water right in front of Morris with a slap, and he lunged for it.

"Got it!"

"Okay, now hang on!" Morris wrapped the vine around his

wrist, and grabbed hold of Shirley's life jacket. Morris just caught sight of Solly as his head dipped under the water. The dog was running out of steam.

"Solly! Shirl, grab Solly!" With her good arm, Shirley reached into the water and grabbed a handful of hair, yanking up with all the strength she had left. She hooked her hand around his collar, keeping his head above the water, and pulled him along beside her.

Bobby dug his heels into the squishy ground and pulled on the vine, hand over hand, as hard as he could. Finally they reached the shallow water, and Morris was able to stand. He turned and helped Bobby pull Shirley and Solly onto solid ground, where all four of them flopped, exhausted.

The little group lay there on the tiny strip of mud between the forest and the river, panting and coughing, unable to speak. Shirley had her injured arm cradled against her, and Solly lay sprawled on his side, chest heaving as he gulped in air, and expelled some of the water he had swallowed. Morris was flat on his back, spread-eagled as he tried in hitching gasps to catch his breath. Bobby sat up, and surveyed the people and dog that he had rescued, giving them time to recover. When he was sure that they were alive and coming to, he started the conversation.

"Hi, I'm Bobby Boyle."

"Boy, are we glad to meet you, young fella," answered Morris, still panting. "We're the Candlemans, and this brave old guy here is Solly."

"Hello, Solly. Good thing I came along when I did. Looked like you guys were losing." At the mention of his name, Solly raised himself and sat up, still panting with his tongue hanging out the side of his mouth.

"Do you know what's going on here? This doesn't look like any part of the river I've ever seen," said Morris.

"Well, all I know is that Hester has disappeared."

"What do you mean Hester has *disappeared?* You mean the people have all gone somewhere? Did we miss some big disaster while we were out fishing this morning or something? An earthquake, a tornado, what?"

"No man, I mean *Hester,* the whole town, people, buildings, streets, *everything!"*

"Now, come on son, you're pulling my leg. I asked a perfectly logical question, and now I expect a perfectly logical answer. What's going on out there that we don't know about?"

"No Mr. Candelman I'm serious. Look around."

Looking skeptical, and somewhat annoyed, Morris and Shirley did.

Bobby continued. "All I know for sure is that Hester has disappeared. One minute I was in Hester Hospital visiting my girlfriend, and the next I'm here. I'll tell you though, after that elephant thing at Mom 'N Pop's, nothing would surprise me."

"What elephant thing?"

"You didn't hear about it? Whoa. Me and my girl Cindy, were at Mom 'N Pop's this morning, shopping, when an elephant came in and tore the place apart. I mean it must have been an elephant, because it sounded just like one. We could hear it doing that trumpeting thing they do. But we couldn't see it; it was invisible you know? Killed three people and scared Cindy out of her mind. That's why I was at the hospital. She's out of it. No wonder though, seeing those ladies squished like that. Yuk!"

Morris was having trouble taking all of this information in, and Shirley just stared at Bobby with a mixture of horror and disbelief. She and Morris exchanged stunned glances, then turned back to Bobby. Shirley fervently wished that she could accuse him of being on drugs, but the improbable rain forest beside her, as fantastic as it seemed, told her otherwise.

"But . . . but how is that possible? I mean, how can an *elephant* be invisible? We didn't hear anything about it, did we Morry?" Morris shook his head. "And where are we? What is this place? How can a whole *town* disappear!"

"Beats me, all I know is that it has. What I'm wondering is how come we can see those hippos?" They all turned to watch the beasts for a minute. They seemed almost completely solid now, and very real as they ducked beneath the water, and then reappeared, only their large nostrils sucking in and expelling air, and tiny, flicking ears showing. When Morris turned back to ask another question, he noticed Shirley cradling her arm for the first time. "Are you all right, Shirl?"

"I think my arm's broken."

"Here, let me have a look."

"Ow!"

"Damn," said Morris as he gingerly examined Shirley's arm. "It's broken alright my darling. We'd better get it immobilized."

"Here," said Bobby. "Will this do?" He was wearing a Blue denim shirt open over a white cotton tee shirt. He took the shirt off and handed it to Morris.

"Thanks, that'll do nicely." Morris folded the body of the shirt, fashioning a make-shift sling, and carefully placed Shirley's wounded arm into it, tying the sleeves around her neck.

"How's that feel? Is it comfortable?" Morris asked as he tied and adjusted it.

"Let's just say I'll manage. Thank you. But it seems to me that we've got a bigger problem on our hands. For instance, where do we go from here?"

"Good question." Morris looked lost, and concern for his wife was etched deeply into the creases of his face as he stared at her broken arm.

"Can I make a suggestion?" Morris and Shirley looked at Bobby a little skeptically.

"Please do."

"Well, I say we follow the river. I'm sure not crazy about the idea of blundering around in that forest. Are you?" He glanced fearfully over his shoulder, and then back at the couple expectantly.

"No Bobby, can't say that I am. Okay, the river it is. Shirl, do you feel up to it?"

"No time like the present. It's only a broken wing, it could have been worse. And a little pain never killed anybody. Solly, how about you? Ready to go boy?" Solly got to his feet and wagged his tail to show his approval.

"All right. We're off." The four then brushed themselves off and set out walking along the slim strip where the jungle stopped and the water lapped at the shoreline.

# Chapter 45

## Isolde Packs A Lunch

Mickey was outraged. In fact he was more than outraged. He hated Beau's guts, and had reached the end of his tether.

*Well,* he thought, *if the mountain won't come to Mohamed, Mohamed will go to the mountain.*

Erin had not returned to her body for at least a day and a half, and Beau had shown up only sporadically, acting mysterious and looking disheveled. It was time, and Mickey knew it.

He had a gnawing feeling of impending doom in his gut, and his nerve-endings were doing the Macarena. *I can't just sit here and do nothing. I'll go completely crazy.* The die was cast, and he knew he had to venture out and find Erin, come hell or high water. So he went to tell Isolde his plans.

She was not surprised. When two people were as tuned in to each other, as Mickey and Isolde were, very few words were needed.

"You're going after her aren't you?" asked Isolde over her shoulder. It was a statement more than a question, because she knew the answer. She didn't even turn around as Mickey entered the kitchen. At the stove, preparing something for dinner, she felt him coming up behind her.

"Yes."

"Just . . . just be careful."

"Isolde." Mickey took her by the shoulders, and turned her around to face him. "Isolde, look at me. *Look at me.*" She squirmed in his grasp, resisting, and tried to look anywhere but into his eyes, but she lost the war of wills. When she finally gave in and did face him squarely, there were tears in her crystal blue eyes.

"Mickey, I've got a bad feeling. Real bad."

"Me too. But you know it's something I have to do. Don't you? Not just for us, but for Erin too."

"I know. I know. But I'm afraid."

"Isolde, I promise you this. I *will* be back. Okay? I swear I will. And then, me, you, and the baby are going away. Somewhere far. You have my word."

Isolde hugged him hard then, not wanting to let go. And she trusted him, because Mickey had never lied to her. They held each other, loathe to let go. Then Isolde broke the spell. "I've packed you a lunch. And some clean clothes. You may need them."

"But honey, I'm not going for a week. I'm only going to look for Erin."

"I know, I know. Indulge me okay? Put it down to overactive hormones or something. I have a feeling . . ."

"Okay love, if it makes you feel better. Wouldn't want those hormones out of control." He appeased her, and it made them both feel better. One last quick hug, and Mickey headed for the front of the house, leaving Isolde wistfully watching him go.

Mickey slung the backpack that Isolde had prepared for him over his shoulder. As he shut the front door, he tested it once to make sure it was locked. Lost in thought, he strolled purposefully down the flagstone path, and opened the gate between the towering cedar hedges.

He no sooner heard the gate latch snap closed behind him, when the heat hit him.

*What . . .?* Spinning on his heel, he turned back to the house, but it was gone. Mickey stared, incredulous. He looked ahead and behind him several times, confused, looking like a spectator with his eye on the ball at a tennis match, but nothing changed. The house was gone, as was all of Dalton Street, and he was in the jungle.

He stood for a moment, getting his bearings. *So this is where Erin goes. Well, so be it.* Mickey started walking.

"Looks like a game trail." He said to himself. "As good a place to start as any."

Mickey was flabbergasted and his mind was reeling as he made his way down the path that used to be Dalton Street. The jungle was teeming with life. He could hear the birds and bugs, mingled in with the occasional scream of a feline predator, as it presumably made a kill. *Wow.*

He continued his solitary trek without incident, until he noticed that the landscape was changing, *had* changed.

He seemed to be passing from one environment to another. One minute, he was drenched in perspiration because of the humidity in the air. And the next, a dryness made itself felt. The deep, dense jungle foliage gave way to a vista of unbelievable dimensions. There was an ocean of waving, rippling golden grass as far as the eye could see. Mentally, Mickey judged the distance from home to the downtown section of Hester, and his mind made a note. The dividing line seemed to be Morgan Street, the main thoroughfare of the town of Hester. *It's like crossing from one world to another!*

In the distance, Mickey could see there were mountains, with filmy white clouds ringing their pink and mauve peaks, with snow-capped summits. The heat was intense, but was not the same kind of heat as the rain forest that he had just traversed. It was a dry heat that evaporated the slick sheen of perspiration that had oozed out of his pores and coated him, plastering his clothing to his body, while he had been in the moist, tropical jungle. As he scanned the view, he could see a wavery shimmer skimming over the surface of the miles of dry savanna grass. It looked like the microwave icon that you'd see on frozen food packages, but it was much more ethereal. Like the Aurora Borealis in reverse.

The sun was a giant fried egg in the sky, directly overhead, and relentless in its blazing intensity. Mickey had an almost uncontrollable urge to remove all of his clothes and run naked through the grass, just to get cool. He was incredibly stirred, and wished that Isolde was with him just then. *I wonder if this is how Erin feels.* Erin. He mustn't forget what he was here for.

As Mickey passed from the rain forest into the African Savanna, the path ran out. He was now wading nearly waist-deep through the dry, whispering grass. The sheer size and vastness of the open plain made him feel very small indeed. Awestruck, he watched a family group of giraffes wandering by in the distance. Then a small herd of zebra passed very close to him, and he hunkered down to observe their progress. They appeared to be heading in the same direction as the giraffes had a short time before. When the last of them were almost out of sight, Mickey again started walking. The heat was becoming increasingly oppressive, and his legs were tiring. Shading his eyes with a hand, he squinted up at the sun which was now directly overhead, and decided that this was a good time to stop for a rest and some lunch. Clusters of baked and weary-looking deciduous trees and shrubs were scattered about, and Mickey chose a relatively shady spot beneath one of these for his break.

He tucked himself in under the branches of a scrubby savanna bush and plopped down with a sigh, pulling the heavy pack off of his back. *What did she put in here, rocks?* As he began undoing clasps and zippers on the pack, Mickey smiled to himself at Isolde's thoughtfulness.

There was a large thermos of iced tea, as well as a variety of fruits, cold cuts, and cheeses, along with a whole loaf of her delicious homemade bread.

"*What a woman,*" he said aloud, smiling. Digging in to the meal with relish, chewing contentedly, he caught a flash of movement out of the corner of one eye. He stopped with the food still in his mouth, and remained absolutely silent as he surveyed the landscape. An alarm bell went off in his head, and his body went rigid when he spied the pride of lions. They were ambling along in a group, following roughly the same route that the giraffe and zebra had taken. So well did they blend in with their surroundings, with their light brown and beige coloring, that he had not noticed them at first. He stared, enthralled. The thought crossed his mind that he could be looking at Erin without knowing it. When the lions were far enough away that it felt safe, Mickey hastily packed up the remnants of his meal and stealthily replaced the pack on his back. *I'll follow them.* Staying what he felt was a safe distance behind, Mickey kept the pride in view and continued to trudge through the grass. He could see their tails flicking here and there above the grass through which they moved. Mickey was weary but determined as the hot African sun made its inexorable journey across the sky into the late afternoon. He lost sight of the pride a couple of times, and he stopped to get his bearings, feeling the skin on his sweaty neck prickle at the thought that they may have doubled back and were coming up behind him. But then the lions would again come into range, and he continued to follow. Eventually he saw the reason for the exodus of the giraffes, zebras and lions. It was water. Far ahead through the shimmering heat he glimpsed a body of water, and many animals clustered around it. As he got closer, he watched the lions begin to crouch down and spread out. Now and then, a zebra would raise its head and sniff the air, as if it scented something menacing. Then it would change its mind and continue to drink. Closer now, Mickey could see that the watering hole was actually a river, apparently flowing down from the distant mountains, and cutting across the grassy plain. There was something odd about the other side of the river though. Whereas the side he was on was dry and had relatively sparse vegetation, the other side appeared to be dense, lush, and green.

# Chapter 46

## To Get To The Other Side...

As Mickey ate, Bobby Boyle and the Candlemans made their way alongside the river that bordered the rain forest and began to take notice of the other side. It was a complete contrast to the dense and steamy foliage that bordered their side of the river.

"Look at that!" exclaimed Bobby. Morris and Shirley looked.

"Look Morris, zebra. And giraffes!"

"Good Lord!"

"Wait, look in the grass there!" All three had stopped now, and were staring across the water.

"Why it's lions!"

"And what's that!"

"What?"

"There, in the grass, behind the lions. I . . . I think it's a person! There's a person over there! Hello!"

"Bobby! Shut up!" It was too late. As if they all belonged to one animal, the heads of the zebras and giraffes shot up suddenly and looked toward the far shore. The lions, too, were on the alert and fastened their attention on the spot across the water where the voice had come from.

"Now you've done it!" said Morris, with a tremble of fear in his voice. Then as if by some invisible signal, the entire zebra herd bolted and ran. The lions tore their eyes away from the river, and took off after the herd. Mickey, from his side, and Bobby and the Candlemans from theirs, watched in horrified fascination as a huge male cat separated a zebra who was lagging behind, and tackled it to the ground. It didn't have a chance.

The observers watched as the pride converged upon the meal. The big male getting first pick while the females and young ones sat back impatiently. When he had eaten his fill, the rest of the pride dove in and fought with each other for the rest.

While the lions were preoccupied, Mickey took his opportunity to move downwind, signaling to the people on the opposite side to do the same. When the animals were out of sight, and far enough behind him, Mickey called out.

"Hello!" They were the first people he had seen all day, and he was surprised at how happy he was to encounter them.

"Hey there! Can you come across?" called Morris.

"How?"

"Hang on! Let's see what we can find!" yelled Bobby. Bobby immediately began combing the riverbank and forest floor for any materials he could utilize to get Mickey across the river. "Help me!"

"What do you need, Bobby?"

"Um vines, and . . . driftwood. Yeah, driftwood. Maybe we can make a raft. He doesn't look too big."

"Yes, that might just work," agreed Morris. "C'mon Shirl!"

Mickey watched as the three set about gathering up materials to work with. He noticed they had a dog with them too, and was suddenly infinitely glad that they weren't on his side of the river, because even though he was afraid of dogs, he still didn't wish them harm.

"*Those lions would make short work of him,*" thought Mickey with a shudder.

"Okay, that oughtta do it." Said Bobby with satisfaction, his hands on his hips. "Help me, Mr. Candleman?"

"Absolutely."

First, they tested the driftwood to see that it indeed floated, and then with Bobby's trusty penknife, began cutting lengths of the thick, sturdy vines, and lashing the wood together. It didn't take long for them to fashion a rough raft-like device. Then, they tied several vines end to end, and secured one end to the raft. As Morris and Bobby stood back to admire their handiwork, Shirley burst their bubble.

"Looks great fellas, but there's only one problem." The two looked up at her then in surprise, as if they had forgotten that she was there.

"What's that?" Asked Morris.

"How do we get it over there?" Bobby and Morris looked at each other sheepishly, and a little crestfallen.

"Oh, yeah. Good question."

"Well, I guess one of us will have to ride it over." You could hear a pin drop, as they all remembered the hippos. After a weighty silence, Bobby spoke up. "I'll go."

"Are you sure, son?" Morris looked into Bobby's face as he asked the question, and looked none too happy about sending the boy that had saved their lives out into the perilous stretch of water.

"I'm sure. Anyway, I'm the smallest."

"Morris, don't let him!" said Shirley, her maternal instincts kicking in.

"Well, I don't like it. You're only a boy." At that, Bobby raised his chin in defiance at being called a boy, and made up his mind.

"Don't worry, I'll be fine. Besides, if I get into trouble, you can tow me in."

"Well, all right then. Just let me check these vines one last time." Morris tugged on all the knots to make certain that they were strong and secure, and then Bobby stepped out onto the bobbing raft.

It held, and it floated.

Morris watched Bobby drift farther and farther away, as he used a stick and his hands as oars to propel himself to the other side. Mickey stood up to watch the progress of the little driftwood raft as Bobby paddled it closer to where he stood on the opposite shore. No one noticed the female lion's head suddenly pop up out of the grass, its small beard dripping zebra blood, as it observed the tableau being enacted down the river. Its eyes then fastened on Mickey. Beautiful, sea-green eyes, containing the glint of recognition.

Miraculously, Bobby made it all the way to where Mickey waited on the other side of the river.

Bobby could see the humps of the hippos backs here and there as they dozed or grazed under the water's surface, and was careful to maneuver the raft around them as best he could, causing as little disturbance with his paddling as possible. Mickey waded into the shallows at the river's edge and reached out to Bobby's outstretched hand. They were close enough to each other now to be able to lower their voices, and communicate in whispers, so as not to push their luck and disturb the foraging hippos.

"Here, grab my hand and climb on."

"I'll try." Mickey's reach was short, and Bobby had to bring the small craft right into the sticky mud, and the forest of thick bulrushes that made up the shoreline. Realizing that Mickey couldn't reach him, Bobby stepped off the raft and waded through the water to him. He towed the raft behind him and brought it even closer, praying that it wouldn't get mired in the muck .

"Can you swim?"

"No."

"All right then, hop on." Bobby turned his back to Mickey, indicating that he intended to piggyback him the short distance to the raft.

"Wait. My pack."

"Give it here." Bobby removed Mickey's backpack, and placed it on the raft. Then he hoisted Mickey onto his back, waded through the mud and rushes, and deposited him on the driftwood vessel too.

"Whoa!" The weight of Mickey and his pack set the raft to bobbing and rocking, and he grabbed hold of the logs on either side of him with both hands.

"Whew! Close one. Now hold on, I'm coming out." But every time Bobby tried to climb aboard, the raft dipped dangerously low in the water.

"Wait. Let me think." He still had hold of the vine with one hand, and it was awkward trying to board the thing and hold it steady at the same time. On the opposite shore, Morris and Shirley kept a tight grip on the vine that stretched across the expanse of water, and held their breaths.

They were not the only ones watching the display of acrobatics.

The female lion with the bloody beard and the green eyes had lost interest in her zebra meal now, and was creeping silently and low to the ground toward the would-be sailors. But Bobby and Mickey were so engrossed in trying to complete their mission that they didn't notice.

Every time that Bobby leaned on the edge of the raft, it practically tipped over and Mickey had to hang on for dear life.

"This isn't going to work. We're too heavy."

"It has to work. Keep trying. Maybe we can distribute our weight more evenly."

"Sorry, but I think the pack has to go. What's in it anyway?"

"Clothes, food, you know, stuff. My girl packed it for me." Mickey gazed wistfully at the backpack, remembering how adamant Isolde had been that he take it with him. Noting the reluctance on Mickey's face, Bobby asked, "Okay then, will it float?" Mickey brightened up.

"You know, I bet it will! Let's see." He lowered the pack into the water beside the raft, and sure enough, it did.

"Great. Alright, now let's try this again, we're taking way too long and we don't know what's out here." Bobby swung his leg up again, and this time the raft tipped only slightly and he was able to pull himself right up onto it, settling himself beside Mickey. Then he undid one of the straps on the backpack and reattached it to a log at the rear of the craft so that it would float harmlessly behind them. When they were relatively balanced in the center of the raft, Bobby waved his arm, signaling to the Candlemans to begin towing them back to the opposite side of the river, which they proceeded to do.

Guided by the vine, the little raft glided uneventfully across the surface of the river, and Bobby was careful to use his hands once again to paddle them around the ominous humps of the hippos backs, knowing full well how quickly disaster could strike should one of them decide to surface unexpectedly.

With Bobby in charge of navigating, Mickey sat perfectly still in the middle of the raft and kept lookout for any signs of danger. As he surveyed the river, he chanced to glance in the direction of the savanna.

There, standing on the shore looking straight at them was a huge female lion. Suddenly it lifted its head, opened its jaws, and let out an earthshaking roar. Bobby jerked in surprise and the raft tilted to one side, so that he had to make a grab for the logs on either side to hang on. Then, as if the rug had been pulled out from underneath them, the whole raft was thrown into the air, and Mickey and Bobby were tossed like plastic bathtub toys into the river.

When the lion roared, a hippo that had obviously been resting right underneath them had raised its mighty head, and upended the tiny craft as if it weighed nothing, sending the occupants flying. The raft came back down with a huge splash, right on Mickey's head, knocking him unconscious.

Bobby, who was heavier, had sunk further into the water, and came back up gagging a few feet away, waving his arms to stay afloat. He was just in time to see Mickey sink into the murky water, as the raft settled back down, so he dove under the water and caught him by one of his arms.

The offending hippo was moving away, apparently unconcerned with the damage he had done. Kicking his feet, Bobby dragged Mickey over to the raft and unceremoniously rolled him onto it face-first. They were halfway across now, and the Candlemans watched in horror, helpless. Bobby knew he had to get Mickey back to shore in a hurry and didn't even attempt to climb back onto the raft. Again he waved at Morris to start pulling on the vine rope, knowing that time now was of the essence. Grabbing hold of the raft from behind, where Mickey's backpack was still attached, he propelled the craft by kicking his legs as hard as he could, and soon they were on the opposite shore, being pulled onto dry land by Morris and Shirley.

They dragged Mickey's motionless body up onto the tiny muddy beach, and Shirley began administering first aid. Almost immediately, Mickey began to splutter, and then rolled onto his side coughing and vomiting dirty brown river water.

"Thank God!" breathed Morris, relieved.

While Shirley sat with Mickey and Morris, Bobby used the rope to pull the raft and Mickey's backpack to safety.

"That was good thinking, son." Morris was gaining more respect for young Bobby by the minute.

"Thanks Mr. Candleman," Bobby said, blushing. Mickey was coming to now, and some of the color was returning to his face. He sat up, under Shirley's protestations.

"Thanks for saving me." He was strangled for a minute by a coughing fit, and then continued. "My name's Mickey."

"You're welcome. I'm Bobby, and these are the Candlemans. And that beast trying to lick you to death is Solly."

"Hi Solly," Mickey said, trying to defensively cover his face with his arms and hands in an attempt to dodge the dog's enthusiastic welcome. His life-long fear of dogs manifested itself even as he tried not to show it. Morris was the first to notice Mickey's discomfort.

"Solly, come!" he ordered. "Let Mickey *be* now you big galute!"

Solly obeyed immediately and galloped to Morris's side, where he plopped down at his feet, tail swishing happily back and forth, and looked hopefully up at him for further instructions.

"Are you alright Mickey? Solly can be a bit overpowering at times. He's very sociable," said Shirley, affectionately scratching Solly's blonde head.

A little red in the face, Mickey lowered his arms and answered Shirley, still looking warily at the dog.

"I'm sorry, I didn't mean to act so goofy. I'm sure Solly is a very nice dog. It's just that I've kind of been afraid of dogs ever since I was little, and I haven't gotten over it."

"We understand Mickey. And so does Solly, don't you boy?" said Morris, at which point Solly jumped up merrily to his hind legs, with his front paws on Morris's chest and began licking him wildly as if in agreement. Everyone broke out laughing, dispelling the momentary tension, and taking the focus off Mickey, for which he was grateful.

The laughter relaxed him, and finally even he had to smile. "Well, I'm glad to meet all of you. But how did you get here?"

The little group formed a circle and proceeded to tell their stories as they rested from their exertions with the river. While the Candlemans recounted their harrowing ordeal with the hippos, and the subsequent fortuitous meeting with Bobby, Mickey thoughtfully looked back to the African side of the river, and could see that the lion was still standing stock-still, watching. He knew that it was Erin. And it knew that he knew, just as Erin had always known what he was thinking.

*Somehow she is the key to all this. It has to end.* Mickey shivered inwardly as he recalled the carnage at the grocery store. *And I think I'm the only one who can convince her to stop it.*

"Mickey, I said what do you think?" They were all looking at Mickey expectantly, and he realized that he had not been listening.

"Sorry, what did you say?"

"Are you sure you're all right?" Shirley looked concerned.

"Yes I'm fine, really. Now what were we talking about?"

Morris continued. "Well, we don't know much, so it's difficult to plan a strategy, but we feel, that is, Shirley and Bobby and I, that we should just keep following the river, and see what we find."

"Sounds like as good an idea as any."

"It's settled then."

Mickey didn't tell them about Erin. Or make any mention of the fact that he pretty much knew what was going on, and why. He kept his inside information, his knowledge of Erin, the twins, and the paintings, to himself. For now.

"Well . . ." Began Morris, looking up at the sun which was still suspended over them like a ball of fire in the sky, although it was lower now, "I think we'd better get moving."

"Yeah, I'm getting pretty hungry," said Bobby.

"Hey, I can fix that," replied Mickey. "Hand me my backpack." Bobby untied the pack from the raft and handed it over to Mickey.

"I hope nothing got wet." Mickey began unloading edibles

from the buckled and zippered compartments, while everyone's mouths started to water. "All right! This things waterproof! Good old Isolde!"

"Isolde?" asked Shirley.

"That's my girl!" Mickey said proudly. "She said this might come in handy."

"You're a lucky man," commented Bobby. And they all dug in to the mini-feast with gusto. When they were coming to the end of the food, Shirley said, "Hold it. We'd better save something for later, we might need it."

"Good thinking Shirl," said Morris. "No telling when we'll get to eat again. Okay everybody, let's get this show on the road." Refreshed by the rest and the meal, the little group packed up with a renewed vitality, and set off again on their plotted course along the river's edge.

# Chapter 47

## Solly In The Bushes

Alongside the game trail upon which Mercy had been attacked by Beau in his python form, and parallel to the Amazon region, but deeper into the jungle, Ed, Jesse, and Mercy were trying to recover from the jaguar attack.

Jesse had a couple of deep gashes and some smaller slash marks, but otherwise seemed okay. Ed was breathing heavily from his assault on the cat's back as he tried to pull it off of Jesse, but otherwise wasn't hurt. They regrouped as they sat together under the still dripping fern leaves, and discussed their next move.

Ed did most of the talking. Jesse was preoccupied and miserable as he dwelled on the terror and pain that Dawna must have endured before she died.

"Okay, let's review," said Ed, taking charge. "Mercy can't walk, and that crutch is no good, it's too slow. And we don't know where we are, or how to get back to civilization, if there is a civilization to get back *to.* "

Mercy looked alarmed at this statement, but said nothing.

"Now obviously, this jungle is full of predators, and we'll have to be extra careful. I don't want to be ambushed like that again."

"But how can we be careful if we can't even see them?" asked Mercy.

"I could be wrong, but I think they're getting more visible. We couldn't see the thing that bit off your toes, *but,* the cat did have an outline, remember?"

"Yeah, actually it did. I could sort of *see* it."

"Alright then, we'll have to go on that assumption, and that should make it a little easier. If we can see something coming, we can take evasive action. What do you think Jesse?"

"Huh?"

"Jesse, snap out of it. Please? I understand, really I do, but we have got to get out of here."

"Sorry. You're right. I just keep thinking about Dawna . . . ."

"I know. But stay with us okay partner? We need you right now." That seemed to break through Jesse's grief, and he shook himself, turning his full attention to his best friend.

"I'm here."

"Good. As I was saying, Mercy can't walk, and the crutch is useless, so I think we should build her a travois."

"A what?"

"You know, a travois, a sling . . . thing. Something we can pull her in."

"Oh right. I know what you mean. A litter. We'll need some long sticks, and something to weave into mesh strong enough to hold her. Well, no shortage of materials around here." Jesse peered into the jungle all around them, and at the abundance of thick branches, leaves, and vines. "Well, let's get started."

He bent down to start looking for thin vines pliable enough to bend, so that they could be woven. He stopped for a minute, still bent over, and looked over his shoulder at Ed. "A *travois?"*

"Shut up." Jesse smiled faintly and kept searching.

Ed pulled a long stick out of the underbrush, and then a second. "These should do." He began to strip off the small branches that stuck out, until he had two roughly the same size and length. Then he helped Jesse gather up thin vines, until they had a fair-sized pile.

"Great. Now let's weave them, fairly tight."

Mercy watched them fumble with the project for a few minutes, and then said, "Oh, give me that!" Within half an hour she had a tightly woven mat that was strong and durable.

"Gee Mercy, you *can* do something besides play pool and drink," Ed teased.

Mercy shot him a withering look, and a friendly, "Fuck you copper."

"Atta girl."

Once the materials for the litter were prepared, it took no time for Ed and Jesse to lash the two long sticks to the vine mesh that Mercy had constructed, and they had themselves a serviceable litter. Ed lifted Mercy onto it and instructed Jesse to take up one stick while he lifted the other. It held nicely, and now all they needed was a direction to go in.

"Well Mr. Livingston, which way?" Jesse asked.

"I suppose we should keep to the path. This jungle looks pretty dense and we'd have a hard time dragging this thing through it. And that's DOCTOR Livingston to you."

"The path it is." And off they went.

All Mercy had to do now was lay back and enjoy the scenery. She marveled at the wild beauty of her surroundings. It was like time had stopped about a million years ago, before man wore shoes and worked nine to five. Hundreds of species of birds raised their voices in songs, protests, and mating calls. And the primates in the canopy were just as vocal. It was a primeval wonderland, with plants and trees bigger and more exotically lush than any she had ever seen.

After about an hour of relatively easy going, the trail seemed to be petering out, and Ed and Jesse decided to stop for a short rest. There was jungle as far as the eye could see, and Jesse was slightly disappointed.

"Damn. I thought by now we might see something resembling Hester, or at least a clue as to how we get back to it." He was rubbing his muscular arms, which were aching from pulling the litter with Mercy in it."

"I've been keeping my eyes peeled, but so far nothing looks even remotely familiar," agreed Ed, as he flopped tiredly down beside Jesse.

"I've been rolling this whole nightmare over and over in my

mind. Trying to pinpoint when it started. First there was the so-called elephant incident downtown this morning."

"Yeah, I know, at the grocery store. I wanted to talk to Bobby Boyle about it, since he was the only real witness. His girlfriend's practically a vegetable, so she's no help." As soon as the words were out of his mouth, Jesse wished he could snatch them back.

Mercy looked stricken.

"Sorry Mercy, I forgot she's your sister. I didn't mean it."

"It's okay," replied Mercy, but she didn't look okay.

"No really, I am sorry. I'm just trying to make some sense of all this. Trying to put things in order in my mind. All right. After Mom 'N Pop's, Rowdy's was leveled. Again by something no one could see."

Mercy whimpered at this, thinking of Shiv.

"God, you've really been through the grinder, Mercy. Now for some reason, I keep coming back to that midget we saw running through the field behind the bar . . . remember Ed?"

"Dwarf."

"Whatever. Anyhow, for some reason I've got this feeling that he's involved somehow, and I can't shake it."

"I thought we settled that. No way could he have caused damage like that."

"Hey I'm not saying he caused it *directly,* of course not. I'm just saying that I think he knows something about it."

"What did this dwarf look like?" asked Mercy.

"Midget."

"Whatever. Did he have red hair?"

Ed and Jesse's heads swung in unison toward Mercy, with identical looks of surprise.

"How did you know that!"

"I know that guy. Rowdy threw him out of the bar one night, about a month ago."

"Well, what happened! Why did he get thrown out?" Both of the cops' attention was riveted on Mercy now.

"It was no big deal at the time. At least I didn't think so. I only just remembered it now, as soon as you mentioned you saw a midget."

"For the last time, he's a dwarf. Now tell." Ed was excited now. He hadn't thought to ask Mercy before.

"Okay, let me think for a sec. I was kinda pissed at the time. Oh, yeah, he was in the bar, being kind of obnoxious, you know? A real aggravating little prick. The guys were making fun of him because he was drunk and started coming on to a couple of the girls. Everyone just thought it was funny at the time, but the little bastard had a mean streak, you could tell. He went too far when he bit Wendy Hargrove on the ass. You know Wendy? Little miss prissy pants."

"Yeah yeah, go on," prodded Ed impatiently.

"Anyhow, Bull got mad. He liked the little bitch, God knows why, so he picked red up by his pants and ponytail, and threw him out. And Rowdy told him he was barred and to never come back."

"Then what happened?"

"Well, I do remember this. As Bull carried him to the door, everybody was laughing, and the little puke was cursing up a storm, and swore revenge. He never came back as far as I know."

Ed and Jesse stared at each other, a dozen theories bouncing around in their cop minds like pin balls.

"You know, it was right after we had investigated the damage at Rowdy's that we saw him running through the field. And when we were leaving was when the patrol car quit, and we ended up here. It seems just a little too coincidental for my liking."

"So what exactly are you saying? He's got magical powers or something?" asked Ed.

"No, I'm simply saying that I've got a gut feeling, that's all. Who is he anyway?"

"All I know is that he moved into town a couple of years ago, and lives on Dalton Street with a couple of other midgets, and that fat girl. What's her name, Erin something?"

"Yeah, come to think of it, I haven't seen her around town for a long time now. Wonder what she's been up to?"

Ed's brow furrowed as he reached back into his mental filing cabinet for something that suddenly nibbled at his brain and seemed to want to squirm its way out.

"Hmmmm."

"What hmmm? C'mon, share," prodded Jesse. He knew the expression on his partner's face too well. He was onto something for sure.

"Well . . . remember last week when we ran into Doc. B.?"

"Yeah, so?"

"Remember the Violet Stringer thing he mentioned?"

"Oh yeah. Something ate her cat. So?"

"Well, Doc said something strange, now that I think about it. I didn't take it seriously at the time, the old doll being so advanced in her years, so to speak. Figured she was pretty far along on the twilight express, you know."

"I wasn't paying a whole lot of attention. Refresh my memory."

"Well, Doc said she was babbling about animal noises coming from the fat girl's house at weird hours."

"Animal noises? Like what?"

"Oh you know, growling and such."

"So . . . what . . . you think the fat girl and the midget are keeping wild animals on the property illegally? If they are, we'll bust their asses."

"For the last fucking time, he's a dwarf. But let's put it this way. I wouldn't jump to conclusions, but I think a closer look is in order. It seems a little too coincidental that ol' lady Stringer's cat got munched right before the Rowdy's thing. For Mercy's sake he left out the elephant incident, as well as what had happened to poor Dawna.

"The little red-headed puke lives next door to the cat lady, *and* we also saw him running away from the roadhouse."

"But you went over to Violet's house to have a quick look around that day, to calm her down and exhibit some serving and protecting. You said you didn't see anything suspicious."

"No, I said there was no obvious sign of a predator of any kind. I did however examine the perimeter of the property and couldn't resist a peek through the hedge. Did you know that fatty and shorty have a God-Damn circus wagon in their back yard?"

"A circus wagon? What kind of circus wagon?"

"Well it was kind of hard to make out, being overgrown with bushes and all, but it's one of those old fashioned kind, like you see in the movies, with big spoke wheels."

"Fine. One circus wagon. Quite the theory Watson. There's just one problem. With the numbers of people who have been disappearing over the past few months, those weirdoes would have to be hiding an entire bloody *zoo*. And if they *are* keeping dangerous wild animals, and if they *are* letting them run loose, one lousy old wagon isn't going to cut the mustard, size-wise."

"As I said, it's just a theory."

"Well, I say that if and when we get out of this craziness, we make a trip over to Dalton Street." Jesse nodded in agreement.

"Shh, guys. Listen!" Mercy was sitting bolt upright, and was holding her hand up in a warning to them not to speak. "Hear that?"

Silence fell upon the group as they listened intently for any sign of intrusion. As soon as they heard the shuffling sound of something moving about in the foliage, the cops automatically went for their guns. Then there was a sniffing, snuffling sound along with it. A creature of some kind was definitely near by, and was unconcerned about concealing its presence. It was coming right for them. Ed gave Jesse a hand signal, three fingers which he folded down to indicate a count of three, and then shoot. As he folded down first one finger, then the second, he mouthed silently, *one . . . two . . .*

Then the bushes parted in a wild rustle of branches, and Ed was thrown backwards by the force of a body which slammed him to the ground. He let out a surprised "Jesus!" when he hit the dirt.

"Hey, it's a dog!" shouted Mercy, laughing out loud with a huge expelled breath, which she had been fearfully holding.

"It *is* a dog!" exclaimed Jesse with vast relief. Solly was straddling Ed with all four paws and licking his face wildly, his tail a blond blur as he wagged it happily.

"Hey, whoa! Hey, fella, give me a break! Where did you come from?" Ed was laughing too, as he wrestled with the big friendly ball of fur. "Let me up!" All three were chuckling now, as Ed struggled to his feet. Solly ran merrily back and forth, from one person to another, getting in as much petting and licking as possible.

"Well, what do you know? Wonder who he belongs to? Doesn't look like he's suffered any. Where'd you come from boy?" Ed smiled as he watched the dog's antics. When Solly heard the question however, he pulled up short, right in front of Ed, as if he understood. Then he started bouncing up and down, and barking, while throwing glances over his shoulder.

"What is it boy? What's up?" It was obvious that the dog was trying to tell them something.

"I think he wants us to follow him!" said Mercy.

"I think you're right," agreed Jesse.

"Well it's definitely the best offer we've had all day. Let's go! All right big fella, show me!" At Ed's command, Solly let out a happy yelp, and took off down the trail.

"Hey, wait for us!" Solly stopped in his tracks, tail wagging and looked back at them impatiently as if to say *hurry up!* The cops each quickly picked up a handle of Mercy's litter and set out after Solly.

Within minutes the trio saw patches of blue sky up ahead, something they hadn't seen since entering the rain forest with its dense overhead canopy.

Then they heard a voice.

"Solly, here boy! Where'd you go off to?" In another minute, the underbrush petered out, and the river and the rest of Solly's party came into view.

"Well I'll be a monkey's uncle!" said Morris when he saw the two cops emerge from the forest with Mercy in tow.

"Hello!" Morris rushed forward to help Ed and Jesse drag the litter onto the strip of muddy beach. Shirley bent down over Mercy, who looked like she'd just survived a tornado. In fact they all did. It took a minute for Bobby to recognize her in her rumpled, bloody clothes and her sweaty, mud-streaked face and hair. "Mercy? Is that you?"

"Bobby? Bobby Boyle? What the hell are *you* doing here?"

"Same as you, I guess."

"How's my sister?"

"She's in pretty bad shape. Still in the hospital."

Mercy didn't answer, but lowered her chin and bit her lower

lip, remembering the cold reception she had received from her parents when she went to visit.

Morris used the awkward silence to initiate introductions all around. As the group shook hands and chattered amongst themselves, Mickey hung back, unnoticed.

The story-telling got very animated as everyone proceeded to relate to each other their various adventures and close encounters. There was much exclaiming and oohs, aahs, and wows. When Morris, Shirley, and Bobby got to the part about the hand-made raft and subsequent escape from the hippos, Morris turned to Mickey for his contribution to the story.

"That sure was hairy wasn't it Mickey? Mickey?" But Mickey wasn't listening. He was standing off from the group, staring across the river at the opposite bank. The bank where he had seen Erin as she watched him cross with Bobby on the raft. Finally, Morris seemed to get his attention, and when he turned around to join his new friends he plastered a grin on his face.

If Isolde had seen the grin, she would have made a remark about the Academy Awards or something, because it was as phony as a three-dollar bill. Morris introduced Mickey to Ed and Jesse, and no one caught the subtle, suspicious look that passed between them, quick as an eye blink, and then was gone.

As the sun sank slowly but surely below the horizon, the shadows thrown by the dense shaggy palms in the steamy, looming rain forest were long. By general consensus, everyone decided to bed down for the night right where they were, and chores were delegated accordingly.

Mickey shared what was left of his food rations with the newcomers, and Mercy produced a lighter from the pocket of her shredded jeans, for a fire. Ed and Jesse gathered dry wood and began to build a pile for burning, while Shirley fussed and clucked over Mercy's foot, trying to make her as comfortable as possible. Morris collected large palm fronds and fern leaves to fashion beds for later.

By the time the chores were accomplished, the sun had just about set, it was almost fully dark, and Morris lit the bonfire. The group gathered around it, as much to keep the eerie sounds and shadows of the jungle at bay, as for the heat and sense of safety it provided. The chit-chat settled into an easy companionable drone, as everyone got acquainted and swapped information and personal experiences from the past macabre and unbelievable twelve hours.

Ed and Jesse saw their opportunity and went for it. Working their way around the fire, and adding their own bits here and there to the talk, they positioned themselves on either side of Mickey before he knew what was happening.

Jesse got the ball rolling. "Hi."

"Hi." Mickey was trapped between these two man-mountains, and he was thinking really fast, trying to anticipate their questions and how he would answer them. He felt as guilty as hell, even though he believed that none of this was his fault, and that he was as much a victim as anyone. But the two experienced interrogators had him in their sights now, and were determined to bag him.

"You live over on Dalton Street don't you?" Ed's innocent gray eyes and sincere expression betrayed nothing of his suspicions.

"Yes I do. Why do you ask?"

"Oh, just making conversation. Doesn't that red-headed guy live there too?" probed Jesse.

The creases in Mickey's forehead were so furrowed as he looked up from one to the other, that in the flickering firelight he appeared to have one long eyebrow stretching right across his forehead, partially shadowing his eyes. He was grateful for the shifting shades of darkness and light created by the bonfire, and hoped that it concealed his discomfort.

"Uh, yes, you mean Beau? Yeah, he lives with us."

"Us?" *Oh oh.*

"Um, yeah. Me, my girlfriend Isolde. Oh, and the twins."

"What about the chubby girl . . . what's her name . . . Erin? And who are the twins?"

Having caught him dead in their sights, the cops were zeroing in, and Mickey shifted uncomfortably on his log seat, squirming under their intense gazes. Jesse's blue eyes, and Ed's gray ones felt like electric drills boring into him, into his brain, his mind. As if they could see inside him.

*I'm just being paranoid,* he cautioned himself.

"Erin? Um, she doesn't go out much. We all pretty much take care of each other. The twins are her sister and brother. Older sister and brother. They live in the back. They don't go out much either." *Shut up! Too much information!*

"In the back of what? Where?"

Mickey was starting to sweat now. "The house. They live out in back of the house. In a cottage. They live in a cottage. Behind the house."

"Mmmhmmm. Interesting." Mickey interpreted all kinds of ominous meanings attached to the word *interesting*.

"Do any of you keep any pets. You know, animals?"

*Oh my God!* "A . . . animals? Why, no, um, no. Why do you ask?"

"No reason. Forget it." There was that look again, over Mickey's head, and Ed nodded imperceptibly to Jesse. *He's lying.*

"Hey listen fellas. It's been a, you know, a long day, and I'm really bushed. If you don't mind, I think I'll turn in now." Mickey quaked inside as he tried to extricate himself from the third degree.

"Yeah, sure Mickey. It *has* been a long day, and we've all been through a lot. Get a good nights' sleep, and we'll talk some more tomorrow."

"Great, well, good night then." Mickey was visibly relieved to be let off the hook, and he almost jumped off his log, heading for the mat of leaves on the other side of the fire, prepared by Morris.

"Good night," said Ed. The cops watched him go. Then they rejoined the rest of the group, and made a last check on Mercy. Exhaustion was written across the faces of everyone, and after saying their goodnights, they all began to move off to their respective sleeping places, each anxious about what would greet them when the sun came up.

\*\*\*

In the morning Mickey was gone, and so was the raft.

# Chapter 48

## DAY TWO

As the dawn painted the early morning sky above the steamy, stagnant Amazon/Hester River with brilliant brush strokes of purple, pink, and watermelon, the Candlemans, along with Ed, Jesse, Bobby, and Mercy awoke to find Mickey had fled during the night.

Their first thought was that he had been attacked and dragged away while they all slept, but closer inspection revealed that the little makeshift raft was now banked among the bulrushes in the sticky mud on the other side of the river. He had somehow made it across and was long gone.

"I hope he'll be all right," worried Morris.

"I think he knows what he's doing," replied Ed. Jesse blinked at his partner. Ed's voice was so nasal that it was almost unrecognizable, thanks to his broken nose.

During the night it had swelled to nearly twice its normal size, and the angry puffiness that squeezed both of his eyes nearly out of his face were the color of burgundy-black, over-ripe plums. Jesse couldn't help wincing in sympathy as Ed continued speaking, seemingly unconcerned about his mashed nose. "So why don't we break camp and keep going, see what we find."

"Listen," said Mercy. "Do you guys hear that?"

"What? I don't hear anything." Shirley didn't notice the change.

"Exactly. The jungle. It's quiet as a cemetery."

"You're right!" agreed Bobby, excited. "What do you think it means?"

"I don't know, but the forest seems empty."

It was true. The myriad and unmistakable noises of the tropical birds and chattering monkeys were now absent and had been replaced with an eerie silence. It had a creepy un-nerving quality to it, as was evidenced by the facial expressions on the different members of the group, which ranged from confused trepidation to outright alarm. An involuntary shudder raced through Mercy as she propped herself up on her elbows and peered into the thick foliage.

"I think I liked it better noisy. Now it feels like an overgrown graveyard," said Jesse as he looked into his partner's blackened eyes. Ed nodded.

"So what now?" asked Morris.

"Well, all we can do is keep going, but let's not take anything for granted. Everyone keep on your toes. Except you Mercy."

"Ha ha. You missed your calling copper. You should have been a comedian."

"Yeah well, maybe if I get outta this alive, I'll make a career change. In the meantime let's not take anything for granted. And everybody stick together. Ready? Let's go. C'mon Solly."

So the little group, Cops, Candlemans, Mercy, Bobby, and Solly, now minus Mickey, continued on their way, following the strip of land between the river and the now silent rain forest.

They trekked for almost an hour and then began to feel a subtle metamorphosis in the air around them.

"Brrr. It's starting to get cold," said Mercy from her litter.

Ed and Jesse had been taking turns with Bobby pulling her along the mucky beach. But the beach had been turning from mud to a more gravelly surface, and was now covered with small rocks and stones. "And look at the forest!"

They looked. What had been steamy, dense jungle vegetation only a short time before, was now thick with conifers, pines, and firs.

"Well we're out of the jungle," said Morris. "And it's definitely getting chilly."

The group was shivering now, as the temperature dropped. They were wholly unprepared for the cold weather, as it had been a lovely June day when the now two-day adventure had begun. Solly, as usual, was exploring way up ahead of the rest, and now he had started to bark insistently. Shirley who was in the lead said, "Now what's got into that dog?"

Then Mercy had her arm out, and was pointing up ahead. "Is that smoke?"

Shading his eyes, Morris agreed that yes, it did indeed appear to be smoke. "And where there's smoke, there's fire," he said decisively.

They stepped up their pace. Solly's barking was louder now as they got closer. Sure enough, now they could spot red, orange, and yellow flames among the tall pine trees, shooting into the sky. It appeared to be a large bonfire.

Then a figure materialized out of the cold, low-lying mist and began waving. Then another, and another.

As the group got closer, they could make out three people waving and shouting. Shirley and Morris waved and shouted back. Solly came barreling back down the path to make sure they followed, and then loped off again toward the strangers. The surroundings had completed their transformation now, and Morris and crew found themselves wading almost knee-deep in snow.

"Hey! Over here!" called Ratch.

Ed and Jesse didn't recognize the guys until they were almost at the edge of the clearing that had melted from the big campfire.

"Well, lookee here. Fancy meeting you guys," said Jesse.

"If it ain't *Officer Friendly* and company," replied Stink. Ratch, Stink, and Crunch were so tattered, bloody, and battered, that they resembled bomb blast survivors.

"Jesse, Ed, do you know these guys?" Without waiting for an answer, Morris began his usual courtesy of introductions all around, and set about to see that the women in his charge were settled by the fire where they could warm up.

Mercy's face lit up like a holiday sparkler when she recognized her friends. "Oh God, Ratch! Stink! Crunch! Is it really you? What happened to you guys! Find a fist with your name on it or what!" She was laughing as Morris carried her to the fireside.

"Or what," said Ratch, laughing too. "Not looking too good yourself Mercy girl!"

"Hi I'm Bobby!" Bobby advanced upon them with his hand held out and a big grin.

"Welcome Bobby! Grab yourself some fire!"

"Thanks!" Ed and Jesse hung back a little, unsure of what to make of this new development.

"Hey coppers, get your butts over here and get warm. Sorry there's no coffee and donuts," joked Stink.

"Ha ha, very funny," said Jesse sardonically, his teeth chattering, but the ice had been broken.

Once again, the group, with the new additions, warmed themselves by the fire and exchanged war stories. They compared notes on various injuries, and Shirley was kept happily busy, with her one good arm, tending to the three Sabres' wounds whether they liked it or not. Mickey's first aid kit was really coming in handy, and Shirley made excellent use of the contents.

"We've been camped here for over a day now," explained Ratch. "Those grizzlies are still out there, and besides it's so cold, and we've been trying to figure out what to do. So far we've come up empty-handed." He looked around at each of his companions in turn, for confirmation.

"Empty-headed is more like it!" giggled Mercy.

"Fuck you Mercy girl, or we'll feed *you* to the bears," threatened Ratch, chuckling. Mercy found this uproariously funny, and Bobby joined her in a good belly laugh.

"Feed . . . to . . . ha ha . . . the . . . bears . . . ha ha!" The two of them were doubled over with mirth now, and everyone else had to smile too. *This is good for them,* thought Morris, *these young folks have been through a lot.* He joined in the laughter, knowing that it was a release of tension that was sorely needed by them all.

The warmth of the blazing fire, as well as the companionship, did much to raise everyone's spirits, but Ed could not stop thinking about Mickey and Beau. In his mind they were definitely linked to the bizarre never-never land that Hester had become, and he knew that when he found them, he would find the way back to reality. He also knew in his gut that it wouldn't be pretty.

When the giggling subsided, Crunch spoke up. He was a little more sober than the rest, with the carnage at the clubhouse and the bloody fate of his friends still fresh in his mind.

"We have discovered *one* thing. They're afraid of fire. We scared them off with lit torches."

"Afraid of fire?" echoed Ed.

"Yeah. I have a theory," said Ratch. This statement sent Mercy off into another gale of giggles.

Ratch fired a disgusted look in Mercy's direction, and continued. As he recounted his conversation with Mavis Whitfield at Rowdy's Roadhouse on the day of its destruction, he gained everyone's rapt attention.

Mercy became somber as his story brought the images of the horrible massacre, and Shiv's gory death, crashing back into her mind. He repeated what Mavis had said about her granny being witness to the long-ago fires in New York City in which many creatures had died such agonizing deaths.

*Another piece of the puzzle,* thought Ed, as he mentally compiled a composite picture of events, people, and components that had, here-to-fore, seemed unrelated. *It all leads up to one group, one house, one street. The arrow points one way. Dalton Street!*

"Well, is everyone warmed up?" There was a chorus of yes's to Ed's question.

"Okay then, it's time to go."

"Where to, Ed?" Morris had learned to trust Ed's judgment in the short time he had known him, and was prepared to follow any instructions the young cop gave.

"I say we go back the way we came. At least it seems to me we'd be heading toward Hester, instead of away from it."

"Makes sense to me." Jesse was already on his feet and ready to go before Ed had finished speaking.

"We'll take turns pulling Mercy," said Ratch. "Crunch, you

and me'll take first shift."

"Great. Thanks." *Adversity sure makes strange bed-fellows* thought Jesse to himself, and he allowed the luxury of a little smile to turn up the corners of his mouth. But he turned away before anyone could see it. Now they were nine people and a dog, headed into an unknown future, and unknown fate.

Ed instructed everyone in his entourage to find a suitable stick to serve as a torch. While Bobby and Morris tore whatever clothing could be spared into strips, Crunch and Stink wrapped them securely around the ends so they would burn for as long as possible. No one was dressed for the snow and cold, and the torches would provide heat as well as protection in case the bears or other predators returned. Although Ed didn't think they would, considering how quiet this forest too had become; it was best to be prepared. There were just four aspirin left in the first aid kit, so Shirley gave two to Mercy, one to Ed, and took the last one herself.

When the torches were lit, the group agreed that they were as ready as they would ever be. It was slow going through the snow, especially with the litter, but the security of knowing they were not alone, and a feeling of determination drove them on. For a while the monotonous trudging lulled the group, and each became lost in their own thoughts. Jesse silently prayed for Donna and his baby, and mourned his loss.

Bobby's thoughts took him back to the carnage in the grocery store, and he was sorrowful at the memory of Cindy languishing in a hospital bed, unaware of her surroundings.

The Sabres dwelled sadly on memories of happy times with their fallen comrades.

As dawn fell behind them and the sun rose higher, they began to emerge from the freezing climate into a warmer one. They came upon the river path once again, and as the now familiar rain forest reappeared, everyone was grateful for the rejuvenating warmth of the sun.

The different environment was new to Ratch, Stink, and Crunch, and they were dazzled by it. The altered scenery was a welcome change, serving to bestir the members of the group out of their individual reveries. It was a relief to be out of the snow, and having had very little sleep, everyone was exhausted from plodding through the high snowdrifts, so Ed suggested they stop for a short rest, which they did.

They didn't linger long. For one thing, Mickey's food had been finished off the previous night, and stomachs were growling. Also a feeling of urgency had descended upon the group that made them want to keep moving. So after the brief respite, long enough to catch their collective breath, and time for Shirley to check on wounds and dressings, they were once again on the move, their sodden clothes drying on their bodies.

Not having to deal with drifted snow and numb feet, they made much better time. Within another hour they came to the spot where Bobby had rescued Mickey, and they could see that the little raft still rested where he had deserted it on the far shore. Morris pointed to it, and informed the three new members of the party that they would have to cross the river.

"Piece of cake," said Ratch.

"You wouldn't have said that yesterday," interjected Bobby, "if you had seen the hippos."

"Don't see any hippos now." It was true. The river now appeared placid and serene.

"So what are we waiting for?" asked Crunch.

"Who can swim?" inquired Jesse. Several people raised their hands.

"Well, I can't," said Shirley, nodding at her arm, now a nasty shade of purple, which was still in the sling crafted by Morris from Bobby's denim shirt. "And neither can Mercy."

"Well Bobby my boy, I guess we make another raft," said Morris.

"Okey-doke Mr. Candleman."

With the added help of Jesse, Ed, and the bikers, a new, larger raft was constructed in short order, complete with vines with which to tow it.

Without the obstacle of the hippos to worry about, it was much easier to reach the opposite shore. Those who could swim went first, leaving Solly to guard Shirley and Mercy, until they could be towed across using the strong jungle vines.

Ed, Ratch, and Jesse were the first to make it to the other side, carrying the vines with them. They made it to the far shore in record time, now that they didn't have the huge river dwellers to navigate around. Morris sat down to catch his breath, and watched as the younger men hauled the raft to safety. Solly rode over with Shirley and Mercy, standing on the front of the craft and proudly looking like a ship's figurehead, tail wagging happily and snout pointed straight ahead.

As he waited for his wife and her little party to arrive, Morris was awestruck by the unspoiled beauty of the untamed domain in which they found themselves. It was a glorious golden world, wild and pristine in its simplicity. Africa in all of its natural splendor. He laid back for a few moments and closed his eyes, enjoying the feeling of the warm sun which buttered his body, and the cushion of soft, fragrant grass beneath him.

He had almost dozed off, as comfortable as a fetus in the womb, when he heard Shirley call his name. He sat up as the men were helping the women off of the raft and onto dry land.

"Look at this place!" Crunch was standing with his hands on his hips, surveying the landscape with wonder.

"This is in . . . *fuckin'* . . . *credible!*" added Stink, who had moved up beside him to take in the exquisite, wild glory of grasslands, mountains, and endless blue sky for himself.

Big stocky Crunch, in his torn grease-covered jeans, and the more compact Stink, with his mop of jumbled black hair, made an incongruous addition to the scenery. As the bikers paused to absorb the beauty of their surroundings and gaze in awe at the distant mountains shrouded in a filmy pastel mist of gray and mauve, Ed and Jesse busied themselves with arranging Mercy's litter for the remainder of the journey.

Ed had made sure that all their torches were extinguished in the river before they started across, but they carried them along to the other side, and now he and Jesse were stowing them at Mercy's feet, in the space at the foot of the litter.

As he worked, Jesse scanned the savanna. "It should be pretty easy to follow Mickey's trail. See that?"

Ed looked. "Yeah I see what you mean."

The lions had left a trampled path in the dry grass. This worried Ed some. By all appearances it seemed that the animals were no longer around, but he wasn't about to take any chances, and he kept his handgun at the ready just in case. As they placed the last of the torches on the pile and tightened up the lacings on the makeshift conveyance, Shirley fussed over Mercy and shot Ed a worried look. When she had his attention, she placed her finger over her mouth and made a shush sound, as she nodded for him to follow her as she tip-toed quietly away from the litter.

"What is it Shirley?" he asked when they were out of earshot.

"Mercy's passed out. I'm worried about her."

"What's going on?" Ratch had taken in the little scene and the concerned expressions.

"I'm afraid Mercy has a fever," said Shirley, her brow furrowed with worry.

Ratch really looked at Mercy now, and the anxiety in his eyes portrayed more than just casual affection. He was at her side in two steps, and he bent down to closely examine her still face. As he tenderly brushed a stray strand of blond hair from her sweaty forehead, he cast a pointed glance over his shoulder at Ed and Shirley. His jaw was set firmly, and his handsome dirt-streaked face was grim. He locked his hazel eyes with Ed's gray ones and no words were needed for Ratch to convey the growing fear he felt for the girl.

Watching them, Shirley had a crystal clear revelation that didn't require her woman's intuition for her to realize that Ratch was in love with Mercy.

By now the others started to notice that something was happening.

"What's up partner?" asked Jesse, as he sauntered up to the intense little group.

"I hope to God we're going the right way. Mercy needs medical attention. And soon," answered Ed.

"Oh no, is she bleeding again?"

"No, she's unconscious."

The group now clustered around the litter where Mercy lay prone and still as a cadaver.

Ratch pulled a ragged scrap of fabric out of his pocket, a leftover from his torch, and ordered Bobby to soak it in the river. "Hurry!"

Bobby returned on the run and handed the dripping tee shirt to Ratch who began tenderly swabbing Mercy's feverish face. Morris and Shirley stood off to the side and watched, quietly holding hands.

Jesse was the first to notice the faint humming sound in the distance. He tore his attention from the little drama in front of him, and nudged Ed with an elbow. But Ed had heard it too. They looked at each other and turned toward the sound, straining to hear.

Just then Solly, who had wandered off with his nose to the ground, came charging back to his friends barking hysterically. He stopped dead in his tracks in front of Ed and Jesse and was fairly bouncing up and down with excitement, while throwing anxious glances back over his shoulder.

The humming was louder now, and sounded like a giant lawnmower that had been left running. Solly was trembling, his whole body quivering.

"Solly, what's up boy . . . oh, shit!" Jesse spotted the black cloud just as Ed hollered, and at that moment, the humming drone grew deafening. In seconds the bees were on them, launching a savage attack.

Solly barked and squealed in fear and pain as the swarm of huge African bees descended, obliterating the landscape. Ratch threw himself bodily over Mercy, in an attempt to protect her with his own flesh, while Shirley, Morris and Bobby screamed and whirled like pinwheels.

Although he could barely make himself heard above the din, Ed shrieked at the others to grab up the torches they had stashed in the litter.

Crunch and Jesse dove for the pile while Stink fumbled for his lighter. He was quickly becoming disoriented from the ear-splitting roar of the bees and the agony of dozens of needles filled with poison being stabbed relentlessly into every part of his body. But just as Jesse, Ed, and Crunch reached him with the retrieved torches, he managed to yank the lighter out of his pocket and snap the flame into life.

As Stink crumpled to the ground, the torches caught, and the badly stung men began to wave them frantically at the dive-bombing insects. As they madly tried to fight them off, Jesse screamed at the others to run for river.

But it was too late for Stink who had lost precious seconds digging his lighter from his pocket and now lay sprawled on the grassy ground surrounded by dozens of bee carcasses.

Morris managed to grab a torch from Jesse and headed for Ratch where he lay spread over Mercy like a large denim blanket. He waved his flame over Ratch who was barely visible under the layer of crawling, undulating bugs, like a live slug icing on a giant cake. As he shook Ratch's still form, he screamed at Shirley and Bobby to go without him. Morris was keeping the bees at bay somewhat with his flame, but Shirley was sobbing and trying to make it to her husband's side.

Bobby took control then, and wrapped his hand around Shirley's good arm, wheeling her around and dragging her behind him. Ed and Crunch kept up their defensive maneuvers with the fiery weapons, and they appeared to be winning. Jesse led the way to the river, fending the bees off of the others as he charged toward the water.

With large back and forth swiping motions, he created a corridor through the deadly swarm, so that the others could make it to the relative safety of the river. He helped herd Shirley, Bobby, and Solly into the water up to their necks, and then turned back to see what was taking the others so long to follow.

Jesse felt his heart stop and his mouth go dry for a second when he glimpsed Morris struggling toward him with a burning torch and a limp body in his arms. He knew it was Mercy when he saw the blond hair swinging over Morris's shoulder. *Oh no! Ratch!* He sprinted out of the water and rushed forward to aid Morris.

As the two clumsily placed Mercy on the bobbing raft, it dawned on Jesse that the deafening hellish humming seemed to be easing off, and he looked up in time to see the pulsating black cloud moving off into the distance. *Thank God!* He thought to himself. Out loud he yelled, "They're leaving!"

It was true. As Ed and Crunch approached, still batting away stray bees from their swollen red bodies, a monstrous black cloud was retreating toward the horizon. Their faces were grim as they waded with relief into the tepid brown water of the river. Shirley wore an expression of shocked disbelief as she asked a question.

"Where're Ratch and Stink?"

Ed and Crunch glanced at each other with trepidation, and neither one wanted to be the one to answer. But Ed squared his shoulders and steeled himself as he turned to answer Shirley.

"They're in bad shape. We've got to get them into the river." With that he and Crunch wheeled around and hurriedly began sloshing their way through the reeds to the riverbank to retrieve the men where they had fallen under the vicious onslaught of the bees. Bobby and Jesse were right behind them.

"Hurry! I'll see to Mercy," cried Shirley, as she and Morris huddled over the still, unconscious girl, on the raft where she had been placed. Solly waded over and slipped his bleeding nose into her good hand. The dog had weathered the horror slightly better than the others, thanks to his heavy blond coat which had kept the stings to a relative minimum compared to his human companions.

Ed, Jesse, Crunch, and Bobby waded out of the river and darted over to where their friends lay motionless. Ratch was closest and Crunch knelt down beside him. Jesse joined him a moment later.

"He saved my life. Him and Stink. I wouldn't be here now, if it weren't for them."

Jesse couldn't see his face because his long matted dirty-blond hair fell in a curtain around his bent head. But from the tight, choked sound of his muffled voice, Jesse could tell that he was practically weeping.

"They've been a big help to all of us. No matter what happens from here on in, we'll never forget that. That is if we get out of this nightmare alive. Here, help me carry him."

Crunch raised his battered face to look Jesse in the eye and his big fists were clenched as if he was ready to start swinging.

"What the hell is all this anyway? Why *exactly* are my friends dead or dying? Can you tell me copper? Because I fucking *really* want to know." The big man sounded miserable and irate at the same time.

Jesse had been crouching on his heels, and fell backwards onto his butt at the angry vehement demand. It was almost as if he had been physically struck. He didn't know what to say.

"I've been trying to figure it out," said Ed. Ed and Bobby, carrying Stink between them, had come up behind the two and caught most of the exchange. As Crunch and Jesse hoisted Ratch up off of the ground, Ed continued.

"It seems that somehow Hester has been trapped in some kind of weird time warp or something. Some sick anomaly of nature. The animals doing the killing are dead."

"Dead! What do you mean they're dead? Those bears seemed pretty lively to me!" Crunch was roused out of his misery by Ed's comment.

"By dead, I mean they're no longer alive."

"Duh. I know what *dead* means smart ass. I wanna know *how* people can be killed by dead animals."

"Apparently they're *spirit* animals." Jesse spoke up as he and Bobby stopped for a second to get a better grip on Stink. Now let's get these guys to the river."

"You mean to tell me we're being attacked by *ghosts?*" Crunch was incredulous.

They had reached the water now and the four waded in with the two badly damaged men. Shirley met them as they entered the river.

"Guys I've got an idea. Everyone scoop up some mud from the river bottom and smear it on." She demonstrated on herself and the survivors followed suit, after laying Ratch and Stink on the bank, half in and half out of the water. Pretty soon they all looked like creatures from the black lagoon.

"You're right Shirl, it helps," said Morris.

"Yeah, it does help. It feels a little better," agreed Bobby, as he lavishly splashed and slathered himself with the muck. The relief was small, but it was better than nothing. They watched as Crunch,

Ed, and Jesse smeared mud on the faces of their two unmoving comrades.

As they applied the cooling sludge to Stink and Ratch's ravaged faces, Crunch continued his interrupted grilling of Jesse.

"Anyways, about this *ghost* thing," he said, glaring at Jesse.

"Well, from what I've been able to figure out, Mickey and his little red-haired friend have somehow brought wild animals back from the dead."

"Huh? What red-haired friend? You don't mean that obnoxious fucking midget that comes to Rowdy's sometimes?"

"Dwarf," Jesse mumbled as he continued to smear the soppy mud onto the dozens of swollen and bleeding welts covering Stink's body.

"Whatever," said Crunch, who was almost out of patience. Ed shot Jesse a sarcastic sideways look and then turned back to Crunch. "That's him. And from what I gather, these ghosts, when they were alive that is, were once burned up by fire over a hundred years ago and now they've come back. For revenge or something. The how or why, I haven't figured out yet."

"Well gawwwwwwlly," said Crunch in a pretty fair Gomer Pyle impression, "that tells me exactly diddly-squat. Thanks a fuck of a lot." Crunch's annoyance and grief were now turning to anger. And frustration at having no one to vent it on.

Ed was up to the challenge, having pretty much reached the frazzled end of the rope himself, and stuck his chin in Crunch's face. "Hey, what do you want from me asshole? Have you got a better explanation?"

Jesse, sensing the potential for violence, got to his feet, and subconsciously felt for his weapon in the front pocket of his pants. He took a step closer.

"Guys, guys, this isn't going to help anybody . . ." he began, hoping to diffuse the situation.

Suddenly there was a shout from the river, and all three snapped their heads around. Bobby was pointing in the direction of the bees departure, and shouting, "Look! Look over there!"

Just as all eyes fastened on the spot in the distance to which Bobby was excitedly pointing, a monstrous *CRACK* seemed to rip the very fabric of the air around them in two. The fading dark smudge that the bee swarm had become winked out, leaving a gigantic wisp of smoke in its wake, and a crack of thunder so loud that the very earth beneath their feet seemed to vibrate.

"What the hell is that!" exclaimed Morris.

"What?" Shirley was vigorously shaking her head in an effort to stop the ringing in her ears, a souvenir from the swarm.

"I said, what the . . ." *SPLAT*. A huge raindrop the size of a small grapefruit slapped Morris smack in his upturned face. Then, as if someone had pulled the drawstring on a mesh bag of blown up balloons on New Years Eve, the skies opened and released a solid sheet, a veritable torrent of water.

The unexpected deluge seemed to have a mind of its own, bent on driving everyone to their knees. Solly let out a frightened "*yip*" and crouched on the ground, with his shaggy front paws over his eyes.

Barely able to make himself heard above the din of the wall of water pummeling the earth, Ed shouted to everyone to form a tight group. But Crunch was having none of it.

Slipping and sliding on the suddenly slick surface, he raced for his two friends, who still lay sprawled on the riverbank. So thick was the downpour, the inert forms of Ratch and Stink were almost indistinguishable in the gloom. Fighting against the incredible power of the pounding water, Crunch reached out blindly and caught hold of Stink's tattered shirt with his left hand. Ratch was harder to get hold of since he had torn off the last of his raggedy apparel to use as a sponge on Mercy's face. With Stink's collar in his left hand, Crunch slid his right arm under Ratch's armpit and pulled. The men were dead weight and it took every bit of strength he had to maneuver against the rain. He felt as though he was being pelted with rocks, and the sheer volume of falling water was so dense that it was getting suffocatingly difficult to breathe. Combined with the exertion of trying to drag the bikers out of the river, Crunch couldn't get a deep breath and was practically drowning. Just as he felt he was about to pass out, he slid his two friends all the way out of the suddenly rapidly rising river and slumped down beside them. Once situated, he raised his meaty forearms above his head and tried to form an eave over his face for the thickest of the water to run off of so he could catch his breath. He was so preoccupied with seeing to Ratch and Stink that he barely noticed that he was now sitting in six inches of water.

The muffled shouts then began to infiltrate his disorientation. Peering through the glittering, gray sheet of monster-rain, he could barely make out the forms of people slogging toward him and calling his name.

"Crunch! Fwuu . . .!"

"What!" *Fwuu?* The others were closer now. Just then a resounding sonic boom of thunder deafened him, followed by a massive flash of lightning so dazzling that for a crazy moment he thought a nuclear explosion was ending all of his problems right then and there. *Some asshole finally pushed the button,* he thought distractedly.

But the electric spider webs raced like white-hot demons across the black sky, pulsing frenetically like a giant beating heart and then flickering out. And in the surreal oscillating light he saw what he believed for a second to be a bizarre hallucination.

It was the classic image of the four friends from the Wizard of Oz racing toward him. Except that Dorothy, the tin man, the cowardly lion, and the scarecrow were hideous parodies of themselves, ragged and melting in the hammering rain and strobe-like lightning. Even Toto was there, charging ahead of the others and coming right at him. *We're off to see the Wizard* . . . It took a second for his brain to register what his eyes were seeing, and then it clicked in.

It was Ed, Jesse, Bobby, and Shirley with the masks of river mud flowing from their faces which made them look grotesque and terrifying, with Solly *Toto* out in front. And in that moment he realized what they were trying to tell him. *FLOOD!* Anxiously he looked down at the foot of water he was now sitting in.

# Chapter 49

## Going Home

It was still dark when Mickey crept out of camp during the night while the others were asleep, and headed for the river. Thanks to his clandestine departure he had given himself a good half days head start. The night was as quiet and soundless as death and he was very careful not to make even the tiniest noise which might wake the two nazi cops. They were a little too alert for his liking. The little log raft was right where they had left it the day before. He climbed onto it and pushed off from the shore, then paddled away using only his hands for oars, gently dipping and thrusting, propelling himself forward. After what seemed an eternity, he finally reached the far side, leaving the raft on the riverbank, and scurried off into the grasses of the savanna. Mickey was driven by an overwhelming sense of urgency. He knew for sure that Beau would beat him home, and he was desperate to get there to protect Isolde. He was positive that Beau knew as well as he did that Erin was no longer around to see to her welfare. Beau had waited for a long time for his chance to take over the household and wreak whatever havoc his demented, warped little mind could devise. *I'm coming Isolde, I'm coming. Please God, please keep her safe until I get there.* As the sun made its morning appearance over the mountains, in a dazzling display of red and orange glory, Mickey became aware that he was not alone on his journey. He could feel eyes boring into his back, and he was pretty sure he knew whose whey were. But he didn't look back. *I have to lead her home.*

The pride followed Mickey from a short distance behind, led by the beautiful big lioness with the sea-green eyes.

It took the better part of the morning for Mickey to retrace his steps of the previous day. Every so often, as the sun got hotter and higher above him, he stopped to rest under whatever meager shade presented itself in the form of a bush or shrub. And whenever he did, a glance backwards told him that the lions too were pacing themselves to his speed. They would stop and lie down in the grass, never taking their eyes off of him. *Good.*

By mid-morning, Mickey knew that he and the lions had left the savanna behind, for the landscape was dissolving and swirling around him like an image out of a kaleidoscope. And now he and the lions padding along a short distance behind him were on the tropical jungle path that he knew would lead him home. He walked faster, thinking of nothing now but getting to Isolde.

A growing sense of foreboding engulfed Mickey, and he barely noticed the incongruous little details that were beginning to emerge beneath his feet.

Every few yards now, the squishy, moist carpet of leaves upon which he trudged were displaying small patches of a bare surface underneath that appeared to be asphalt or concrete. And every so often, part of a street sign or light pole stuck out from among the trees.

Then suddenly through the foliage, Mickey stood staring at the gate to his house on Dalton street. It appeared out of the greenery so unexpectedly that he was momentarily taken aback. But the reality slammed into him like a punch in the gut and he rushed to the gate, throwing it open. Mickey was almost drooling now in his terrified haste to reach the love of his life, praying she was alive, and well. *If Beau's hurt a hair on her head, I'll kill him with my bare hands!* Fumbling in his pants pocket for his key as he ran, he reached the porch, stabbed the key into the keyhole, and frantically heaved open the front door. "Isolde! Isolde, it's me. Isolde!"

# Chapter 50

## The Beginning Of The End

Isolde had spent a sleepless night. She and Mickey had never slept apart before, and she was worried sick about him. Beau had arrived home in the afternoon of the previous day, and only grunted at her as he passed the kitchen on his way out to the twins' cottage. She didn't think he had noticed the various coolers and containers that were strewn about the room half-filled with provisions. But just to be on the safe side, and so as not to alert suspicion, she began to transfer the cartons of food up to her and Mickey's bedroom. There she added a first aid kit, and carefully chosen clothing items to the growing pile on the bed. *Mickey where are you?*

Periodic checks on Erin produced a certainty in Isolde's mind that she was gone for good. There was no sign of life anymore in the huge mound of flesh. No flicker of eyelids, no twitch of fingers. Just a great, fat body with oxygen tubes in its nostrils to keep the oxygen going in and the carbon dioxide coming out. Erin had disconnected her telephone recently, Isolde wasn't sure when, and it never rang anymore. She knew that Erin, the essence of Erin, was never coming back. It was the beginning of the end, and Isolde was determined that when *"that"* end came, she, Mickey, and their baby would be prepared and ready. Exactly how or when the happy life they knew would crumble around them all, she couldn't predict, but she would see to it that they survived.

# Chapter 51

## Beau Loses It

Beau's eyes flashed like lightning bolts when he burst unannounced into Sarah and Patrick's cottage. Several hyenas had been lounging around the place, but the sound of the slamming door startled them and they scampered back into their frames. All except two. In seconds, the remaining two furry and speckled animals morphed into the shapes of Patrick and Sarah, and became solid.

"Don't you have the common courtesy to knock anymore?" demanded Patrick angrily.

"Shut up!" barked Beau. The twins blanched at the venom in his voice.

"We've got problems. There's a bunch of nosy bastards out there and they'll be coming, so we'd better be ready for them." He began frenetically racing from frame to frame. For the most part they were empty. Beau spun around to face the twins, and advanced upon them with a murderous look in his eyes.

"Call them in!"

"Call them in? You know we can't d . . ." began Sarah.

"Well I know you CAN! Now CALL . . . THEM . . . IN!" He was livid, and his face was now the flaming color of his hair. Patrick and Sarah reared back in fear, as Beau spit his order into their petrified faces, with his fists clenched.

His teeth were bared and an amorphous image was alternately appearing and dissolving upon his enraged face. A python's head, fangs and all, was being superimposed over his own for seconds at a time. Now you see it, now you don't. Sarah thought it was the ugliest and most horrific thing she had ever witnessed. The head was huge and almost heart-shaped, covered with grayish scales. Between the deadly looking pointed white fangs, a long wet tongue snaked in and out of its leathery lips. When Beau's face appeared momentarily, the tongue was transparent but still there, whipping up and down, and the sight of it coming out of a man's mouth was surreal and sickening.

The twins had no choice. They threw their heads back and howled, emitting a series of growls, yips, cackles, whoops and roars.

Within minutes the frames began to fill. Where only moments ago there had been bare landscapes, now animals of every description appeared. Scores of them, whole herds and groups, milling about uneasily, waiting for what came next.

Beau closely examined the paintings. "Wait a minute. Where are the lions?" The lion canvas remained empty.

"I . . . we . . . don't know Beau. They don't respond to us anymore. Not like the others. We think it's Erin. She tells them what to do now. We have no control over the lions anymore." Beau turned on the shivering and frightened pair with blazing snake-eyes filled with hatred.

"You little BASTARDS! How did you let this happen?!"

The twins panicked then and evaporated right before his eyes, joining the hyena pack in their frame, and blending in with the others in their African landscape so as to be indistinguishable from all the rest. Beau was on his own and crazed with rage.

***

In her mind, Isolde flashed back to the evening before, when Beau had returned home with a murderous gleam in his eye. Isolde swore that she could smell the putrid stink of hatred and malevolence that poured from him. He was furious and frustrated that Mercy had survived his attack on the jungle path, and he was intent on venting his killer rage.

Isolde's feet froze to the kitchen floor as she watched him skulk by on his way to the cottage out back. When the screen door slammed she released the breath she had been holding, and accelerated the pace of her preparations for flight. Keeping busy with her packing and provision lists also served to take her mind off of Mickey and her concerns for his safety.

As she scurried back and forth from the kitchen to the bedroom, Isolde trembled at the sounds emanating from the twins' home. Beau the python was in a full-blown fury as he railed at Patrick and Sarah to call the animals in. Isolde had never seen the serpentine abomination that the evil little man had become and so couldn't imagine what was producing the nightmare shrieks that were carrying across to the big house from the back yard.

When the twins panicked and jumped into the picture frame with the rest of the hyenas, Beau squealed and thrashed, impotent and out of control.

It was when the sounds of bedlam coming from outside quieted that Isolde locked herself in her bedroom, determined to wait for Mickey. She pushed the sliding bolt into place, and heaved a wooden dresser up against the door for good measure. Then her adrenaline faltered, and she slumped to the floor with her back to the wall and shut her eyes, saying a silent prayer.

She listened with her eyes closed and her ears sharply tuned to any untoward sound, no matter how minute. The waiting was ghastly, and visions of Mickey torn to bloody scraps with his entrails gushing out of his body kept creeping into her thoughts, no matter how determined she was to remain hopeful. She squeezed her eyes tight shut and willed the grisly images from her mind. Somehow the night passed in periods of fitful slumber. She slept sitting up with her back against the bureau that she had shoved across the bedroom door. In the morning she blinked herself awake and was confused for a minute at finding herself on her bedroom floor. Then it all came back in a rush. Mickey was still out there somewhere. Beau was doing God knew what out back with the twins. She closed her eyes, folded her hands together, and pleaded with God to bring Mickey home. That was when she heard it. *Swiiisssssh swiiisssssh sssssss . . .*

Isolde's blue eyes popped open, perspiration burst out on her skin, and a vibration of dread turned her nerve endings into tuning forks. *Oh my God NO! Swiiiisssh swiiiiish . . .* "Isolde, Isolde it's me." It was Beau's voice, silky and wheedling. *He's outside the door! But what's that swishing sound?*

"Isolde, open up. Please? Don't be afraid, I'm your friend. I just want to tell you something." His voice oozed with insincerity, his words like droplets of pus dribbling out of a festering untended wound.

Isolde was familiar with the thin vocal veneer he was able to manufacture like cheap furniture. She knew that when he used it, it was generally intended to mask some kind of malignant motive. After three years of sharing a living space with him she was well aware that he wasn't normal, and she and Mickey referred to him as "psycho-dwarf" behind his back.

But as wary as she always was of him, this time there was an added edge that she had never heard before, and it scared her silly. It was the thinly disguised voice of a cruel, ruthless monster.

"I'm busy now Beau, and I'm not dressed. Come back later okay?" She tried to sound calm and reasonable, but was quivering inside with a chill that went right down into her bone marrow, and refrigerated her nerve endings. As she spoke Isolde desperately scanned the room for anything she could use as a weapon if Psycho-D decided that he'd just as soon not come back later. *As if!* She thought wretchedly to herself. *Yeah right, maybe he'll bring me a nice cup of tea and a crumpet!* BAM! Something heavy smashed against the door. *There goes my tea and crumpets.*

"Fuck you bitch! Now open this door!" Something inside of Isolde snapped then, and she knew what she had to do. Isolde was a survivor and now she had a baby to protect. Her maternal instincts took hold and booted her fear right in the ass. *Alright Beau you sick little hillbilly dick! I'm not afraid of you.*

"Get away from my door Beau, I mean it." She had scooted around the bureau until she was crouched down alongside it. BAM! BAM! It sounded to Isolde like Beau was using a battering ram on her bedroom door, the sound reverberating like thunder. And she was sure she heard the unmistakable sound of splintering wood on that last one. *The door's not going to hold out very long.* There were several cardboard boxes of varying sizes stacked around her into which she had been packing her belongings. At the first sound of shattering wood, Isolde dropped her palms to the floor and quickly scooted over to one of the larger cartons on her hands and knees. She fished around inside it as the pounding on the door increased and the object being used to batter a hole in it appeared momentarily. She caught just a glimpse of the thing over her shoulder as she frantically sought what she was looking for. She almost toppled over in her shock and amazement at what she saw and for a second she questioned her own sanity, not to mention her usually dependable baby-blues. *It can't be!* It looked like the tail of a gigantic snake, scales and all that slithered back through the raggedy and growing opening in the wooden door, and Isolde knew that it was back on the other side, preparing to take another whack. Shirley Temple curls jiggling and jumping, Isolde found what she was searching for and backed up as far into the room as she could go, ready to do battle with whatever ghastly nightmare was out in the hallway. Her eyes didn't leave the disintegrating portal as she bumped up against the wall and felt something dig into her back. *Of course! The windowsill!* Just as she quickly fired a glance over her shoulder to see if the window was closed and locked a freakish scream of triumph shredded the air to rags around her. It was a piercing shriek straight from the bowels of hell itself and her hands flew to cover her ears. It was the sound that she had heard the previous evening coming from the cottage out back that up until now she hadn't understood. But now comprehension hit her like a brick in the face. And at exactly the same moment that realization dawned, Beau's mammoth and horrible snakehead entered her room through the splintery hole in the door. Screeching and flicking his long shiny tongue in and out at her, she could swear that he—*IT*—was grinning.

As if shot from a cannon the hideous hissing head burst triumphantly into the room, followed by the rest of the twisting writhing body of the giant serpent. Isolde cowered against the windowsill, her hands behind her back. She thought she would die dead away from fear until the thought of her baby gave her the psychological strength to stand her shaky ground. *Just another minute, just anoth . . .* the snake had toyed with her up until now, hissing and snapping at her, then rearing back so it towered over her.

Beau was enjoying her stark terror immensely. It hung back for a second, with Beau's fiendish grinning face alternately appearing and dissolving, and then a small hiss was accompanied by that long sinuous snake-tongue covered in mucus. It slipped from between the scaly lips slowly and stretched out longer and longer. It twitched almost prissily from side to side and up and down at the tip, as if tasting the air, seeking her out. Isolde's eyes got wider and wider as it got closer to her face. *Hold on hold on . . .* she coached herself.

Then, just the very tip of the odious thing tickled her bottom lip. It retreated for just a second and then slithered back for another taste. Isolde felt her gorge rise and she desperately wanted to retch. She fought the urge to slap the disgusting thing away as it sensuously and lasciviously tried to thrust itself between her clenched lips, minutely licking and testing sickeningly for an opening. Every agonizing second seemed like an hour as it stroked and probed. Slithering away from her trembling mouth, the vile and hateful squirmy projectile began to explore further. Beginning to quiver, it traced a slow course along the curve of Isolde's chin and down her neck, the pointy nib flicking to and fro. Leaving a thin trail of mucousy slobber the tongue slid ever more lazily down to her breasts where it hovered for an excruciating few seconds, first circling one, then the other. Isolde was screaming inside and felt as though she were being raped, but she knew it was imperative for the survival of she and her baby that she let the loathsome monster have it's *his* fun. After a few minutes of this torture Beau grew impatient, as she knew he would when he didn't get the reaction he had hoped for. The tongue withdrew slightly and the great snakemouth opened, advancing upon his small victim. *NOW!* Isolde timed it perfectly. She withdrew her right hand from behind her back and with a deadly aim worthy of any major league ball player alive or dead, hurled the open peppershaker right into the foul creature's face. It's outraged scream of pain rattled the walls, and as the beast writhed in agony, temporarily blinded, Isolde spun, twisted open the latch, heaved the window up, and was gone.

Landing with a thump outside the window, Isolde realized three things. One, the pepper wouldn't hold Beau off for long. Two, she was on the precariously slanting shingled roof that overhung the large front porch of the house. And three, Mickey was right below her frantically calling her name.

# Chapter 52

## O Savanna, Won't You Dry For Me?

Just as the Wizard of Oz gang had almost reached him, Crunch lurched to his feet and promptly toppled back again with a tremendous splash. A wicked current tore the feet out from under him and almost swept him away. At that moment the illumination from another massive burst of lightning revealed that Stink and Ratch were gone.

"NO!" he howled into the storm.

The water had now risen more than knee deep, and Crunch gained his footing with difficulty.

The others reached him, and Solly was dog-paddling to stay afloat because the river was now over his head. Crunch dove underwater. He desperately flailed and thrashed around under the surface trying to locate the missing men. He struggled up for air every couple of minutes and saw that there weren't four Ozians but six. Shirley, Morris, Bobby and Jesse had been the ones out in front that had created the weird illusion he had experienced. Now he could just make out Ed behind them carrying Mercy in his arms. As he was gasping for air during his third breach out of the water Crunch sensed that the violent storm was abating somewhat. Someone was trying to make himself heard over the noise of the rain and he was just barely able to make out the words. To Crunch they looked like a bunch of drowned rats washed out of a slimy sewer pipe. He could see this because the sky seemed to have lightened considerably since the onset of the storm. Suddenly everyone was calling out at once.

"Are you all right?"

"Where are the others?"

"The storm's letting up!" But all Crunch could think about was finding Stink and Ratch. He dove under again. Minutes later, half-drowned and mad with fear for them he stood thigh deep in the water, his chest heaving, and his filthy and soaking bandages hanging off of him like huge chunks of rotting flesh.

"I can't find them, help me!"

Jesse could tell that Crunch was losing it. He sloshed up beside him and took hold of both shoulders, forcing the distraught man to look at him.

"I'm sorry buddy, but we have to face it. I think they're gone."

"No! I won't believe that you sonofabitch!"

Shirley moved up and put her arms around Crunch.

"I'm afraid Jesse's right honey. We're all so sorry about your friends, but we've got to think of Mercy. She needs help and we're going to need you if the rest of us are going to survive. What do you say, are you still with us? Please Crunch, we need you."

The big man allowed Shirley to hold him and even rock him a little as a mother would soothe a small child.

"All right," he mumbled miserably. "I'm with you."

"Thank you love."

Bobby had been holding Solly around the middle to keep his head above water and now hugged him tight, looking heartbroken and forlorn. Suddenly from somewhere behind them came a shout.

"Hey!" Everyone turned. Two moving figures were just visible in the distance.

"Hey everybody, look what we found!"

"Holy shit, it's them!" Crunch broke free of Shirley and began splashing his way toward the approaching forms. Stunned, Jesse and his group stared in disbelief as Ratch and Stink came into view towing something behind them.

"Well I'll be Damned, it's our rowboat!" shouted Morris. "Well what do you know!"

"It *is* our rowboat! Morry it's our rowboat!" Shirley was laughing and crying at the same time.

"And what's that behind it?" asked Bobby.

"Don't tell me, it's the raft." Ed was astounded. His jaw hung open and he looked like he'd been whacked with a crowbar.

Crunch had reached the guys and was helping tow the vessels towards the bedraggled crew. Everyone seemed to talk at once as they joined forces once again. Ratch and Stink had both regained consciousness as they were being washed away by the current back to the river's edge. There on the shore was the Candleman's fishing boat and the larger raft the men had constructed to get them to the African side of the river.

Still carrying Mercy in his arms, Ed moved forward to place her in the rowboat. Ratch immediately occupied himself with trying to make her as comfortable as possible. Bobby waded over to the raft and placed Solly on it. The dog was none the worse for wear and stood up to give himself a mighty shake which made everyone duck and laugh.

There was much back-clapping and bicep-punching, and Crunch looked like he had died and gone to heaven. The monsoon-like rainstorm had now faded down to a misty trickle, and a damp grayish daylight had returned. Ed took this as a sign to start organizing.

"Okay, Morris and Shirley, you ride in the boat with Mercy." The Candlemans didn't answer.

"Morris, Shirley, Helloooo . . ." The pair were staring off into the distance. "Would you look at that," Shirley said.

"Don't think I've ever seen a prettier one," replied Morris. It was a rainbow arcing across the African sky, multi-colored and beautiful.

"Wow," breathed Bobby.

"Hm. Wonder what we'll find at the end of it," said Ed thoughtfully.

"Pot of gold maybe?" replied Bobby with a smile.

"With our luck it'll probably be a bucket of shit," cracked Stink, chuckling at his own joke.

"Okay everybody wagons ho! Let's get this lost cause on the road," said Ratch. Ed shot him an amused dirty look.

"Speak for yourself shithead," Stink answered. "*Lost cause* my rosy water-logged ass. By this time tomorrow I for one intend to have a beer and a smoke in one hand, and a babe and a steak in the other. Not necessarily in that order." This sparked giggles from Bobby.

"Amen," from Crunch.

Smiles between Shirley and Morris.

And silence from Ed and Jesse.

"Here Solly." When Morris called him Solly leaped lightly from the raft into the rowboat where he settled happily at Morris's feet, wagging his sopping wet tail.

Ed instructed Ratch, Crunch and Stink to climb aboard the raft, reasoning that they had suffered the worst of the flood. Ratch refused. "I wanna stay with Mercy. The water's not that deep, I'll walk alongside." Ed could see from the determined expression on his face that there was no sense in arguing.

"Fine. Alright then, Stink you, Crunch and Bobby get on it and Jesse and I'll walk. It won't hold five."

"No way," answered the three in unison. It was a Mexican stand-off. Ed and Jesse looked at each other in exasperation.

"Now look here you macho buggers, somebody better get on the damn thing because we're going nowhere fast." Morris figured he had better take control or no one was going anywhere.

"Okay okay, we'll take turns then. C'mon Bobby up you go. Crunch why don't you keep him company?" Ed saw that the deep slash wounds across Crunch's torso had opened up again and his dirty soaking bandages were stained with fresh blood. Bobby was looking at him hopefully and Crunch acquiesced.

Ed then turned to Stink. "C'mon pal, you too. I promise when we get tired we'll trade places."

"Okay copper, what the fuck." Stink climbed aboard.

When everyone was situated the little flotilla set out across the expanse of swollen river. Since the strong jungle vine was still attached to the raft, Ed and Jesse took up positions out in front and used it to tow the raft, and Ratch waded alongside the rowboat, keeping a worried and watchful eye on Mercy for signs of distress. The oars had been lost during the encounter that Morris and Shirley had had with the hippos, but it was fairly easy going without them, albeit slow. After about a half hour it was obvious that it was time for the switch. The two cops looked exhausted and didn't argue when Bobby and Stink jumped into the water to take the tow-line from them. Crunch was on his back and appeared to have dozed off, so they let him be. His bunched up, saggy wrappings were now solidly drenched in blood which Ed eyed with growing alarm. Alongside the rowboat Ratch rebuffed Morris's repeated offers to trade places, and they amused themselves with some good-natured verbal volleyball.

"Just relax you old fart."

"Old fart! I'll show you who's an old fart. You couldn't outlast me on your best day you beer-swilling motorcycle-riding punk."

"Oh yeah? Care to make a little wager on that pops?"

"Now kiddies play nice," said Shirley, smiling. Suddenly there was a scraping sound from underneath the boat. Bobby said, "Hey look, the water's getting shallower."

"You're right. Check it out."

"And what's that?" asked Ed pointing. "It looks like a street sign."

"Morgan street. It *is* a street sign." The rowboat stopped completely, snagged on the bottom. Solly hopped from the craft and landed in six inches of water. The cops shook Crunch awake and stepped off of the raft.

"Well what do you know?" Said Morris happily. The water was receding rapidly now and they could actually see bare ground ahead. Everyone clambered from boat and raft and stood upright, enjoying the feeling of firm ground beneath their feet again.

"What about Mercy?" Shirley looked very worried as she peered down at the girl in the bottom of the boat.

"I'll carry her," said Ratch, and he reached down to do just that. They had had to leave the litter behind when the water rose, and even after all he'd been through Ratch looked big and strong enough to haul an entire girl's pep squad under each arm without much trouble.

Carefully he hoisted Mercy out of the boat and settled her in his arms like a baby-doll. He lowered his battered face to hers and whispered, "She's light as a feather." He kissed her softly on the cheek.

It was kind of an embarrassing moment for the others so they all bustled about a little more than was called for with much throat-clearing and adjusting of damp clothing.

"Well, let's push on shall we?" said Ed.

"Lead on McDuff!" answered Morris. Solly romped on ahead as usual and within minutes they heard him barking. And they saw why. A few hundred yards ahead appeared a solid wall of trees. Or almost solid. As they drew closer an opening in the foliage appeared. They encountered the path that had led Mickey away from home and into the tropical rain forest on his quest to find Erin. This forest was just as silent as the jungle they had left behind on the other side of the river. No one spoke now as a macabre feeling of foreboding enveloped the group.

When Ed looked behind him he saw that the entrance to the path had vanished and the forest was closed up tight behind them, as if they had been swallowed alive *like Jonah and the whale.* His skin began to prickle and tingle all over and it was scary and exciting all at the same time. Absurdly he remembered the first time he had ever had sex—*Marybeth Brigante under the bleachers*—and it had felt very much like this. Fear of the unknown and the danger of being discovered over-ridden by his raging teenage hormones and the anticipation of finally realizing a schoolboy fantasy. *Where did THAT come from?* Ed was horrified to discover that he was actually enjoying himself. He had to admit to himself that he truly loved the danger. *What kind of lunatic are you?* he asked himself. But he loved being a cop. *Maybe when this is all over, IF this is ever all over, maybe I'll put out some feelers to a bigger city, a more exciting Police Force.*

Crunch and Jesse led the way for the others, clearing away stray vines and debris from the trail to make it easier for the others to maneuver their way along.

Bobby stuck close to the Candlemans, *just in case one of them trips or something.* He had come to think of them almost as his parents and was feeling very protective.

Ratch's emotions were obvious as he cradled Mercy in his arms, with her head resting on his bare muscular shoulder, tangled blond hair spread out on his back like a badly crocheted shawl. Then he stumbled and almost dropped her on the ground as the shrieks of pain and rage issuing from the python penetrated the forest. Ratch and his friends had almost reached the gate to Erin's house.

"Oh my great Lord above!" exclaimed Morris.

"What the fuck . . ." Crunch and Stink were already reaching reflexively for weapons in the pockets of their raggedy pants.

Mercy's eyes fluttered open when Ratch stumbled in surprise at the unexpected heart-stopping caterwauling, so shrill that it felt like steak knives stabbing into his skull.

"Ratch? Ratch what's going on! Oh my God what's happening!"

"I don't know, honey! Just hold on to me! Don't let go!"

The screams of the outraged snake-dwarf were now accompanied by the deafening booming sound of demolition. The colossal reptile was in a frenzy, bodily bashing and walloping the inside of the bedroom to smithereens. Ed and Jesse had the same instinctive reaction at the same time and went for their guns. Gone. Twin looks of horror confirmed their worst fears.

"My weapon's gone!"

"Mine too. Must have lost it in the flood."

"Now what? Whatever that is it sounds pretty aggravated." Everyone instinctively drifted closer together. *Strength in numbers,* thought Jesse.

"Okay," began Ed as he read Jesse's eyes. "Ratch put Mercy down under cover." He looked hastily around. "Over there, under that big fern."

Jesse joined in the serving and protecting. "Morris, Shirl, go with him. Watch Mercy and try to stay out of sight."

As Ratch and Shirley headed for the foliage, Morris asked, "What are you going to do?"

"We're gonna have a look."

"Not without me you're not," warned Crunch.

"Or me," agreed Stink.

"I wanna go too," said Bobby.

"Like hell! Now look. Jesse and I'll . . ." His words were cut short by a feral low-throated growl coming from Solly. It was like nothing they'd heard him emit before. His ears were bent straight back and his damp blonde fur was bushed out and standing on end. With his lips peeled back to reveal a wicked pair of incisors he no longer even remotely resembled the Candlemans loveable and highly socialized canine companion.

Several pairs of surprised eyes turned to him just as he was blindsided by two snarling furry cannonballs. With a screech the savage battle was on and it was two against one. The three combatants rolled and tumbled together, teeth gnashing and fur flying. Without hesitation Bobby dove into the fray to help his friend.

"Bobby NO!" Shirley started screaming. The hyenas were relentless in their savagery and Solly was getting the worst of it, because he was on the bottom more often than not. His squeals of pain were gut-wrenching but he fought on like a tiger defending its young.

Then it was Bobby who screamed. It was impossible to tell where the animals began and the boy left off. The men were mobilized into action. Crunch and Ratch dove right in. By this time, one of the hyenas had Bobby's bloody right arm in a death grip and was shaking him like a rag doll. Solly rolled and tumbled with the second spotted creature and his blonde coat was turning a slippery-looking sickening red.

As Crunch launched himself at the nearest pair, he wrapped his meaty forearm around the hyena's throat and yelled, "Get Bobby!" Jesse swooped in, grabbed Bobby by one of his legs and dragged him free.

As Crunch tore the wild dog off of Bobby, Ratch hurled himself at the other hyena which was trying to turn Solly into coleslaw. He came at it from behind and fastened both large hands on its stubby tail. With an iron grip he tore the slathering hyena off of Solly and flung it as hard as he could into the forest. Ratch used such momentum that the hyena was literally airborne.

It came to an abrupt halt against the hard unyielding trunk of a palm tree. There was the nauseating thwack of tissue and bone caving in, and then, except for an odd *zzzzt* sound, silence. He couldn't see the whiff of smoke that rose up from the gruesome smear of brains and blood on the tree trunk.

As Ed rushed forward to seize Solly and pull him free, Crunch applied deadly pressure to the throat of his twisting, snarling adversary. As he held his head back just out of the way of the deadly jaws, he squeezed. Hard.

The hyena was in its death throes when Crunch used his free hand to grab his other fist, which was as rigid as iron around the animal's neck. One quick twist, a loud crack, and the hyena melted to the ground in a boneless furry heap, its neck broken. Crunch stared down at the crumpled body at his feet, his chest heaving from the exertion. Suddenly there was a *zzzzt* sound, and the dead hyena dissolved into a puff of acrid smoke. Blinking in confusion, he only glanced up when he heard Solly whimper, to see that the others were clustered together, and fanned out around the injured dog.

Exhausted from his skirmish, he joined them and found Shirley and Morris ministering to Bobby and Solly who were laid out side by side and covered in blood. Shirley was clucking over the two of them in the mother-earth voice to which they had all become familiar at one point or other on the journey. He was swamped with relief to find them both beaten-up but conscious.

"Who do you think you are kid, superman? And *you*, Solly the lionhearted. Out-fucking-standing, the both of you." Bobby smiled wanly up at Crunch, his young warrior's face streaked with blood and his eyes shining with pride at the compliment from his hero.

"Thanks, ow, thanks man." Bobby winced a little as he reached over to run his hand over Solly's forehead.

"You okay boy?" Solly gave Bobby a feeble little tail wag and tiredly licked his hand.

Relief was evident as everyone relaxed slightly.

Suddenly a woman screamed in pure unmitigated terror and everyone's blood turned to ice.

"Now *that* was human," said Jesse.

"Definitely. Let's go," agreed Ed. As they swung around

together and bolted toward Isolde's voice, Jesse tossed orders over his shoulder at the others.

"Get Bobby and Solly under that fern with Mercy! Ratch, you and Crunch are in charge. Guard them. Stink, come with us." This time there were no arguments as the three plowed into the trees.

"Hear that?" asked Stink as they hurried away.

"What?"

"Whatever that thing was we heard just before the hyenas jumped us. It stopped."

"Yeah. But wait a minute . . . what's that?" It was a man's voice.

"Hey, isn't that Mickey?"

"I think it *is* Mickey. And I think he's in trouble. Hey Mickey, hang on, we're coming!" The men broke into a run.

"Mickey who? Who's Mickey?" asked Stink as he ran.

"You remember, we told you about Mickey. He was with Bobby and the Candlemans when we met them on the river. Before we found you guys" explained Jesse, legs pumping.

"Oh yeah, the midget."

"DWARF!" barked the cops in unison.

"Whatever." He was breathless now. Suddenly Ed, in the lead, came to an abrupt halt. Jesse and Stink almost slammed into him. It was the gate to Erin's house, tucked between the tall cedar hedges.

Now they could hear Isolde's screams, and Mickey, sounding agitated and desperate, trying to coax her into something.

# Chapter 53

## Showdown!

The python screamed as Isolde scuttered along the slanted, shingled roof, like a terrified spider trying to elude a giant foot. The pain in his eyes from the pepper and the frustration of being thwarted by Isolde's escape enraged Beau to insanity. After bashing around in the upstairs room trying to shake the pepper out of his eyes, he recovered just enough to refocus his attack. He stuck his hideous massive head out of the small window through which Isolde had thrown herself. The blood-curdling screams heard by the group following the hyena event had been hers as she saw that Beau intended to exit the same window and come after her.

*"ISOLDE!"*

*"MICKEY! I'm up here! Oh, Mickey help me he's coming! Please please please!"* Isolde was almost hysterical and trying desperately to think straight, to not let panic take over.

"Isolde, listen to me. You have to jump." Mickey was standing slightly away from the front steps craning his neck, and could see Isolde. She reached the edge of the roof farthest from the bedroom window and clung to the shingles, peering over at Mickey.

"SCREEEEEEEEAAAAAGH!" The snake launched himself through the small window and was halfway out onto the roof, but just as he almost reached Isolde, he got stuck. He shrieked and flopped, an immense and savage figment out of the worst kind of nightmare. His deadly fangs and that disgusting tongue were inches from Isolde's feet, and she had nowhere to go but down. Mickey saw too and his mind was whirling. Then he remembered. He looked behind him.

Just as Ed reached his hand out to unlatch the gate, he froze, as did Jesse and Stink behind him. Coming straight at them from out of the jungle on the other side of the path, was a lion pride, led by a magnificent huge lioness with beautiful sea-green eyes. The men stared in stunned fascination at the incredible sight. The lions didn't hurry and they didn't run, but moved toward them majestically on huge padded feet. The men froze like statues, but the pride paid them no attention. Instead, as one, they veered left and approached the wooden gate. With a toss of her mighty head, the female in the lead smashed the gate open and led her family through it. Mickey felt no fear as they quietly surrounded him.

Erin turned to Mickey and he didn't flinch as she looked directly into his eyes. He stared right back at her with love as he had so many times over the years. The exchange communicated anything and everything that needed to be said between them and then he whispered, "Help us."

As Beau wormed and twisted his way further out of the window, Erin leaped onto the porch roof. She assumed her stalking stance, head down, placing her huge paws with their razor-sharp claws quietly, stealthily, one in front of the other, and inched her way closer.

At that moment, the snake broke free and shook the entire building as his gargantuan writhing body landed directly in front of Erin. The Beau-thing's rantings halted for a split second as he took in the sight of the lioness preparing to spring. Resting on its twitching tail, it elongated itself skyward until it was towering over Erin and then drew back with its mouth open, preparing to strike.

Ed, Jesse and Stink entered the gate behind the lions and rubbed their eyes as they tried to absorb the incredible drama unfolding in front of them.

Ed recovered first and moved forward extending his arms. "Okay, I've got you, now jump."

This mobilized Jesse and Stink out of their stupor and they too joined Ed. "Isolde honey, jump, you can do it." She did. Ed caught her in his arms and deposited her beside Mickey, who grabbed her up in his arms and squeezed her tight.

Then the battle was on.

With an earthshaking roar, the lion sprang at the snake, just as it reared back and opened its massive jaws preparing to attack.

The powerful lioness was on him, ripping and tearing with her killer jaws and claws like razors.

But the constrictor was up for the challenge and began looping himself around and around her tawny body, squeezing tighter and tighter.

The coils, with Erin wrapped inside formed a gray scaly helix which began rolling down the incline of the roof. Bodies locked in mortal combat, they rolled over and over and then right off the edge the roof, landing with a tremendous crash on the ground in front of the house.

Erin had the snake in her formidable jaws and was savagely grinding and chewing a bloody hole in its throat as the snake brutally tried crushing the life out of her. The combatants were now drenched in blood, mostly Beau's. As the lions watched intently, Ed, Jesse, Stink, Mickey and Isolde stared, incredulous.

It was obvious that Erin was starting to have trouble breathing, but the python's life was ebbing away, most of its strength flowing out along with its blood. The deadly coils finally began to loosen and fall away with heavy thuds.

Erin extricated herself from the scaly loops and got shakily to her feet. With a final shake of her mighty head, she stood with the twitching snake in her massive bloody jaws.

She opened them just enough for the serpent to fall lifeless to the ground. Then she raised her head and roared in victory.

No one breathed.

Mickey stepped forward to face Erin, without a word. She was panting and exhausted and Beau's blood was dripping from the whiskers on her chin. She turned to him wearily and stared into his eyes. After a long moment she nodded and then turned to the lion family to which she now belonged completely.

The humans stood back as en masse the pride followed Erin single file up the steps and into the house.

The first doorway they came to was the bedroom where Erin's bloated, empty body reposed, and the lioness stopped for a moment. As she gazed upon it, a tiny tear escaped from the corer of one of the unbearably beautiful sea-blue eyes and trickled down her tawny cheek.

Then with a final toss of her noble head, Erin led her family to their final destination. They proceeded on through the house, past the kitchen, and across the back lawn to the twins' little cottage.

Erin looked around. Once again, the gnarled dead tree in the painting of the Amazon rain forest held a huge snake, only this time it was dead, and hung from the branches limp and lifeless.

She then turned to the frame where a pack of hyenas reposed tranquil and unmoving in their African painting, in a lovely aura of semi-twilight. She didn't see Patrick and Sarah, but she knew they were there somewhere, never again to venture out of the frame.

Isolde and Mickey chose to remain behind in the front yard, but Ed, Jesse and Stink couldn't resist following the lions. They took in the sight of Erin's huge still body lying in the king-sized bed where she had left it behind forever. As they reached the back yard, a switching tail was just disappearing into the cottage. They followed.

As they filled the doorway of the small dwelling, they were just in time to hear several zzzzt's and smell the puffs of smoke, but the lions had disappeared. Awestruck, they moved from painting to magnificent painting, which were now all as still as the day Sarah had rendered them. The most stunning was the picture of a pride of lions, with a huge female in front staring off into the distance, her jaws bloody and red.

After the men disappeared into the house, Mickey took Isolde by the hand and led her up the porch steps. When they reached Erin's room they entered and walked up to her bedside.

Tears coursed down both of their faces as Mickey pulled Mercy's lighter from his pocket and set the bedclothes on fire. In death Erin smiled, free from her fleshy human prison at last. When the bed became fully engulfed, Erin's two loyal companions turned and left the room. They encountered Ed, Jesse, and Stink in the hallway looking stunned and numb. Ed spoke first.

"They were paintings. They were all paintings."

"Yes, they were paintings. And they still are. Only they can't hurt anyone anymore."

Ed didn't know how to reply to this.

Jesse broke in. "What now Mickey?"

Mickey and Isolde were standing with their arms around each other. "We're going away from here. There's a whole world out there for us now." He stepped forward and hugged Ed around the middle. Ed hugged him back.

"Guys, let's go get our friends." Stink had already turned to leave.

Ed nodded and the three headed down the hall and out the front door. When they got to the gate they seemed to take a collective deep breath and walked through. There, on the other side of the tall cedar hedges, Dalton Street was once again part of a quiet suburban neighborhood in a tranquil little farm town called Hester, New York.

"Ed! Jesse!" It was the group of weary adventurers they had left behind under the giant fern, at the scene of the hyena attack, and not far from the opening in the tall cedar hedge that surrounded Erin's home. Ratch had Mercy in his arms, and Solly was limping and bloody, but they were all there, had all survived.

Ed looked at them and said tiredly, "Let's go home."

# Epilogue

Mickey and Isolde returned to the twins' little home in the back yard. It now contained nothing but a multitude of lovely paintings.

The magic and the terror it had wrought was over now, the cottage was once again just an antique menagerie circus wagon. With Erin and Sarah's help, the painful longing embedded in its wooden walls had been fulfilled. The animals had had a chance to be free just one more time.

Only one painting was removed and destroyed. It was the pathetic depiction of a large snake hanging bloody and limp on a dead tree branch in the Amazon jungle.

The two made several trips back and forth from the big house, arms loaded with the supplies that Isolde had prepared for them to take along. Although Beau had pretty much trashed the bedroom and everything in it, they were able to salvage most of their belongings.

While Isolde chopped away the foliage from around the wheels of the wagon, Mickey went to Erin's bedside one last time.

The fire he had set was only smoldering now, and all that was left of Erin's body was a charred, blackened spot on the king-sized bed where she had spent so many years of her life.

Tears coursed down his face as he remembered the day she had saved him and brought him home. Through his tears, a sparkle caught his eye. He moved closer to the bed.

There on either side of it, were several small objects also blackened by the fire.

*Erin's rings!*

Reverently, one by one, Mickey picked them up. The last one was the largest. It was the huge golden lion's head created by Rudy the jeweler, and Mickey wiped the soot from its glittering sapphire and emerald eyes. He stared into them for a long time, and he heard Erin's voice in his head.

*"Don't worry about me Mickey darling. Please. I'm happy, and you must be happy too."*

Aloud, his voice breaking with emotion, he answered, "I'll always love you. Goodbye Erin."

Gently he closed his hands over the rings. Without looking back he turned and headed out to the garage.

As Mickey checked on their transportation, Isolde made sure that the twins' wagon was packed with everything they would need to move on for good, and start a new life somewhere far away.

That night under cover of darkness, no one noticed the old-fashioned circus wagon leaving town by way of Route 17, towed by a small exotic sports car, specially equipped for little people.

## THE END

# A Spectral Visions Imprint

## Now Available

# The Apostate

By
**Paul Lonardo**

An ancient evil is spreading through Caldera, a burgeoning desert metropolis that has been heralded as the gateway of the new millennium. As the malevolent shadow spreads across the land, three seemingly ordinary people, Julian, Saney, and Chris, discover that they are the only ones who can defeat the true source of the region's evil, which may or may not be the Devil himself. When a man claiming to work for a mysterious global organization informs the trio that Satan has, in fact, chosen Caldera as the site of the final battle between good and evil, only one questions remains…

Is it too late for humanity?

**Ask for it at your local bookseller!**

**ISBN 193140132**

**www.barclaybooks.com**

# A Spectral Visions Imprint
## Now Available

# Riverwatch

By
## Joseph M. Nassise

From a new voice in horror comes a novel rich in characterization and stunning in its imagery. In his debut novel, author Joseph M. Nassise weaves strange and shocking events into the ordinary lives of his characters so smoothly that the reader accepts them without pause, setting the stage for a climactic ending with the rushing power of a summer storm.

When his construction team finds the tunnel hidden beneath the cellar floor in the old Blake family mansion in Harrington Falls, Jake Caruso is excited by the possibility of what he might find hidden there. Exploring its depths, he discovers an even greater mystery: a sealed stone chamber at the end of that tunnel.

When the seal on that long forgotten chamber is broken, a reign of terror and death comes unbidden to the residents of the small mountain community. Something is stalking its citizens; something that comes in the dark of night on silent wings and strikes without warning, leaving a trail of blood in its wake. Something that should never have been released from the prison the Guardian had fashioned for it years before.

Now Jake, with the help of his friends Sam Travers and Katelynn Riley, will be forced to confront this ancient evil in an effort to stop the creature's rampage. The Nightshade, however, has other plans.

## Ask for it at your local bookseller!

## ISBN 1931402191

## www.barclaybooks.com

# A Spectral Visions Imprint
## Now Available

## Spirit Of Independence

By
### Keith Rommel

Travis Winter, the Spirit of Independence, was viciously murdered in World War II. Soon after his untimely death, he discovers he is a chosen celestial knight; a new breed of Angel destined to fight the age-old war between Heaven and Hell. Yet, confusion reigns for Travis when he is pulled into Hell and is confronted by the Devil himself—the saddened creature who begs only to be heard.

Freed by a band of Angels sent to rescue him, Travis rejects the Devil's plea and begins a fifty year long odyssey to uncover the true reasons why Heaven and Hell war.

Now, in this, the present day, Travis comes to you, the reader, to share recent and extraordinary revelations that will no doubt change the way you view the Kingdom of Heaven and Hell. And what is revealed will change your own afterlife in ways you could never imagine …

### Ask for it at your local bookseller!

### ISBN 1931402078

### www.barclaybooks.com